Touch Me Again

JAX BURROWS

BOOKS

Vinci Books

vinci-books.com

Published by Vinci Books Ltd in 2026

1

A CIP catalogue record for this book is available from the British Library.

Paperback ISBN: 9781036708122

The EU GPSR authorised representative is Logos Europe, 9 rue Nicolas Poussion, 17000 La Rochelle, France contact@logoseurope.eu

Chapter One

Colleen O'Shea stood on the pavement gazing up at the block of flats. Next to her was her suitcase on wheels that she had pulled along beside her for what felt like miles from the tube station. London wasn't a complete mystery to her; she'd visited plenty of times, with her mother and sometimes on her own. But she'd never been to this part of London before. She loved the centre with the Houses of Parliament, Big Ben, Buckingham Palace and the art galleries and museums. Especially the art galleries. She was on a mailing list and was notified of interesting exhibitions that were to take place and occasionally she found the money for a trip.

She glanced down at the piece of paper in her hand containing Nora's address then back up to the building. It was the right place. But it wasn't as she'd imagined. Nora had given her the impression that she was living the high life with friends, parties, and men. Just one mad social whirl is how Colleen had pictured it. She'd imagined her living in a smart, bijou apartment with a balcony, and a lovely view of one of London's many parks. But this building was dirty, dark, and cold looking. The small patch of grass at the front was littered with dog dirt, broken bottles and even a super-market trolley with no wheels lying abandoned on its side.

A man came out of the front door, letting it swing shut behind him. He stood on the patch of grass, swaying slightly, and trying to make a roll-up cigarette. He had a tin, presumably for the tobacco and dropped it twice on the grass. He cursed each time and on the third time he dropped it, he tried to kick it, swearing loudly. He missed and landed on his backside then noticed Colleen watching him.

'Don't just stand there you bitch, help me up.'

Colleen was frozen to the spot. She watched him strug-gling to get to his feet, then, swallowing her fear, went to help him. He was a big man, heavy and drunk as a lord. He stank of beer, sweat and nicotine, and his clothes were grimy with dirt. Colleen took hold of his arm and tried to pull him up, but he was too heavy for her. Somehow the man ended up on his hands and knees and Colleen backed off.

'Leave him, love, he's not worth your efforts.' A younger man stood in the doorway of the flats, holding the door open. 'Are you coming in or what?'

Colleen retrieved her suitcase and moved towards the front door.

'Thanks,' she said as he held the door open for her.

'You're welcome,' he said and hurried off down the street.

Nora's flat was number five, which meant it was on the next level. There appeared to be four flats to each storey, making twelve in all. There was a lift which had tape across it and a sign declaring it to be out of order. The sign was written on a piece of paper in blue biro and was so faded Colleen could hardly read it. The lift had obviously been out of action for a while.

Colleen started towards the stairs, dragging her case with her. There was a strong smell of urine, and the stairs were filthy. Colleen tried not to breathe in too deeply as she hurried to get to Nora's flat. At least it'd be clean and tidy. Nora had always been a stickler for cleaning her room. She had kept it spotless. Until she reached the age of fifteen when she suddenly lost interest in everything.

Colleen knocked on the door of number five. There was no answer, so she knocked again. It had never occurred to her that Nora wouldn't be home. Friday evening at teatime. Everyone was at home then. Nora would be back from work and looking forward to the weekend. Colleen intended to join her in whatever activities her sister engaged in on a Friday evening. She knew she'd be welcome; Nora would be delighted to see her, she was sure.

Colleen pushed the door carefully and it swung open. That was bad, not locking her door. She'd heard about London and the crimes that went on. Manchester was bad enough, but London would surely be worse. Nora should be more careful.

'Hello,' she called. No answer. 'Nora?' she called again, louder this time. Still no answer. Oh to heck with it. Something was very wrong, and she needed to help her sister. It was a good job she'd come.

Colleen went into the flat and was hit by the stench.

Weed. Dope. Cannabis. Whatever you called it, it was bad news. Nora had started smoking it while she was still at school but when their mother had found out, had promised faithfully that she wouldn't touch the evil stuff again. Well, so much for promises.

The flat was cold. Although it was May, there was a nip in the air and, despite the heavy smoke-laden atmosphere, the cold and damp were obvious.

A man lounged in an armchair, a spliff in his hand, his head back and his eyes closed. He wasn't quite as dirty as chummy outside with his roll-ups but wasn't far off. Colleen stood in the middle of the room, not daring to move, but the man looked as if he was asleep, or unconscious. The spliff had burnt down, the hot ash dangerously close to his fingers. Should she wake him up and tell him? And, more importantly, where was Nora?

Colleen looked around the room for signs of her sister. Maybe she'd wandered into the wrong flat. Perhaps she lived at number seven or three. Then she heard the sounds of someone retching, then groaning. Was that Nora? Whoever it was needed help.

'Nora? Are you okay?'

Colleen left her suitcase and moved towards the bathroom. Nora was lying on the floor with her head in the toilet. She was almost unrecognisable from the pretty young girl who had left the family home in Manchester to make her fortune in London. She had told them that, without her father, there was nothing for her in Manchester anymore and she was moving on.

This comment had stabbed their mother in the heart, and it took all Colleen's powers of persuasion to convince Mum that she didn't mean it, she was grieving and didn't know what she was saying. Eventually, her mother accepted that Nora needed to go, and she hadn't tried to stop her, although she wept buckets the night Nora left.

Colleen knelt down on the floor and took Nora's hand. It was cold and clammy. She wanted to envelop her in a hug and take her back home, but Nora was struggling to stand up and she wasn't looking pleased.

'What the fuck are you doing here?'

'I've come to visit. I've not seen you for ages and just wanted to see for myself how you're doing.'

'Well, as you can see, I'm living the dream.' Nora was pale and she avoided eye contact.

Then Nora pushed past her, and Colleen had no choice but to follow her back to the living room. With one last glance at the bathroom—no bath or pedestal mats, no shower curtain, and the bath looked like it was used for everything but washing—Colleen followed her sister.

The man was awake now and had lit a new spliff.

'Hello, darlin',' he said.

'Hello,' said Colleen trying to avoid looking at him.

Nora collapsed onto the sofa and accepted the spliff from the man.

'Manners,' said the man. 'Perhaps your guest would like a drag.'

'Oh shut up, Maggot.' Nora took a deep drag and offered it to Colleen.

'No thank you. You know I don't take drugs.' Colleen was horrified and heartbroken at the same time. This was her baby sister, the girl she loved more than anyone, and she was living in a slum and doing drugs. She needed to help her but felt completely out of her depth.

'Please yourself,' said Nora and continued to smoke defiantly.

'Let me make you a nice cup of tea,' Colleen said cheerfully, 'I'd kill for one, not had anything for hours.' She'd had a stale sandwich and a can of orange on the train but had been hoping for a nice meal sometime that evening.

Nora and Maggot burst out laughing.

'Tea? Is that still your answer for every problem in life? You poor sad old woman. You'll be living with cats soon and taking up knitting.' Nora was staring at her with contempt in her eyes. This wasn't the baby sister she knew and loved. Colleen wanted her back and vowed to help her in any way she could. Nora needed to stop the drugs and start looking after herself. And it would be their secret, not a word would they breathe to Mum. It would break her heart.

'Nothing wrong with cats or knitting. And yes, tea can help in any situation. That's why, when people have had a shock, they give them sweet tea.'

'I'm a coffee man myself,' said Maggot.

'Oh shut up, Maggot,' said Nora. 'Anyway, we haven't got either.'

Colleen went into the kitchen which was littered with drug paraphernalia. A tin on its side spilt its contents onto the kitchen table. Needles, spoons with a black sticky substance caked on, dimps. Ash littered the table and the floor.

Colleen braced herself as she slowly opened the fridge door. Half a bottle of milk looked as if it had turned to cheese. No food, but strange packets pushed to the back. She shut the fridge door and looked in the cupboards. Mice droppings and dirt.

'Right. I'll just nip out and get you some supplies. I noticed a supermarket on the corner. Shall I buy something for our tea as well?'

'Fish and chips, darlin', with salt and vinegar.' Maggot grinned at her with a mouth full of broken, brown teeth.

Nora said nothing, so Colleen left the flat and hurried down the stairs to the outside and fresh air. She breathed deeply and suppressed the sob that rose to her throat at the thought of the way Nora was living. Her poor baby sister.

She took her time strolling to the supermarket, dreading going back to that flat with the putrid air and the filth. Even as a child, she'd hated getting her hands dirty or sticky. Where was she going to sleep? She hadn't even seen the bedrooms but if they were anything like the rest of the place, she couldn't stay there overnight, she just couldn't.

After buying milk, tea, coffee, bread, butter, and jam, she went to the chippy and bought fish and chips three times with plenty of salt and vinegar.

Her footsteps dragged as she approached the block of flats. Never had she been so reluctant to enter a building as this one. But the fish and chips would get cold if she didn't hurry up and her stomach was rumbling and if she didn't eat soon, she'd get the shakes from low sugar. She took a deep breath and pushed the front door which, despite it being a security door, wasn't locked.

After she handed out the fish and chips, she perched on the edge of a chair, dreading to think what the stains on the upholstery were. The food was hot and delicious, but she was the only one who finished the lot. Maggot ate about half and left the rest on the floor in its polystyrene tray. Nora said she'd have hers later. She looked unwell and, before Colleen had finished eating, she was in the bathroom again throwing up.

'You need to eat something, Nora, that's why you're being sick, because you've got no food in your stomach.' Colleen knelt down next to her sister and stroked her hair.

'I've got a stomach bug, that's all.'

'Then you should be in bed. Shall I ring a doctor?'

'Yes to the first, no to the second.' Nora tried to get to her feet, but she was weak, so Colleen helped her up. She put her arm around her, shocked at how thin she was.

'Come on, let's get you into bed.'

Nora let her lead her to the bedroom and help her onto the bed. There was only one bedroom in the flat and it contained a double bed, a wardrobe and little else. The duvet was filthy, and the room smelt rotten.

'You need to drink some water, you'll be dehydrated after all that vomiting.'

'Fine.' Nora sounded lethargic as if she didn't care anymore.

Colleen went back to the kitchen and found a glass. She washed it as best she could despite the fact there was no washing up liquid, ran the tap until the water turned cold, then filled the glass and took it back to Nora. Maggot seemed to have succumbed to sleep again; he was slumped in the armchair snoring heavily.

'Here you are. Drink this and you'll start to feel better.' Nora took the glass and drank.

'Now. Listen to me. You need help to get yourself out of this situation. I'm here to help you, Nora. I hate to see you like this. You're a bright girl and can do so much better for yourself.'

'How do you know I don't live like this from choice? I might enjoy it.'

'I don't believe that for a minute. You're clever. You could have the world at your feet if you went to college and learned a skill…'

'So, if that kind of life is so wonderful, why don't you go to college?' Nora was watching her, and Colleen felt she deserved the truth.

'I'm not as clever as you are. A secretary is all I'll ever be and I'm content with that. But you take after Dad. He was clever and he wouldn't have wanted to see you in this mess.'

Colleen was dismayed as tears fell from Nora's eyes and traced a path down her cheeks.

'Oh my darling girl, I'm so sorry, I've upset you. I didn't come here to do that, I want to help you. You know I love you, don't you?'

Nora nodded and wiped her face on the pillowcase. 'There is something you can do if you really want to help me.'

'Oh? What?'

'I've got a job tonight, but I'm too sick to go. Could you go in my place? We can share the money.'

'I didn't know you worked. Well done, you. Tell me all about it.' Colleen imagined she was a waitress or worked behind the bar in one of the swanky wine bars or nightclubs.

'I work for an agency. They text me when they have a job for me. I never know when and they don't give me much notice. Anyway, this is a good one. A stag night at the Spice Club.'

'Okay. What do you have to do?'

Nora looked embarrassed but defiant at the same time.

'Don't judge me. It's hard getting work when you're not qualified. At least you've got secretarial qualifications. I've got nothing.'

'Well, that's more reason to consider going to college. Learn something that'll earn you a wage.'

'Whatever.' Nora lay down and put her arm over her eyes. 'Do you want to do this job for me or not?'

'Yes. Sorry. Of course I do. Tell me.'

'I'm a stripper. They want me to burst out of a box shaped like a present and then strip.'

'A stripper! You have got to be joking. I can't do that. It's degrading. Why are you doing this, Nora? I don't understand you.'

'No, that's the problem, isn't it? You don't understand. Anything.'

Nora turned her back on Colleen and pulled the duvet over her head. Colleen put her head in her hands and shut her eyes. This day was going from bad to worse. Her sister was taking all kinds of drugs and keeping herself alive by taking her clothes off in front of men. And now she was asking her to do the same. Well, not the drugs, of course. But if she really wanted to help her, maybe she needed to stop being so judgemental and do as she asked.

Colleen sighed, a sound that came up from her boots. She was tired and heartsore. Mum had asked her to ring her and let her know how Nora was. But how could she tell her the truth?

Nora was still. Had she fallen asleep?

'Nora? Listen to me. I'll help you all I can and first thing tomorrow I'll go out and find a job. But please don't ask me to strip, I can't do that, okay?'

Nora turned over slowly. 'Can't or won't?'

'Both.' The thought of taking her clothes off in front of strange men made her shudder.

'Okay. If you won't do it, I'll have to do it myself. I'm not throwing away the chance to earn two grand.'

'How much? Did I hear right? They're paying you two thousand pounds? Who are these people?'

'They're rich knobheads that's who they are. They pay well to ogle women.'

'I can't believe it. It's incredible.'

'No, Colleen, it's London. Now, if you aren't going to

help me, can you leave me alone to get some sleep so I can get through tonight?'

'I can't let you go, you're not well enough.' Nora lay still with her back to her. 'Nora, talk to me, please. Tell me why it's so important to do this job.'

'I owe people a lot of money. Bad people.'

'What people? How much do you owe?'

'I owe five thousand pounds. And if I don't pay, they'll…'

'What? How did you get yourself in so much debt? What have you been doing? And what will these people do?'

Then the penny dropped. Drugs. Oh God, this was far worse than she'd realised. She owed drug dealers five thousand pounds.

'They're coming back for their money. You shouldn't be here, or you'll be a target. You need to go, Colleen. Trust me, you don't want to mess with these people.'

'But if you owe them five and the stripping job is only paying two.' *Only*, what was she saying? What kind of world had she become involved with? 'What about the other three thousand?'

'If I can give them two, it'll get them off my case for a while, but they'll come back. They always come back. And every day they add more and more interest. I'm trapped but as long as I work, they let me be.'

'Oh my darling girl, what are we going to do?'

'*You're* going to do nothing, it's not your problem. I'm going to work as much as I can and pay it off gradually. What else can I do?'

'Meanwhile, the interest is making the debt impossible to pay off. They've got you for life, Nora. We have to do something.'

Colleen knew she couldn't let Nora go out feeling so ill.

She was worried sick about her but the thought of drug dealers turning up and frightening her baby sister made her sick to her stomach. She wasn't leaving London until Nora was off the drugs and clean again. That money would just keep them sweet for a short while. And then what?

'Okay, I'll do it.'

Chapter Two

Adam arrived at the Spice Club before any of the others. As best man, it had fallen to him to organise Jeremy's stag night. Adam had known Jeremy since their university days, and he considered him one of his closest friends. In fact, the closest, as most of his other "friends" were work colleagues and CEO competitors from rival companies in the city.

Adam was determined that Jeremy would enjoy himself tonight as he had waited a long time for his fiancée, Lady Theodora Blakely, to agree to marry him. She had kept him dangling for days when he proposed and even after she had agreed to wed him, he had to wait an inordinately long period of time before she agreed to make the announcement official.

'She likes to do things properly,' Jeremy had said to him with a smile.

'We know who wears the trousers in that relationship,' said his friends.

Everyone in their social circle despaired of Jeremy and Theo ever tying the knot and most of them had lost interest in the couple, with the exception of Jeremy's parents who were desperate for an announcement so they could boast to everyone who would listen, of the wonderful match their son had made.

Jeremy had a lot of friends and even more acquaintances, being one of the richest, most eligible bachelors in the country, who was also unusually generous with his money. Consequently, Adam was ruthless in choosing only people he knew to be genuine friends of Jeremy to invite to the stag night. The gold diggers and hangers-on would be denied entrance.

Jeremy Baxter was considered to be an odd fish by people who didn't know him as well as Adam did. He came across as a bit of a hooray henry and could be a bumbling oaf on occasions, tactless and outspoken, with a loud, braying laugh and a penchant for dirty jokes. Adam had quickly seen through his outer persona to his quirky sense of humour, sharp business brain and almost infallible talent for picking winning horses. In fact, Jeremy had won more money on the races than anyone Adam had ever known.

Adam hated stag nights. They were all the same; a group of men who were old enough to know better, getting drunk and boasting of how many women they'd shagged while trying to get off with every waitress, bartender and female customer who was unfortunate enough to stray into their orbit. They got louder and more obnoxious as the night went on. And the nights usually went on a long time after the club had closed, well into the early hours. He flatly refused to go to any stag night that was taking place in Amsterdam, or weekends in Scotland for the shooting, hunting and other upper-class obscenities.

This stag night would be different. Adam had spoken to the manager and told him that there would be no strippers and no raucous or unseemly behaviour. It would be a civilised occasion of friends having a few drinks to celebrate Jeremy and Theodora's nuptials.

The manager had grinned and nodded. 'If you say so,' he said.

Adam was checking over the venue when the manager came into the bar.

'Just the man I wanted to speak to.'

'Really? Okay. What is it?' Had he missed something important?

'You know what you were saying the other day about there being no strippers?'

'Yes.'

'Well, who ordered that then?' He pointed to a large cardboard box in the corner, wrapped up in shiny paper and tied with a blue bow.

Adam hadn't noticed it before. Someone must have delivered it when his back was turned.

'Well, it wasn't me. What's in it?'

'Nothing at the moment, but there'll be a stripper in it later, waiting for her cue to burst out of the box and do a strip in front of your friend.' The man was grinning, no doubt at the thought of a woman taking her clothes off. Lecherous old sod.

'I'm sorry I have no idea who ordered it. I certainly didn't.' Damn, it must have been one of Jeremy's moronic friends having a laugh. 'Can we get rid of it?'

'We could. But the stripper will be showing up any time now. She has to hide in the box before any of your guests arrive.'

'Couldn't we just apologise and say there's been a mistake?'

'She'll want paying. Are you prepared to pay her? What if she makes a scene?'

Adam was flummoxed. The man was right, of course, he couldn't expect the girl to go away empty-handed but his strict instructions from Theo had been no strippers or someone would be in trouble. He wasn't sure if she meant himself or Jeremy. Maybe both. Theo took no prisoners if her demands weren't met exactly as per her instructions.

'It's not very big,' Adam said staring at the box. 'And it sticks out like a sore thumb wrapped in that shiny paper.' He felt sorry for anyone who had to spend time crouched in such a small box.

'It'll be covered until the moment the stripper bursts out of it. I'll put the cover on when she turns up if she ever does. She's late.'

Adam sighed. 'I guess we'd better let the show go on.' Jeremy and his mates would love it. They seemed to enjoy tacky entertainment. So much for his idea of a civilised stag night. Perhaps there really was no such thing.

'What's this?' Colleen stared in dismay at the pile of red ribbon the manager of the Spice Club had shoved in her hands.

'It's your outfit apparently. That's what the man from the agency told me anyway.'

'It's just a handful of ribbon. What the heck am I supposed to do with it?'

'Why are you asking me? You're the stripper, you should

know how these things work. And don't shoot the messenger. If you're not happy, take it up with the agency, it's nothing to do with me.'

The manager was smirking in an unpleasant way. She hoped he wouldn't be watching when she stripped. He gave her the creeps.

Colleen had no idea what she was letting herself in for. Nora had been non-committal telling her it was a straight-forward job. Wait for the cover to come off the box, which was her cue to jump out of it, then do a quick strip and go. No physical contact of any kind was required. It sounded straightforward the way her sister told it. But now, standing in front of this big, smirking man who looked as if he despised her, but would watch the show anyway, she was having serious reservations.

Two thousand pounds she was being paid. Just to jump out of a box and wiggle around a bit. There had to be more to it than that. Was it too late to back out? Then she thought of Nora being threatened by drug dealers. She had no choice.

'Well, are you just going to stand there or are you going to put your *costume* on?'

The man's voice dripped sarcasm and Colleen marched off in the direction of the Ladies. She took her clothes off and put them in the plastic carrier bag that she had brought the groceries home in. It was the only bag she could find as there were none in Nora's flat and she didn't want to lug her suitcase all the way there and back.

She started to wrap the ribbon around herself, trying desperately to cover her breasts and pubes. Fortunately, there was a lot of ribbon and she managed to cover up most of her private places, tying a massive bow at the front that looked ridiculous but did offer her a modicum of protection.

After covering herself as best she could, she scrutinised herself in the mirror to see if she'd missed any important bits. Good God in heaven this was ridiculous! What was she doing? She tiptoed out of the Ladies.

Finding it hard to walk naturally as she'd had to put some ribbon between her legs to cover her pubes properly, she shuffled back into the lounge area where the action would take place. The manager was leaning on the bar with his back to her talking to a customer. Luckily, there was no one else in the place.

The customer stopped in mid-sentence, his mouth hanging open and his eyes on stalks. The manager turned around to see what he was staring at and did the same.

'What's the matter? Have you never seen a woman wrapped in ribbon before?' Colleen wasn't usually so outspoken, but the adrenaline was flowing, and she just wanted to get this pantomime over with so she could get dressed and collect her money. Which reminded her. 'When do I get paid?' she asked the manager.

'Take it up with the agency. You better get in the box, the guests will be arriving soon.'

'Right.' Colleen still hung onto her plastic bag. She wasn't prepared to let it out of her sight as it held all her worldly goods at that moment. The most important ones being her clothes and phone.

The manager took the lid off the box and stood back, watching Colleen struggle to climb inside. Not a gentleman then, but maybe that was a blessing, she didn't want any man near her while she was dressed in nothing but ribbon. His gaze moved over her like strobe lighting which caused her to hurry so she almost fell inside the box. There wasn't enough room to stand up, so she crouched, trying to cover herself from his penetrating eyeballs as best she could.

'You better make yourself comfortable, you could be in there for a while,' said the manager.

'Okay.' How the heck she was supposed to get comfortable in a box while trussed up like a festive turkey she didn't know.

'The holes are in the front. You'll know when the cover's taken off as you'll be able to see through them. Do you understand?'

'Yes, of course. I'm not stupid.' Although her present situation might prove otherwise.

'Right. Wait for the cover to come off, then jump out.'

'Yes, thank you, it's perfectly clear.'

The man was starting to get on her nerves. Did he treat all women as if they were imbeciles or just the strippers?

It went dark as the cover was put on over the lid. Colleen didn't think she suffered from claustrophobia but had never been stuck in a box before. How long would she have to stay there? The manager had said a while. How long was that? A few minutes or a few hours? Oh God, no, not hours. She'd have to get out before then. What if she wanted the loo? She took a deep breath and breathed out slowly. Think of the money. Just concentrate on two thousand pounds. Don't think about anything else.

Not only could she not see through the holes in the box, but she couldn't hear anything. Were they still there? They hadn't just gone away and left her like this had they? As some kind of joke?

Colleen willed herself to calm down and concentrate. She listened intently and then breathed a sigh of relief when she heard voices. Men's loud voices, sounding as if they were out for a night of fun. The stag party. There was one man in particular who had a loud voice and an even louder laugh. She wondered if he was the stag. Would he expect her to remove the ribbon? Well, he could think again, it was staying put.

At one point she thought she heard someone doing something to the box. There was the sound of rustling nearby, but it must have been her imagination as it stayed dark, so the cover must still be on. She had been hoping that it was her cue to leap out and strip. She might just remove a tiny bit of the ribbon as a tease, but no way was she going to do a full strip. She just wanted to get it over with now, she was growing more anxious by the minute.

Colleen crouched in the hot, stuffy atmosphere of the box. Her long legs were starting to grow numb, but she couldn't turn around or stand up to ease the discomfort. How much longer would she have to be in here listening to the sounds of men getting drunk? Their voices were growing louder and there was more laughter.

Maybe she should just burst out now and get it over with. Colleen pushed at the lid to see how easily it moved. It didn't. She pushed again, harder. It was completely immobile. The cover must be heavy. So, she was totally reliant on someone to get her out of her prison. What if they forgot she was in there and the party just continued into the early hours? No, that wouldn't happen, she was just scaring herself witless and needed to calm down.

She did her deep, slow breathing again, but started to feel dizzy so stopped. There was no air in the box. She felt around the lid, trying to find the holes that the manager had told her about, but couldn't find them.

Music started up, sounding a lot like "The Stripper" which was presumably her cue to jump out of the box.

Then she felt and heard something as if the cover had been dragged off. She looked frantically for the holes to see if it was time for her to exit but couldn't see them anywhere, the box was completely sealed.

Chapter Three

Adam didn't like it, not one bit, but he wasn't going to be the party pooper and say something, spoiling Rupert's little joke and Jeremy's stag night. But it was cruel, and Adam didn't like cruelty. It reminded him of the pranks boys used to play on each other in school. Adam had been the victim of bullying and had been expected to treat it all as one big joke.

Adam had watched as Rupert and two of his cronies, had carefully covered up the holes in the front of the box and taped the lid with masking tape, so whoever was inside stood no chance of being able to get out on their own.

He hadn't seen the stripper before she got in the box, but the manager had told him in graphic detail about the "costume" the woman was wearing, which consisted entirely of ribbon wrapped around her. He had told Adam that he had almost caught a glimpse of the promised land when she was clambering into the box.

Then the manager pulled the cover off and the stag

party shouted louder, trying to drown out the music that had been turned up to full volume.

Rupert was beside himself with glee and his two friends were nearly wetting themselves and clapping each other on the back.

'Let her out,' said Adam to Rupert.

'What?' said Rupert cupping his hand behind his ear as if he couldn't hear him.

'I said, let the woman out. You've had your fun, now get her out of that box or I will.'

'Oh, don't be such a girl,' said Rupert swaying slightly, 'this is Jeremy's stag night, he's here to enjoy himself. Don't ruin it before it's properly begun. It's just a joke and she's just a stripper.'

Adam scanned the room glancing at all Jeremy's friends, most of whom he only knew slightly. They were all drunk, red in the face and shouting 'strip, strip, strip' in time to the music. This stopped now.

Adam cut the masking tape with his car keys and yanked the box open. The woman climbed out and stood, looking like a deer caught in the headlights. She was blinking in the sudden light and trying to cover herself with her hands. And she was crying.

Rupert made a lunge for her and tried to tear the ribbon off. She screamed as she backed away from him.

'Strip, you silly bitch, what do you think we're paying you for?'

'Take it easy, she's upset,' said Jeremy. 'Would you like a drink?' he asked the woman.

But the stripper was nearly hysterical and still trying to fight Rupert off, which inflamed the rest of the men to egg him on.

'Take your hands off her, Rupert, or you'll be sorry.'

Adam pulled Rupert off the woman and he fell to the floor. Adam stood over him with a clenched fist, so he got the message.

'Want her for yourself do you Turner?' shouted someone behind them.

'Oh come on, chaps, no fighting, please. We were having such a good time. It is my stag night, after all.'

Adam moved away from Rupert who had scrambled up and dusted himself off. He accepted the drink that Jeremy held out to him.

Just as Adam was about to take his jacket off to cover the stripper's embarrassment, a woman's voice stopped him in his tracks, the familiar tone commanding, and he turned as Lady Theodora Blakely entered the room.

Theo was chic in a cool, sophisticated way. Her wide-eyed look and finely chiselled features belied a strength of character that people found surprising when they got to know her. They expected her to be sugar and spice and all things nice, whereas, in reality, people crossed her at their peril. She was forthright and didn't pull her punches.

'What,' said Theo her voice echoing around the room, 'the hell is she doing here?' She pointed at the stripper who cowered in the corner, whimpering.

'Hello, darling,' said Jeremy who looked genuinely pleased to see his fiancée at his stag night. 'This is a lovely surprise. Would you like a drink?'

'I was right not to trust you, Jeremy. As soon as my back's turned you're getting cosy with sluts and prostitutes.'

'I'm sorry darling, I had no idea this would happen. Some of the chaps have arranged it. Not a proper stag night without a stripper.'

Theo ignored Jeremy and rounded on Adam. 'I said no strippers, Adam, and you promised there wouldn't be. So why is that woman in the corner dressed in nothing but a ribbon? And when I say dressed I use the term lightly.'

Jeremy sidled up to his fiancée and tried to take her hand.

'It's just a bit of fun, dear, nobody got hurt.' He laughed, which sounded like a donkey braying.

'Was this your doing?' Theo was a pretty woman, even when she was angry, with a soft bob of blonde hair that curled around her perfectly made-up face. She wore diamond earrings that sparkled in the light.

'No, it wasn't my doing.'

'But you, as best man, were responsible for arranging the stag night were you not?'

Adam sighed. 'Yes, but some of Jeremy's friends arranged the stripper, not me.'

'Who?' Theo stood with her arms crossed and a frown creasing her forehead. They would never hear the end of this, and Adam had a feeling he would be blamed for the whole sorry business.

'I don't know, Theo—does it matter?'

'Yes, of course it does. I want to know who is responsible.'

The stripper was still having a meltdown in the corner and Adam wanted to rescue her. Theo could wait.

'I'm sorry, I don't know, now if you'll excuse me.'

'Don't just walk away, Adam, I'm talking to you.'

Adam ignored her and went to the stripper who was shaking, tears still rolling down her cheeks. She clutched a white plastic bag as if it contained the crown jewels.

'Hi. Look, I'm sorry about all that. Are you okay?'

'Yes,' she said, wiping the tears away with the back of her hand.

'I'll take you home.'

'Thank you.' Adam slipped his jacket over her shoulders and they left the club. He could hear Theo's voice all the way down the stairs to the front door.

It was dark in the car and Adam instructed his driver to go back to his penthouse apartment. The woman couldn't go home in this state. He'd let her recover and then take her home later.

'Is that okay with you? You can freshen up and get changed, before going home.'

'Okay.' The woman seemed numb as if she was in shock. She'd probably say yes to anything. Adam felt responsible for what had happened. He should have stopped it from the beginning and not let it go that far. She must have been terrified if her present state was anything to go by.

'What's your name?'

'Colleen.'

'That's an unusual name. Gaelic I imagine.'

Adam had never made small talk with a stripper before, but he was curious about this one. She was still upset and wiped her eyes periodically with a tissue. He had always imagined that women in that type of profession were quite tough and able to handle themselves. This one, however, looked fragile, as if a loud noise would shatter her into tiny pieces.

'It's Irish. It means woman or girl.'

'Right. That's nice. I'm Adam by the way.'

'Hi. Thanks for… well, for rescuing me.'

'That's okay. You looked as if you were having a breakdown.'

'I couldn't get the box lid open. There were supposed to be holes for me to see out of, so I'd know if it was time. I couldn't find them.'

'That was because someone taped them over. In fact, I'm surprised you didn't suffocate in there.' Adam silently cursed Rupert, the stupid prick.

'I did find it hard to breathe. And it was hot, and I felt dizzy.'

'You should never have been subjected to that and I'm so sorry.'

'It's okay. It wasn't your fault.'

Adam studied her surreptitiously. She was pretty and looked quite innocent. But that could just be her stage persona or whatever strippers had. He was trying not to stare at her as, wrapped in that ridiculous ribbon, he could see more of her body than he should be able to.

'Have you been stripping long?' Great conversation starter. He cursed himself for his tactlessness.

'No.'

'Are you a student?' Some of the more attractive female students used their looks and figures to earn money as pole dancers, strippers, and the like. At least, they had when he was at university. It paid off the student loan quicker.

'No. I'm a secretary.'

Ah, a poorly paid office worker, stripping to supplement her income. He couldn't blame her, some people had to resort to these things to get by.

When they arrived at the luxury apartments, Colleen hurried out of the car and Adam led her to the private lift before anyone saw her, admiring her figure as she leaned against the wall, looking down. She had long legs and smooth skin. He wanted to touch her skin to see how soft it was. An idea was developing in his mind.

When the lift reached the penthouse apartment, Colleen stood back and waited for Adam to open the door. Then he stepped back and let her enter first.

'Oh, it's so big.'

'I like space.'

Colleen wandered into the apartment, gazing around at everything opened mouthed.

'Look at that view, will you? You can see the Thames. The lights reflected on the water. Oh, it would make a beautiful painting.'

'Are you an artist?'

'Well, not really. I do draw a bit.'

'Right.'

'Can I use your bathroom? I need to get changed.'

'Of course. Make yourself comfortable and I'll make us a coffee.'

'Okay. Where's the bathroom?'

Adam showed her, thinking she was cheering up a bit now. Maybe it had all been an act. Being locked in the box was genuine enough, but her reaction to it had been a bit over the top.

As he made the coffees he wondered about her. She was an extremely attractive woman and he wanted to take her to bed. Would she be insulted if he offered her money? Only one way to find out.

Colleen came out of the bathroom, wearing jeans and a sweatshirt. She'd washed the make-up off and looked younger, wholesome, and sweet. He wanted to kiss her.

'Are you hungry?'

'Starving. I couldn't eat before I was so nervous.'

'I'm not much of a cook but I make a mean cheese and tomato toastie.'

'That sounds wonderful. I'll just go and look at the view while you're making it.'

Adam set to work while Colleen went onto the balcony. He wondered if she'd gone out there for a smoke as he didn't allow smoking in his apartment. He peeked at her, but she was leaning on the security rail, gazing out at the vista spread before her. It was quite a view. Adam had grown used to it, so he took it for granted. But he could still remember the day he moved in and also stared wide-eyed at the luxury the apartment offered.

When the toasties were ready, he took them out to the balcony, and they sat on the wicker chairs eating them and gazing at the lights of London.

Colleen must have been hungry as she finished her toastie well before he finished his.

'Would you like another one?' he asked.

'Oh, no thanks, I really should be getting back. My sister isn't well, and I need to be there for her.'

'Your sister?' Was this another story or did she genuinely have a sick sister?

'Yes. I'm staying with her for a while.'

'How long have you lived in London?' Adam was intrigued by Colleen. She seemed quite innocent and was obviously not a stripper. What was she hiding?

'Not long. But my sister has been here for a year now.'

'You got a stripping job straight away?'

'Yes.'

Her story didn't quite add up, and there were obviously things she wasn't telling him. That wasn't all. Adam was reluctant to let her go. She was an attractive woman, and he hadn't had sex for a while. He wanted to take her to bed and discover if that unblemished peaches and cream skin was as soft as it looked.

'Would you like a drink before you go?'

'No, thank you, I don't drink much. Just occasionally.'

Colleen was an enigma. Surely there were more appropriate jobs she could have done to supplement her income. If she was a secretary she could have worked from home, typing manuscripts. Or done an evening job. He knew the legal profession employed secretaries in the evening to keep up with the mountains of paperwork it generated.

'So… what's wrong with your sister?'

'She has a stomach bug.' Colleen blushed and turned her head away, looking out across the city.

'Is she a stripper too?'

'Yes, she is. Why are you asking me all these questions?'

'Because you interest me. You were scared stiff back there at the Spice Club and not just because you couldn't get out of the box. Why?'

'I don't like confined spaces, that's all. I was having a panic attack and if you hadn't helped me… well, I don't know what I would have done.'

'Strange job to take if you don't like confined spaces, being stuck in a tiny box.'

'We need the money.'

'You and your sister?'

'Yes.' Colleen's cheeks flushed, and she couldn't look at him.

'Fair enough.' It was her business anyway, nothing to do with him.

'Do you think they'll still pay me?'

'I very much doubt it seeing as you didn't actually do anything.'

'Oh God, I went through all that for nothing. I don't believe it.'

'It doesn't have to be for nothing.'

'What do you mean?'

Adam sat back and sipped his coffee. 'Spend the night with me and I'll double whatever you were going to be paid.'

'Are you joking? I was going to be paid two thousand pounds.'

'Two grand? Okay, then I'll pay you four.'

Chapter Four

Was this man out of his mind? Colleen had been so grateful to him for getting her out of an awful situation, but now he was treating her as if she was a high-class prostitute. What was this world that Nora had got involved in?

Then she thought of Nora being under the control of drug dealers, men who showed no mercy to anyone. But he was offering her four thousand pounds which meant that Nora would be able to pay them almost all she owed. It would be better if she could get the full five thousand of course, but she couldn't ask Adam for more.

She couldn't believe what she had almost agreed to do. Have sex with a complete stranger for money which meant she was no better than a prostitute. She couldn't do it. It went against everything she had always believed in. What would her mother say, or her priest? Hell and damnation would be waiting for her, there was no doubt about that.

But Nora had looked so ill. The only way she was going to recover was if she could get away from that flat and the whole drug scene. And the only way that was going to happen was if she could pay off the dealers. Four thousand pounds was a lot of money. How else could either of them get hold of that much? Who was Maggott? Where did he fit into it all? Adam was waiting for her to answer his question.

'I'm not...' Then she stopped before she put her foot in it. Adam thought she was a stripper, so it was a logical conclusion to draw that if she was willing to take her clothes off for money, then she would be willing to have sex with a stranger for money too. Or was that way of thinking an insult to strippers? She was so out of her depth she didn't know what to think anymore. All she knew was that she would be devastated to go back to Nora empty-handed after all she'd been through. And Adam was an attractive man.

'You're not what?'

'I can't stay overnight. My sister needs me.'

'Your sister? Why does she need you?'

'I'm staying with her and she's been ill like I said. I don't like to leave her on her own for too long.'

'Why don't you ring her and find out how she is? Then decide.'

'Good idea, I will.' Colleen grabbed her phone and pressed Nora's number. 'It's ringing.'

Adam nodded but said nothing. He was watching her closely.

'Nora? It's me. Listen, would you be okay if I stayed somewhere tonight and came back in the morning?'

She glanced at Adam and he raised his eyebrows in a question. Nora sounded okay. She wasn't slurring her words and said she'd be fine. Colleen wished she was on her own so she could tell her about the four thousand pounds. It would cheer her up to know that most of the debt would be paid, and she could escape the toxic hold the drug dealers had over her.

Suddenly the thought of spending the night in the hovel of a flat that Nora lived in was too much for her to bear after her experiences in that box. Her nerves were still frayed, and she relished the idea of a soft bed with clean sheets. And if there was a hunky man in the bed wanting to make love to her, all the better.

'Well?' Adam asked, looking as if he was growing impatient. 'Are you staying or not?'

'Okay,' she said quietly. How easily she had agreed to have sex with him. May God forgive her.

'I must say you don't seem very enthusiastic. I'm offering you a lot of money.'

'I know, and I'm grateful.'

'Good. Shall we go inside?'

'Yes.' What had she got herself into now? Did he like kinky sex? BDSM and all that kind of stuff? Maybe she should ask him before they made it to the bedroom.

'Adam?'

'Yes.' He leaned forward and watched her face. He was good looking with his blue eyes and brown hair brushed back in a masculine style. Colleen didn't hold with the modern fashion of men wearing ponytails, she was old school in that respect and liked men to look masculine. But at four grand for one night he could have looked like Quasimodo and she would still be sleeping with him.

'Nothing, it's okay.'

Colleen got up and went inside, Adam following her closely.

When they got to the bedroom, Colleen stood in the middle of the room and watched Adam take his clothes off.

'Aren't you going to strip? I don't expect a performance but it'll be easier to have sex if you're naked.'

'Yes, sorry.' She turned her back and took off her sweatshirt, bra, jeans, and knickers. When she turned back, Adam was in bed, leaning back on a mountain of pillows watching her.

'Is something wrong, Colleen?'

'Um, no… not exactly. I was just wondering what kind of thing do you like?'

'In what way?'

'Well, I'm not terribly experienced and I don't want to disappoint you.' Perhaps he'd refuse to pay her if he wasn't satisfied.

Adam got out of bed and padded towards her. He grabbed the clothes she was still holding and threw them on a chair, then he cupped her face and kissed her.

Surprisingly, he kept his mouth closed and just their lips touched until she opened to him and he kissed her deeply, their tongues meeting and moving away. It was slow, deliciously tender and Colleen felt the wetness start.

Few men had been able to turn her on sufficiently that she became wet enough to enjoy sex. It usually felt uncomfortable at first and by the time she was in a physical state to enjoy it, the man had finished and had turned his back on her leaving her unsatisfied and frustrated.

By men she meant Harold, her only long-term boyfriend. They had been together three years and in all that time, she had never had an orgasm with him.

But Adam had brought her to a state of arousal just by kissing her.

'That's the kind of thing I like,' said Adam kissing her face, her neck and then her breasts. Soft butterfly kisses that woke up every erogenous zone she possessed.

He had an arm around her waist and was holding her up which was fortunate as her legs felt too weak to do the job. He continued kissing her, soft little pecks of kisses, with occasionally a lick.

'Don't worry,' he murmured against her neck, 'I won't give you a hickey. I don't want to mark your beautiful skin.'

Colleen nodded, not understanding the comment. She vaguely remembered girls from high school trying to cover up bruises on their necks then proudly showing them off to their friends as a mark of having had the sexual attentions of a boy. Colleen had never been one of the cool kids and had been ignorant of the things that went on behind the bike sheds.

Adam swept her up into his arms and carried her to the bed. He laid her down gently, then moved over her and continued his kissing spree down her body, while his hands caressed and stroked her sides, stomach, and breasts.

She started to panic as he reached lower and spread her legs as far as he could. No man had ever touched her there, Harold claiming it wasn't something he would feel comfortable doing. Although he had been perfectly happy for her to give him blow jobs on a regular basis.

'Bend your knees,' Adam instructed, and she did, feeling exposed and vulnerable, open to him in a way she had never been before with any man. 'Wider,' he said.

She closed her eyes and waited for Adam's next move. Then she felt his tongue on the most private part of her body; his face was between her legs and his mouth, lips and tongue performed miracles on her quivering flesh and she cried out and tangled her fingers in his hair. She didn't know if she wanted to pull him away or push his head closer. She writhed on the bed and wriggled as a feeling started in the centre of her being, a feeling she had only had once when, as a frustrated teenager, she had played with herself in the bath and brought herself to the only orgasm she had ever experienced. As a good Catholic girl, she had feared hell and damnation too much to repeat the performance.

But that was nothing compared to the feelings that soared through her body now. She felt as if she was flying higher, trying to reach a place that was so high, she'd die if she didn't get there. It was building inside her, and there was nothing she could do to stop it.

Then, with a final stroke of Adam's tongue, she was there. An explosion inside her caused shock waves to flow through her and she cried out in ecstasy and rode the tide of the orgasm, her head thrown back and her hips pumping.

When she eventually came back to earth, she opened her eyes to see Adam sitting between her still opened wide legs, his erection on proud display, watching her.

'Good?' he asked.

'That was wonderful.' Now she knew what all the fuss was about. This was how sex should be and she wanted more. 'Would you like me to return the compliment,' she asked gazing at his erect penis. He was big, far bigger than Harold, but she felt brave, able to tackle anything.

'No, I want to be inside you.' Adam got off the bed and opened the drawer of the bedside cabinet. He removed a box and took a condom out. 'Would you like to put it on?'

'I've never done that before,' said Colleen, straightening her legs and sitting up.

'First time for everything.'

This was a night of first times. First time she'd pretended to be a stripper—and the last—first orgasm, first time she'd had sex for money, and now the first time she would put a condom on a man. What a night.

Colleen opened the foil packet as Adam stood next to

the bed, his cock standing to attention like an obedient soldier. She sheathed him then leaned back, admiring her work with her head on one side.

'Are you sure you've never done that before?'

'Yes, quite sure.'

'You must be a natural.'

Either Adam was impressed with her or he didn't believe her. Perhaps he still thought she was a stripper and a prostitute.

Adam got back on the bed and Colleen opened her legs again. If the orgasm he had given her was evidence of his expertise, then she was in for a good time. She guided him into her body and moaned with delight as he filled her.

'You're tight,' said Adam.

'You're not hurting me if that's what you're worried about.'

She was wet enough that there was only pleasure as he started to thrust into her. There was no pain at all, no discomfort or dryness to sour the experience. Colleen sank into the joy of feeling him inside her. She clenched her muscles and he groaned softly.

'That's good.' So she did it again.

Soon, Colleen could feel the wave building again. Only this time it was better as she was moving in time with Adam. Thrusting her hips up to meet him as he pushed into her. Every time he seemed to go in deeper and she put her legs around his waist and urged him on.

It'd be wonderful if she could come at the same time he did. She'd read about couples who climaxed simultaneously, and she envied them that. But she sensed Adam was being a gentleman and waiting for her to come first, so she gave in to the incredible sensations that were building steadily and urged him to go faster.

In the end, there were only seconds in it. Colleen came first and Adam followed, collapsing on top of her and lying still before pulling carefully out of her. Her heart was beating in a joyous rhythm and she realised she was panting.

'Oh, that was… wonderful.' Such an inadequate word to describe what had just happened between them. Two orgasms in one night. Colleen had finally entered the realm of adulthood.

'I'm glad you enjoyed it.'

'Didn't you?'

'I did. Very much.'

Adam got up and went to the bathroom to dispose of the condom. She heard the water running and then he returned.

So, what now? If they'd been a couple, they would fall asleep in each other's arms. Unless she'd had sex with Harold as he didn't like cuddling.

In this situation, when Adam was paying her an extortionate amount of money for the whole night in her company, he would want more sex. Well, that was okay with her. As soon as he'd recovered, they'd go again.

But Adam was yawning and had got back into bed. She was tired too. It had been an emotionally draining day. She'd take her cue from him.

Adam put his arm around her, and she cuddled up to him. Within minutes she was asleep.

———

Adam had sex with women, lots of them, but he wasn't in the habit of sleeping with them and he never did what he and Colleen were doing. He lay on his back, she lay on her side with her head on his chest. His arm was around her shoulders and her arm was lying across his chest. One of her long legs was across his legs, pinning him to the bed.

And it felt amazing.

The sex had been good, and he wanted more. As soon as he felt rested, he would wake her up and they'd have more sex. This time they'd try different positions. Doggy style was one of his favourites. He also liked the woman on top so he could play with her nipples as she rode him.

Colleen was an enigma. Was she a stripper or wasn't she? Who cared? He certainly didn't, not anymore. When he'd made the offer of four grand for the whole night, he thought she'd refuse on the grounds that she wasn't a prostitute. But she'd accepted, which proved to him that she'd done this kind of thing before. Okay, it was a lot of money and Colleen did say she wasn't experienced, but few women who weren't in the profession would accept money for sex. No matter how desperate they were.

'Colleen?'

'Um…'

'Wake up.'

He kissed her forehead and slipped his arm out from beneath her shoulders, waking her up.

'Is it morning?'

'Take a look.'

Colleen sat up and looked across to the floor to ceiling window and the view of London. Away to the east, the sky was just beginning to lighten as if the sun was slowly pushing the darkness away. Dark indigo blue was changing to light blue with orange streaks.

Adam never tired of watching the sun rise over London. He was a morning person and, even when he wasn't working, would be out of bed at first light.

But he had other business to attend to at that moment and kissed Colleen on the lips.

'I haven't cleaned my teeth,' she said turning her face away.

'Neither have I,' he said kissing her again.

Adam took a condom out of the box and handed it to Colleen, who took it with a smile and rolled it onto his erection. Then he lay back and she accepted the invitation by climbing on top of him and carefully lowering herself down onto him. She must be still wet and ready as he slid into her easily and she started to move up and down. This time he would let the lady do the work and just lie there and enjoy it.

Except that his arousal was growing fast, and he wanted to up the ante. He took hold of Colleen's waist and moved her up and down faster, as if she were as light as a feather. She met his thrusting and came first with him following swiftly behind.

'Wow,' Colleen said, 'I didn't realise I was as turned on as that.'

'Me neither. We're good together.' Now why had he said that? He didn't want to give the lady ideas. He wasn't in the market for a relationship and wouldn't choose a stripper in any case. He'd never paid for sex in his life and had always been scornful of men who did. But after spending a night with Colleen, he could see the attraction.

'I'll jump in the shower, then I'll make us some breakfast, okay?'

'Okay.' Colleen lay on the bed, her blonde hair tousled, her face relaxed and her body a tangle of arms and legs. She was beautiful in a fragile kind of way. She was also easy to be with. Too easy. She could become a habit and he couldn't let that happen. There was too much at stake.

Chapter Five

They were quiet on the way back to Colleen's home. It was still quite early, and few people were around. The car moved smoothly through the London streets. Adam sat and gazed out of the window, as did Colleen. A barrier had sprung up between them from nowhere and they seemed like strangers, which was curious considering what they had spent the night doing.

Before leaving his apartment, Adam had taken four thousand pounds out of his safe and put it in an envelope. Before sealing the envelope, he had offered it to Colleen in case she wanted to count the money.

'Oh no, it's fine, I trust you.'

She had seemed almost embarrassed to take the cash but didn't refuse it all the same. Now in the cold light of day with both of them fully dressed they had nothing to say to each other. Naked they were almost equal; two people enjoying each other's bodies. Now, he was the rich, successful CEO and she was—what? A secretary, stripper, prostitute, all three?

As they got nearer to the address Colleen had given his driver, the streets grew more dismal, more littered and there were signs of poverty and neglect everywhere. There were blocks of high-rise flats, some houses were boarded up and others looked empty with smashed windows. Colleen grew more withdrawn and could hardly look at him.

'You don't have to take me all the way there. Just drop me at the corner.'

'We're taking you home.' Adam didn't look at her. He wanted to see for himself exactly the kind of place Colleen lived in.

'Just pull up here,' she said. 'Right, I'm fine from here. Thanks for the lift.'

Adam put his hand on her wrist to stop her opening the door while gazing up at a block of flats. There was a group of teenagers hanging about around the front door, some on bikes, all of them wearing hoodies in black or navy. They stared at the car and Adam felt a chill run up his spine.

'Right. I'm going to see you inside. Davis? Lock the doors behind us and if that lot come any closer, drive away, okay.' He wasn't going to have his Mercedes messed with by anyone.

'Very good, sir,' said Davis.

'Come on.'

Colleen scrambled out and Adam followed her. He took her hand, and she gave it a quick squeeze.

They walked towards the front door, Adam maintaining eye contact with the biggest boy who looked to be the leader of the gang. He was the oldest and had the best bike. Colleen kept her gaze down on the ground.

When they got nearer to the front door, two of the boys moved out of the way so they could get through. The biggest one, however, stood his ground, directly in front of the door. They had two choices: either squeeze past him which would almost surely mean touching him or asking him politely to get out of the fucking way. Adam favoured the second.

'Excuse me.' Adam didn't add the "please" as he didn't want to appear weak. These street kids had their own code of behaviour which didn't include social niceties.

After what felt like hours, the boy rode his bike slowly to the side and Adam breathed a quiet sigh of relief.

'Thank you,' he said with a blank expression on his face. The boy didn't answer.

'It's upstairs and the lift doesn't work,' said Colleen, as they hurried inside.

'Right. Let's go then.'

Adam kept hold of Colleen's hand and had no intention of letting go of it until she was safely inside her flat. But when he saw the flat, he was tempted to keep hold of her hand and take her back to his apartment.

The first thing that struck Adam was the fact that Colleen just pushed the door of the flat and it opened. An unlocked door in a place like this? Really? The second thing was the stench. As soon as they stepped inside he had to fight to prevent himself from gagging.

'Nora?' Colleen went straight to a bedroom and Adam stopped in the middle of the living room, reluctant to touch anything. He gazed around and shuddered. It was bad. Much worse than he had imagined. Filthy, with unidentifiable stains on the wooden floor, the upholstery and the single couch and armchair. There were no cushions, no small tables, or rugs. No curtains at the windows. The place was probably rat infested.

'Adam!' Colleen's voice penetrated his disgusted brain

and tore his thoughts away from the horror that he was looking at.

He hurried into the bedroom and saw a young woman in the bed. She was unconscious and there was a needle and a tourniquet on the floor. The sheets on the bed were grey and Adam dreaded to think how long ago they'd been washed. If ever.

'I'll phone an ambulance. Is she breathing?'

'Yes,' Colleen sobbed.

'Has she got a pulse?'

Colleen picked up her arm and tried to find Nora's pulse, but she was looking in the wrong place. 'I can't find her pulse!'

Adam, still on the phone, put two fingers to her neck to check for her carotid pulse.

'Hello, ambulance, please. Yes, she's breathing, and she's got a pulse but she's unconscious. Drugs. Not sure what she's taken but there's a needle. Yes, of course.'

He ended the call and turned to Colleen. 'The ambulance is on the way. They've asked us to keep any of the drug paraphernalia around to identify what she's taken.'

'Oh, Adam, thank you. I don't know what to do. What if she dies?'

'Depends what she's taken.' Adam realised how callous that sounded but he had little sympathy for addicts. Surely everyone had a choice on how to live their lives? No one was forced to take drugs. But then, looking around this hovel, he wondered at how a person sank so low that they could end up here.

Colleen felt deep and bitter shame. She had been having a good time with Adam, being paid a ridiculous amount of money to enjoy herself while her poor little sister was overdosing in a dirty, dank, disgusting... she should never have left her alone. All because she preferred clean sheets to sleep in.

Adam was appalled at the flat. He hadn't said anything but didn't need to. It was written all over his face. And who could blame him? This place was the pits. But now they had four thousand pounds to pay the dealers, Nora could turn her life around. She'd get a job and look for somewhere else for them to live. Get Nora away from Maggot and all the other drug addicts that were such a bad influence.

The sound of the ambulance siren interrupted her thoughts. No doubt Adam would go now that he had done his good deed. Would she ever see him again? Probably not.

'Thank you, Adam, for everything you've done for us.'

Adam shook his head as if she didn't need to thank him. 'You stay here with your sister, I'll tell the paramedics where we are.'

'Okay.' Colleen held Nora's hand and stroked her hair back from her face. She was pale and her eyelids had a blue tinge, as did her lips.

Then two paramedics, a man, and a woman, came into the room carrying their equipment and greeting her before moving over to Nora. Colleen stepped back and let them do their job, feeling overwhelming gratitude that they were there and neither had responded negatively to the environment they found themselves in. They were there for one reason and that was to treat Nora and save her life.

As Colleen watched them work, Adam put his arm around her and hugged her to him. She put her head on his chest, relishing the strength of the man, grateful for his presence and his calm demeanour.

'I just want her to be okay,' she whispered.

'She's in good hands,' said Adam.

Once the paramedics had intubated her and were satisfied she was fit to travel to the hospital, they put her on a stretcher and carried her carefully out of the flat and down to the ambulance.

'I'll see you at the hospital,' said Adam as he headed towards his car which was still parked in the same place, with Davis, Adam's driver, waiting patiently in the driver's seat.

'Oh, you don't have to come, Adam, you've done enough. I'm so grateful for everything you've done but I can manage from here.'

'I don't think you should be alone at a time like this. I'll see you there and don't forget to give them the needle and the other stuff.'

'No, I won't. Okay.' Colleen watched him striding back to his car and she hurried into the ambulance to be with Nora.

They sat together on plastic chairs at the side of Nora's bed in the A&E department. The medics had worked swiftly and efficiently to assess her sister and had brought her back from the dangerous place she had been slipping towards.

Nora had overdosed on heroin and judging by the track marks in her arms it wasn't the first time she had taken it. Colleen was still shaking with the implications of it. It was one thing smoking weed, lots of people did it and didn't get addicted, but quite another abusing heroin.

'They asked me if I thought she'd done it on purpose. I didn't know what to say.' Colleen kept her voice low. She'd read that unconscious people could sometimes hear conversations going on around them. She wasn't sure if that would be true in Nora's case as she'd been sedated, but she wasn't taking any chances.

'Has she ever tried anything like this before?' asked Adam who had refused to leave her side on the few occasions she had suggested he go home. She was so grateful for his company, she was glad he was being so stubborn.

'Never. Well, to my knowledge. Not before she came to live in London anyway.'

'Tell me the truth, Colleen, what's the real story with you and your sister?'

'Most of what I told you *is* the truth. Okay, I'll start at the beginning. When my father died of a heart attack last year, we all fell apart in different ways. Nora was his favourite daughter which, I didn't mind as I was and probably still am our mother's favourite. It sounds bad doesn't it to say that your parents have favourite children, but I think it's more prevalent than people think.'

'Yes, you're probably right. My younger sister, Vivien, was always the favourite, but when my father died of cancer ten years ago, I took over as head of the family, so it didn't seem to matter then.'

'How old were you?'

'Twenty-two. Vivien was eighteen. Anyway, go on with your story.'

'When Dad died, Nora and Mum argued the whole time. She was twenty-four so she wasn't a child, but she had been happy when the family had all been together. Then, to make it worse, Auntie May kept coming around; two or three times a week, she'd turn up on the doorstep. She's

Mum's sister and never married so doesn't have a family of her own.'

'And Nora doesn't get on with her,' Adam whispered.

'No one gets on with her, not even Mum. She's lazy. When I left, she was plonked in front of daytime TV, eating her body weight in crisps, and ordering Mum around. My poor mother was run ragged, doing her cooking, cleaning, and washing. She said she had come to help, but never lifted a finger once.'

'Was that why you left?'

Colleen sighed. 'Yes, do you think I'm awful? I was getting too close to telling Auntie May to eff off and Mum would have been horrified. So I decided to come and see my sister instead and have some fun in London.'

'And you ended up stripping at a stag night.'

'Or not stripping.'

'I bet you wish you'd stayed at home. Where is home by the way?'

'Manchester, and no I don't wish I'd stayed at home because then I wouldn't have known about poor Nora and her addiction and...'

'And?'

'I was going to say I wouldn't have met you. I don't know what I would have done without you, Adam. I don't know how to thank you.'

'You don't need to. I'm glad I could help. What are your plans now, apart from getting help for Nora?'

Colleen was tempted to tell Adam about the drug dealers and the debt, but pride kept her quiet. Adam had done a lot already, she didn't want him to think she was asking for more money.

'I need to get a job. I can't go back to that flat, and neither should Nora. The doctor who I spoke to said he was going to refer her to the Drug and Alcohol Liaison Team. Maybe they can get her into rehab.'

'So you'll be sticking around for a bit?'

'Yes, at least until Nora's better.'

'Right. Then maybe I can help you.'

'You've done enough already.' Colleen would never be able to thank Adam for his kindness.

'You need a job, I need a secretary.'

'Really? You're not making this up, are you? Being kind?'

'Not at all. My personal assistant, Doris, who's been with me right from the beginning, is overworked and it will only get worse if my plans to expand into Asia take off.'

'What are you CEO of?' Colleen had never even asked Adam what he did. She'd just assumed he was rich, probably a millionaire if his penthouse apartment was anything to go by.

'It's my father-in-law's business, Meredith Motors. We specialise in classic and vintage cars. China especially is starting to show interest in collectable cars. It won't be long before the demand increases, and I want our company to be one of the frontrunners.'

His father-in-law? So, he was married. Of course he was. A man like Adam wouldn't stay single for long. 'You like your job, obviously.'

'I love my job, Colleen, and I need a junior secretary to learn the ropes and take some of the pressure off Doris.'

'That's a very kind offer.' One she should turn down. She had slept with him for money. A considerable amount of money. How could she now do a reverse turn and be his secretary, albeit a junior one? It would never work. But she liked Adam, a lot, and the prospect of having a respectable job that she would enjoy and get paid a good salary for with the chance to learn about the classic car trade was tempting.

'What's worrying you?' Adam was watching her face.

'Well…'

'Whatever happened between us yesterday is water under the bridge. Nobody at work knows you and I'll make Jeremy swear not to disclose anything about the stag night.'

'What about his fiancée?' Colleen didn't imagine that lady would keep quiet without an incentive.

'Don't worry, she won't say anything.'

'Well, if you're sure. Thanks, I'll accept your kind offer.'

'Good. You won't regret it, I promise.'

Chapter Six

When Nora was settled onto a ward—they were keeping her in for a day or two for observation and a psychiatric assessment and she was still sedated—Colleen took the opportunity to go home for a few hours. Adam had already left with the promise to keep in touch about the job.

Colleen took a taxi as she could afford one now and called in to an estate agents to ask about the possibility of a two-bedroomed flat that they could rent. She knew exactly the kind of thing they needed. Somewhere near to the centre of London, with easy access to the tube station. She had no idea where Meredith Motors was situated but didn't want to live too far away. It had to be somewhere central she imagined. She should have Googled it beforehand, but she'd been in such a hurry to find them somewhere to live that she forgot. The apartment needed to be bright and clean, with plenty of space and, preferably fully furnished.

An hour later, she left the estate agents, her spirits quashed by the reality of London living. Colleen had naively thought that they'd be able to walk into the perfect apartment. But even the more moderate flats and apartments cost an arm and a leg in rent. And that wasn't including the deposit. Furnished flats were a lot more expensive of course.

Even if Adam wanted her to start work immediately, she wouldn't be paid until the end of the month. And asking for an advance seemed cheeky after everything Adam had done for them. And it probably wouldn't be enough to pay the rest of the debt to the drug dealers. And then they had to live; food, clothes, tube fares, the list would be endless.

Colleen gave herself a telling off and after pulling up her big girl pants, stopped off at a supermarket to buy a mop and bucket, scrubbing brushes, detergent, bleach, Marigolds, and other cleaning equipment. She wished they had a steam cleaner and wondered if she could afford to rent one. If they had to stay in the flat, they certainly didn't have to put up with the disgusting state it was in. She would clean it, even if it took several attempts.

Colleen was determined to improve the condition of the flat for when Nora was discharged. Living in squalor wouldn't be conducive to good mental health, and Nora was obviously suffering from clinical depression and needed to be surrounded by beauty, and cleanliness.

She started in the kitchen as that was the most important room in her opinion. Preparing food in the filth and muck would mean instant salmonella and they had to eat.

Three hours later, Colleen was exhausted and near to tears. The kitchen looked marginally cleaner but still nowhere near clean enough. The test was her mum. If Deirdre O'Shea would be willing to cook in it, then it was good enough for her. The problem was her mum would throw her hands up in horror and run screaming from the place.

'What the hell are you doing?'

A familiar voice behind her made her jump. 'Adam. What are you doing here?'

'I've come to save you from yourself, obviously. Why are you cleaning this dump?'

Colleen struggled to her feet, realising what a sight she must look to him. He was dressed casually in smart trousers and an open-necked shirt. She was wearing jog pants with holes and now with an added layer of muck. Her hair was tied haphazardly on the top of her head and she was sweating from her exertions.

'The thing is, I went to an estate agents to ask about flats but there was nothing we could afford, so I decided that I'd make this place habitable, at least as a temporary measure.'

'And how long have you been scrubbing that small patch of the floor?'

'About three hours.'

'Right.'

They looked at each other and then burst out laughing. Colleen, verging on hysteria, laughed until tears ran down her face. Adam's shoulders were shaking, and his eyes were tightly shut.

When the mirth had died down, Adam shook his head. 'What am I going to do with you?'

He said it quietly and with affection. At least Colleen thought it was affection. Unless it was sheer exasperation. But he was right. It was like arranging the deckchairs on the Titanic or whatever that expression was. It would take more than her humble efforts to clean this place.

'I don't know what to do,' she said, wishing she didn't sound so defeated.

'I blame myself for this and I apologise for not mentioning the apartment sooner.'

'What apartment would that be?' Colleen felt drained suddenly as if she was constantly swimming against the tide.

'The apartment that goes with the job.'

'What… my job? The junior secretary job?'

'That's the one.'

'Oh no, Adam, that's ridiculous. You're being kind again, I can't accept it and probably couldn't afford it either.'

'I'm afraid it's in the contract which means if you accept the job, then you have to accept the apartment. But, of course, if you've changed your mind about working for me…'

'No! Of course I haven't. You're a lifesaver, Adam, with that job. I can't tell you how grateful I am.'

Colleen wished she could show him how grateful she was. The sex with Adam had been amazing and she wanted it again. But once she was working for him that couldn't happen, could it?

'Then we'd better go and see this apartment then. Gather your things together, and Nora's, and you can have a quick shower and change in my apartment before I show you the place. Don't leave anything behind now as you won't be coming back here.'

Colleen didn't have to be told twice. She gathered her things together which didn't take long as everything she owned was still in her suitcase. She hadn't taken anything out to hang up or put in drawers as there were no drawers or wardrobes in this place. It was the same with Nora. She collected her clothes and a few meagre possessions, feeling sad that Nora had so little to show for the time she'd been in London.

Then, she turned her back on the hovel and tried to imagine the new apartment. It would be glorious if it had been chosen by Adam. She couldn't believe how generous he was being and hurried out without a backward glance.

———

Colleen was in the shower and Adam was horny. He couldn't get the night they'd spent together out of his mind and wanted her again. He undressed and put on a bathrobe, slipping the box of condoms into the pocket. He didn't want to assume she'd be desperate to have sex with him, especially if she only did it for the money, but his memory of the night before was that she'd enjoyed it as much as he did. Nothing ventured…

Colleen must have the water too hot as the place was full of steam. He could hear her singing softly to herself as he opened the shower door.

'May I join you?'

'Adam.' Colleen looked pleased to see him and he stepped inside, then took her in his arms and kissed her. The water was hot, so he turned it down a notch.

'You'll burn yourself having it that hot.'

'I love it hot,' she murmured as she ran her hands over his chest, stomach and then around to grasp his buttocks grinding herself into his erection.

Adam ran his hands over her wet hair, sweeping it back so her neck was exposed. He loved her neck. It was long and elegant and he kissed it, feeling her pulse beating fast. Then he ran his hands down her back and she lifted one leg and hooked it around his legs. He reached down and stroked her pussy, parting her gently and pushing a finger inside her. She was wet, open, and ready for him.

'Shall we?' Adam asked.

'Yes, please,' Colleen said softly.

He reached behind him, to where he'd left the condoms and took one out of the box, opening the foil packet, then sheathing himself in a smooth practised move. Then lifting Colleen up so she could keep one leg around his hip and securing her against the wall of the shower, he slid into her and started thrusting rhythmically, going in deeper with each thrust.

'Oh that's amazing,' she said. Colleen's eyes were closed, and she had a smile playing at the corners of her mouth.

He was in no hurry. Instead, he stayed in the moment, concentrating on the heat of the water that flowed over them and pooled around them. This must be what having sex under a waterfall feels like. He'd never done that. Maybe he'd put it on his bucket list.

Colleen also seemed more relaxed this time. She moaned softly with each thrust and clung to him, her arms around his neck and one leg still hooked around one of his.

But their arousal was spiking. Colleen groaned more loudly, and Adam felt that familiar clenching that told him he was reaching the point of no return. He thrust faster and deeper, and Colleen moved with him.

'Oh, yes, that's it…'

He couldn't speak and he couldn't have stopped even if his life depended on it. He wanted to make it good for her and held back until Colleen spasmed and cried out, taking him with her and they climaxed together.

'Oh, fuck that was good,' he said, and Colleen moaned softly and put her head on his chest, as he carefully pulled out of her.

He held her for a few minutes, wanting to dispose of the condom safely but not wanting to break contact with her. She lifted her head and searched his face. What was she looking for?

'Adam?'

'Yes, Colleen.'

'We'll have to stop this when I start working for you, won't we?'

Ah, so that was what was worrying her. Maybe he should tell her that he couldn't stop now even if he wanted to, which he certainly didn't. Colleen was special. He'd never enjoyed sex with a woman as much as he did with this one. She was such a mixture of naivety and sexiness. She had no idea of her allure. Good. He didn't want other men to have her, he wanted her all for himself.

'No. We'll have to be discreet about meeting and professional at all times in the office, but what we do in private is nobody's business but ours.'

'You're married aren't you?'

'We're estranged but as I'm CEO of her father's business, we have to be seen together. Keep up appearances for the sake of the company and the Meredith family name.'

'And you're okay about that?'

'If it means I continue to be CEO of Meredith Motors, then, yes, I'm okay with it.'

'But what about—'

'Right, no more questions. Get dressed and we'll get you moved into your new apartment.'

'OMG, this is wonderful!' Colleen looked around the apartment in amazement. She'd expected it to be nice, but she was thinking of a couple of steps up from the hovel. This was as far removed from Nora's flat as anyone could get. It was luxurious.

There were wooden floors throughout, possibly laminate, but they shone as if they'd been polished. The ceilings and walls were white, the floor contained brightly coloured rugs, and there were cushions on the sofas. The fitted kitchen was gleaming white and chrome, with a massive built-in fridge freezer and a gas cooker that her mother would be proud to prepare family meals on.

There was a small dining room with a table and four chairs and then two bedrooms. One was a double with a bed that looked incredibly comfortable. Colleen wondered if she could entice Adam to try it out with her. The other, smaller bedroom also contained a double bed. Colleen was definitely claiming the larger room for herself.

But the two things that impressed Colleen the most were the size of the apartment, which was huge, and how sparkling clean everything was. You could practically eat your meals off the floor. It was so different to the place she had just left that it took her breath away.

'So… what do you think? Will it do?' Adam had followed her around as she looked the place over, obviously wanting her to like it. How could she not?

'I love it,' she said throwing her arms around Adam's neck and hugging him. 'Have we got time to christen the bed?'

He laughed. 'Are you serious?'

'Never been more serious.'

'You're insatiable,' Adam said as he lifted her up and carried her to the bedroom, dropping her onto the double bed and proceeding to undress her.

Colleen lay still, letting him do it, her need for him increasing as her clothes came off. She loved being naked with Adam, skin to skin, their bodies melding together with the warmth of them, holding, touching, caressing and…

In no time she was naked, and Adam was pulling his

shirt off and fumbling with the button on his trousers in his haste to be with her in the bed.

She held her arms out to him and he covered her body with his own, his erection already stiff and magnificent. They kissed and Adam squeezed one breast gently, then took her nipple into his mouth and sucked on it, while stroking her stomach, then tweaking the other nipple which sent an electric current through her and she writhed on the bed.

Adam moved down to her pussy and spread her legs, licking, and sucking her until she felt she was on the edge of her climax. She had never experienced such a spontaneous feeling of lust in her life. All Adam had to do was touch her, with his fingers, or mouth and she exploded like a Roman candle. No man had ever made her feel like this. She was being carried on a slipstream of sensations that spun her out of control and all she could do was go with it.

When she came, she cried out and revelled in the feeling of her whole body being given pleasure in a way she had never thought possible. To think she had spent years with Harold and never realised what she had been missing. Now, with Adam, she was making up for lost time and intended to enjoy every minute they had together.

'I want you inside me,' she said as he moved off the bed.

'No can do, I'm afraid, no condoms.'

'Right,' said Colleen, 'come here to me.' He came closer as she sat on the edge of the bed and she took him in her mouth, one hand holding his balls, then ran her tongue up and down his shaft, swirled it around the head, and then licked and moved her lips up and down gently until Adam moaned and grasped her hair, holding her head in place. Colleen didn't mind this as Harold used to do it when she gave him a blow job, but Harold had been rough and demanding, whereas Adam was gentle, almost massaging her scalp in time to the rhythm of her stroking and the attentions of her lips and tongue.

Everything about Adam turned her on. The way he made love to her—she didn't call it having sex anymore—it had become more than that for her. She loved his smile, the way his eyes lit up when he was laughing, and his hands on her body. And his cock was simply beautiful.

Adam was getting closer to his climax as he had started to thrust his hips in time to her "sucking". She slowed things down so he could enjoy it more and he moaned deep in his throat, so she took her mouth away.

'Are you enjoying it, Adam?'

'Yes, oh God, yes.'

'Do you want it faster, harder?'

'Yes, yes…'

'Anything you want let me know.'

'Your mouth… ahhh.'

Colleen took his cock in her mouth again and resumed the teasing and licking that was reducing him to a mass of need before her. She was loving it, but wanted Adam to enjoy it too, so she grasped the base of his shaft and used both hands and mouth to bring him off.

Adam collapsed with the strength of his orgasm and knelt as she swallowed and lay back to appreciate her efforts. It was clear that Adam had experienced a satisfactory orgasm. Hopefully, it lived up to the ones other women gave him, for she was under no illusions that he had other women. His wife for one. Did they still have sex? Probably. Was it as good as the sex they had enjoyed? Definitely not.

'That was amazing. Where did you learn your technique?' Adam sat next to her on the edge of the bed.

'Have I never told you about Harold, my long-term boyfriend?'

'No, I don't believe you have. Was he the love of your life?'

'No, Adam, he was a selfish bastard who I can't believe I wasted three years of my life on. You may not believe this, but the first orgasm I ever had with a man was with you.'

'You're kidding me? You spent three years with a man who never gave you an orgasm?'

'Yes. He did give me crabs once but don't worry that was in the early days and I'm clean now.'

Adam chuckled. 'I know you are, I would have noticed if not.'

'Of course you would.' Colleen lay back on the bed, wishing she could stay like this, in bed with Adam, for the rest of the day.

'Colleen, I need to go. Things to do. You'll be okay here. You do like the place, don't you.'

'I love it. I can't thank you enough. I need to get to the hospital to see Nora and tell her the good news. You'll come and see me again before she's discharged?'

'Of course. And are you okay to start work on Monday?'

'Yes, I'm looking forward to it.'

'Great. Right. Better be making tracks.'

Adam seemed reluctant to leave her and she didn't want him to go. They'd have to meet in secret, stolen moments and snatched hours together, but that was better than nothing. Adam was beginning to be a habit.

Colleen had never had an affair that she'd had to keep to herself. To be more accurate, she'd never had an affair at all. It was in turn scary and exciting. But for Adam, she'd put up with anything.

Chapter Seven

Adam got a shock when he arrived back at his penthouse apartment. He'd been thinking of the blow job he'd just had and to find Rosamund sitting at the breakfast bar drinking coffee, was quite disconcerting. Note to self; ask his estranged wife to give him back the key. Especially now that he and Colleen were seeing each other, the last thing he wanted was his ex intruding when they were having sex. Although technically incorrect, he preferred to think of Rosamund as his ex.

'Ah, so the wanderer returns. Where the hell have you been? I've tried to contact you umpteen times since that ridiculous stag night. Have you seen Jeremy since? Teddy is livid as you can imagine. Well, don't you have anything to say to me?'

Chance would be a fine thing. 'Which comment would you like me to address first?'

'The first one, of course.'

'Okay. Well, where I've been is none of your business. I don't have to answer to you, Rosamund.'

She glared at him as he made himself a coffee. He knew he should humour her as he had done since their marriage broke down. It made life easier as they kept up the pretence of having a rock solid marriage in public. Hugo, his father-in-law, was a stickler for family and keeping up appearances. And, as the man had terminal cancer and wasn't going to live for much longer, it was in Adam's best interest to keep up the charade, at least until he knew for certain that he would remain CEO of Meredith Motors.

But Rosamund was Hugo's only child and there was every chance that he could sign the ownership of the company over to her. Hugo was being frustratingly tight-lipped about the whole business and stringing them both along.

'And as for your other comments; no I haven't seen Jeremy since, and Theo was gatecrashing the stag night and deserves everything she got.'

Adam leaned against the work surface and sipped his coffee. He knew what this was about, and he hadn't decided yet whether he was going to indulge his ex and give her what she wanted. It was the best way to enjoy a peaceful life, but now that he'd known the best sex he'd ever had with Colleen, he was reluctant to give in to Rosamund's need for rough sex. Because it was a need, something she couldn't help, and it could be off-putting to some men.

'What happened to that slut that Teddy said was there? Not a stitch on but wrapped up like a present in red ribbon of all things. God, I have no idea how some women can sink so low as to do that for a living. You must have seen her.'

Adam put his coffee down carefully in case he was tempted to throw the hot liquid over his silly, entitled, estranged wife, for spouting such utter crap. Colleen was a beautiful, brave young girl, trying to do the best for her sister; a victim of circumstance who had been misused by that prat Rupert.

'Adam, I'm speaking to you. Do you know what happened to her?'

'No idea. Now, I have work to do so would you mind awfully fucking off?'

'There's no need to be like that. What's got into you?'

'I'm busy running your father's business for one thing.'

Rosamund was an attractive woman and could be a beauty with a bit of effort though she was happier in jodh-purs and a riding jacket than a dress and high heels. She had shoulder length red hair that she wore loose with a middle parting and hardly ever wore make-up.

Adam had been attracted to her because she was sexy in a natural way. She was an outdoorsy type, hunted regu-larly, and had taken part in gymkhanas ever since she could walk. He'd accepted her need for rough sex and indulged it because he had loved her at the beginning of their relationship. But not being a sadistic bastard like Max, the man she had been having an affair with since before they were married, Adam had found it difficult to keep up the role play on a regular basis. He was a gentleman by nature in both senses of the word and, as time went on, found it more difficult to satisfy his wife's sexual needs.

When he had found out about Max, he used it as the perfect excuse to tell Rosamund that their marriage was over.

'I'm just going to use the facilities, then I'll go seeing as you're so eager to get rid of me.'

'Fine,' said Adam with his back to her.

Ten minutes later, Rosamund came up to him, her face

like thunder, heavy breathing and looking as if she was about to kill him.

'What the fuck is this?' She held up a bundle of red ribbon. Colleen must have put it in the bin in the bathroom. He should have thought of that. Rosamund had a habit of snooping through the apartment when she got the chance.

'I don't know, what is it?' Playing dumb wasn't going to work; it would stall things a bit, but now he'd have to perform to keep her quiet.

'It's bloody red ribbon. Like the kind that stripper was wearing. You said you didn't know what had happened to her, but she was here, wasn't she?' Rosamund held the ribbon up triumphantly.

'How do you know it's like that other ribbon? You weren't even at the stag do.' Thank God.

'How many types of red ribbon are there? Of course it's the same.'

'How many types? I don't know off the top of my head, would you like me to Google it for you?'

'Did you have sex with her?'

'None of your business.'

'You did, didn't you? I can't believe it. You slept with that slut—'

'She's not a slut, stop calling her that.'

'Did you pay her?' Adam turned away as Rosamund could always tell when he was lying. 'She's a prostitute as well as a stripper. How much did you pay her? Come on, how much?'

'More than I'd pay to sleep with you and I'm not putting up with being cross-examined any further. Isn't it time you were leaving?'

'You think you're so clever, don't you, Adam? The working-class boy who married above his station. And you've been enjoying the perks of the Meredith name ever since. Well, don't think you're getting Daddy's business because you're not. I'm his only child and he'll leave it all to me, you wait and see.'

'Your beloved father once told me that you were a useless, lazy bitch and couldn't manage a tombola never mind a multi-million-pound business. So let's see shall we?'

Adam wasn't worried about the insults being exchanged. It was foreplay as far as Rosamund was concerned. And he knew he'd have to go along with it now that she'd found that damned ribbon. If his affair with Colleen was going to be successful then he would need to be a lot more careful about what he left lying around for Rosamund to find.

'You are such an arsehole, Adam, do you know that? Everyone in my social circle despises you. They pretend for my sake but really they all think you're an ignorant, despicable upstart—'

'Then why is it that several of the women in *your* social circle have come on to me, more than once, at parties and other social occasions? There's more than one or two of them who'd love a session between the sheets with an ignorant upstart, including Lady Theodora Blakely.'

'Teddy would never look twice at you, you poor misguided fool. You're not fit to clean her shoes. Teddy is a beautiful, elegant, lady—'

'You know what I think, Rosamund. I think you fancy Theo. You are the only one who calls her Teddy. Special name from school was it? We all know she swings both ways. Well, maybe you do too.'

'You utter bastard.'

Adam didn't get the chance to reply before Rosamund threw herself on him, screaming obscenities and trying to scratch his face with her long nails. Adam had anticipated this having been through similar scenarios many times before. He grabbed her wrists, forcing her to the floor and pinning her down on the Persian rug, then lying on top of her.

She writhed under him, but just enough so he needed to use the exact amount of physical restraint that aroused her but never so much that she was marked or badly hurt. He played along with her, taunting her, and teasing until she panted with desire rather than anger, real or pretend. Rosamund quite often worked herself up into a frenzy just to initiate this kind of foreplay to the rough sex that she craved so badly. Adam went along with it just wanting it over with as soon as he could manage it.

He held her hands over her head and opened the shirt she wore carefully. He didn't want to rip it as that would just annoy her. He pinched her nipples hard making her cry out. She continued to wriggle and pant but with less conviction now the moment he slammed into her was close. He quickly removed her trousers and panties as she continued to writhe about and moan.

When he took his own trousers off, he knew she was ready for him.

Adam knew her every move, subtle changes in body language and played the game to perfection. He entered her, wishing he had a condom, but not wanting to break the mood. Another note to self: keep condoms on person at all times.

She clung to him as she orgasmed crying out his name. He came soon after and they lay together on the rug, panting. As he lay there, Adam wondered how he could bring an end to these sessions without Rosamund suspecting anything. He only wanted Colleen now and had no patience for Rosamund's fetish anymore.

'I've got some good news,' said Colleen settling herself down next to Nora's hospital bed. She had expected her to have a room to herself but here she was on the main ward, with all the comings and goings past her bed. Maybe the nurses wanted to keep an eye on her. Colleen wondered if she was on an at-risk list having tried to get rid of herself once. Maybe she should have a word with someone and find out what the thinking was.

'What?' Nora was pale. In fact, she was competing with the sheets for who was whiter. She lay still, looking sad and pathetic, and Colleen desperately wanted her chirpy, cheeky little sister back.

'It's great news, in fact. Two pieces of great news.'

'Oh for goodness sake, Colleen, what are you going on about?'

'Sorry.' Nora didn't look well and was probably not up to being cheerful. No matter, despite the threat from the drug dealers, Colleen felt cheerful enough for the both of them. 'Well, I haven't told you about that night, have I? The night I was supposed to strip and didn't, you remember.'

'No, because when you came back to the flat you found me in a heap having overdosed. Yes, I do remember.'

'Yes, of course you do, sorry. Well, I met a man. The best man who arranged the stag night, but it wasn't him who booked a stripper from your agency, it was someone else. A brute of a man. I didn't like him at all. But Adam, the nice one, well he's offered me a job as a junior secretary, a kind of assistant to his PA, and—guess what?'

Nora pulled the sheet over her head which made it seem to Colleen that she was trying to talk to a corpse.

'Colleen, you are doing my fucking head in,' Nora said from behind the sheet.

'Am I? Oh God, I'm so sorry. I'll go if you like but I just wanted to give you our new address.'

'What new address?'

'That's what I was going to tell you. Adam said that as part of the contract for the job, I have to accept the tenancy of an apartment he owns. He said it was so people would see that Meredith Motors looks after its staff. But, between you and me, I think he was just being kind. But the apartment's in Chelsea and is absolutely gorgeous. Just wait 'til you see it. I've got photos on my phone to show you. You're going to love it.'

'Have you finished?'

'Nora, will you come out from behind that sheet, I can't talk to you when you're hiding.'

Nora pulled the sheet down so only the top of her head and her eyes were showing.

'How are you feeling, Nora? I've been so worried about you.'

'Now she asks me.'

'Sorry, I just wanted to tell you the good news.'

'I'm feeling like crap if you must know and what makes you think I want to move? That's my flat and you descended on me uninvited and took over with your cups of tea and stupid advice. I never asked you to find another place.'

'I was just trying to help. Don't you want a nicer place to live?'

'How are we going to afford it?'

'I told you, it comes with the job. And that's well paid.'

'How many bedrooms?'

'Two. And a lovely lounge, dining room, kitchen—wait

'til you see the kitchen—it's all there for us. Look, check it out.'

Colleen passed her phone to Nora under the sheet and five minutes later, Nora's hand came out holding the phone. Colleen took it back and the hand disappeared.

'So—what d'you think?'

'It's okay. Are you fucking him?'

'Fucking who?'

'Your man. The one who saved you.'

Colleen squirmed. She didn't want to lie to Nora, but she also didn't want to tell her the truth. Because telling her sister would bring it all down to the level of drug dealers and prostitutes, and what she and Adam had was above all that. But Nora did need to know about the money that would pay off most of the drug debt.

'He asked me to spend the night. He gave me a lot of money.'

'Right. So now my high and mighty older sister is no better than me. She's come down to my level. Having sex for money. How much did he pay you?'

'Four thousand pounds.'

'Four thousand pounds! What the fuck did he expect you to do? Has he hurt you?'

'No, of course not. It was fine.' More than fine, it was heaven.

'And this man who paid you for sex has given you a job and a posh apartment for what reason? Remind me why he's done that. If you think it's out of the goodness of his heart, you're mad. Away with the fairies.'

'He's a good man. He wanted to help.'

'You didn't tell him about the drug dealers, did you?'

'No, of course not. But he was with me when we found

you collapsed and needles and syringes all over the place. He knew you'd overdosed.'

'But he thought I'd done it to myself?'

'We both did, Nora. At least at first. We didn't know what to think, to be honest. I was so frightened for you. You could have died.'

'But now you've got a job and a place to live, so you've not done badly out of it, have you?'

'Well, neither have you if it comes to that. You're getting the four grand for your dealers and obviously, you'll be living in the apartment too. This is your chance to turn your life around, ditch all the druggy people and clean yourself up. It's a fresh start, Nora. You don't sound at all grateful.'

'Well, I'm so sorry, Sister Colleen. I suppose you'll be reporting me to the Mother Superior?'

'Oh, don't be so bloody stupid. I'm trying to help.'

Colleen was disappointed by Nora's attitude, but she put it down to her feeling ill. They needed to talk about what had happened and Colleen didn't want to annoy Nora any more than she already was doing. But she was the older and therefore, theoretically, the more mature of the two of them. Not that she'd ever felt more mature than Nora. Her baby sister had grown up fast after their father had died.

'Nora? I need to ask you something. I need to know. It's going to make a difference to what happens from now on. I have your best interests at heart, you do know that don't you?'

'The answer's no.'

'I beg your pardon?'

'The question you want to ask me. The answer is no I didn't try to take my own life. I've told the psychiatrist it was an accident even though it wasn't. I don't take heroin, but now I'm probably addicted to the stuff, so there.'

'I don't understand. You took it but didn't accidentally overdose. But it wasn't a suicide attempt?'

'I didn't take it, it was given to me. While you were not stripping, I had a visit from the dealers. I told them I'd get their money to them, but they said they were going to leave me with a little something to make me understand the seriousness of the situation. Two held me down and Big Man injected me with heroin.'

'Oh my God, Nora, that's awful. You nearly died. You have to go to the police. What if I hadn't got home when I did and Adam wasn't there to help, what then? And where was Maggot when this was happening? Did he not try to defend you?'

Nora pulled the sheet down so Colleen could talk to her face again.

'Maggot? Defend me? Have you met Maggot?' Nora started laughing, her whole body shaking and tears rolling down her face.

'Isn't he your boyfriend?'

Nora shook her head, rolling it from side to side on the pillow as the laughter poured out of her.

'Oh my God, that's funny. Insulting, but funny.'

'Nora, will you calm down, you're worrying me now.'

'Do you know why he's called Maggot?' Nora asked once she had stopped laughing enough to look at her.

'No idea. Should I?'

'No, there's no reason why you should. It's because maggots are used as bait to catch fish. He's the one who got me onto drugs in the first place. He works for Big Man, enticing young people, women, and boys, to take drugs with him. He's the go-between until they're well and truly hooked. Then he disappears. Moves on to the next lot of victims. We won't see him again.'

'Was this after I rang you or before?'

'After. If it had been before I wouldn't have been capable of answering the phone.'

'Oh, Nora, I can't believe what you're telling me. He needs to be locked up. They all do. But when you've paid them, they'll leave you alone won't they?'

'Probably not.'

'What do we do?'

'*We* aren't doing anything. You need to go home to Mum and look after her. Don't tell her anything about the drugs, okay. Swear to me.'

'Nora, you can forget all that. I'm not going anywhere.'

Colleen wouldn't leave her sister until the drug situation was sorted out. And while they were thinking of what to do, she had a good job and a luxurious flat and Adam. No, Colleen was going nowhere.

Chapter Eight

Colleen took extra care choosing her outfit for her first day at work. She wanted to create a good impression and look smart, but also had to be comfortable in case it turned out to be a long day. She had no idea how many hours she'd be expected to work; would it be the usual nine to five, or would they still be at their desks when the cleaners descended with mops and buckets?

She chose a navy blue pencil skirt and a white blouse. She didn't have a navy jacket, so wore her white one. Instead of high heels, she chose sling-backs with a wedge heel that were both comfortable and fashionable.

Colleen was delighted to find that the registered office of Meredith Motors was situated in Chelsea and was within walking distance of the new apartment. The showroom was in Wandsworth and Adam had mentioned that he would show her around when he had the time. This delighted Colleen. Although she knew nothing about cars, didn't know a Mini from a Mercedes, and couldn't drive, never having had the inclination to learn, any time spent in Adam's company would be a good thing.

She arrived early at a nondescript office block that listed the companies in it on a plaque set at eye level next to the front door. There was a buzzer next to each name. Colleen pressed the buzzer next to Meredith Motors, then put her ear near to the contraption and listened.

After a few seconds, there was a clattering sound and a female voice said, 'Yes?'

'Oh… hello, it's Colleen O'Shea, I'm starting work today… for Adam Turner.'

Colleen wondered if she should say any more, name the company or something, but the voice said, 'Come on up, we're on the third floor.'

'Okay,' said Colleen but the voice had hung up. She heard a metallic click as the door was unlocked, so she pushed it open and went inside.

There was a lift, and she was the only one around. Normally Colleen hated lifts as she had a fear of getting stuck in one. This had never actually happened to her, but she had watched enough films of people being stuck in lifts with the oxygen running out and women having panic attacks, to make her choose the stairs if there weren't too many floors to climb.

This lift was on the small side but was clean and moved smoothly upwards to the third floor with barely a jerk when it stopped. Colleen hadn't realised she'd been holding her breath until the lift doors opened and she breathed a sigh of relief.

A woman of indeterminate age was standing in the corridor with a smile on her face, obviously waiting for her.

'Good morning,' said Colleen.

'Hello, my dear, I'm Doris and am I glad you're here.'

'Thank you,' said Colleen, 'I'm glad too.'

Doris held her hand out to her and Colleen shook it firmly. She knew that people hated limp handshakes, so she always made sure her handshake was robust.

'I don't suppose Adam has told you what your duties are?'

'Not in any detail, but he said I was to help you as you're snowed under. I'm to learn the ropes and take the pressure off you.'

'Right, well let's get cracking then.'

Doris led her down the corridor and they turned left into a small suite of offices. There were three separate areas. One door had the nameplate, Adam Turner, CEO, another said Meeting Room, and the reception area with two desks with computers, phones and all the other equipment needed, presumably, by Doris and herself. There was a printer, a fax machine and two bookcases, as well as the usual grey filing cabinets and a dusty, dried-up plant in the corner that looked as if it hadn't been watered for years.

Colleen had worked in enough office environments as a temporary secretary to recognise the archetypal office. It could be any office, in any company, in any city of the world. But it was Adam's, and this thought gave Colleen a secret thrill. To think she was here, in Adam's world, and would be working alongside him all day, every day. She couldn't wait to get started.

'Right,' said Doris. 'This is my desk,' she settled herself behind the one nearest to the door, 'and that one over there is yours. There's a drawer for you to put your handbag in and anything else you need to store. There's a key so you can lock it at night.'

Colleen obediently put her handbag in the drawer and shut it again, then waited for further instruction.

'We'll do housekeeping first as that's the most important.'

'Okay.' Colleen grinned. She liked Doris already. Her hair was white and swept back in a modern style, and her eyes were the lightest blue Colleen had ever seen. She wore a wedding ring and there were a couple of framed photographs on her desk. Colleen vowed to have a look at them when she got the chance. She idly wondered where Adam was. The door to his office was closed. Was he in there?

'In case of fire, leave everything as is and make your way down to the street. Don't use the lifts, just the stairs. There's an assembly point on the corner and a book on the ground floor for you to sign in and out. It's not to keep tabs on you, it's only used in case of fire, so the firemen know how many people are in the building. It is important, so do try to remember, dear, won't you?'

'Oh yes, of course. But… I didn't sign in.'

'No matter, you can nip down and do that in a minute.'

'Okay.'

'There's a kitchen, which I'll show you, and the toilets are down that end of the corridor too. We share both with a firm of accountants; nice people, but we have to keep reminding them to do their own washing up. There's a fridge too if you want to risk keeping your sandwiches there. I usually go out for lunch, for a breath of air and a change of scene. We'll have staggered lunches so there'll always be someone to answer the phone.'

'Okay. Can I ask something?'

'Of course, dear, anything.'

'How many people work here?'

'You mean the whole building, I've no idea, but there's five storeys—'

'No, I mean at Meredith Motors.'

'Oh, just you and me, dear. Adam pops his head around the door now and again but spends most of his time at the showroom. He loves the cars, you see, and enjoys talking to the customers. And he also spends a lot of time with the mechanics. You will see him later today, as he has a meeting with one of our regular clients from overseas. You can sit in and listen, but don't worry, I'll take the minutes and type them up. Adam likes to keep a record of everything that's said in these meetings, even the more informal ones.'

'Oh good. I don't do shorthand I'm afraid. I never learned that, just typing and office management.'

Colleen was disappointed to learn that Adam spent most of his time at the showroom but cheered up when she learned that she'd see him later for a meeting.

'Right. Why don't you pop downstairs and sign the book. It's on a table just around the corner from the lifts, then when you come back, we'll have a cup of tea and you can tell me all about yourself.'

'Okay.' Colleen leapt up to do Doris's bidding, thinking that she was going to like working at Meredith Motors.

Adam listened to Franco Alberto Bartolomeo, the owner of an Italian classic car company, describing some of the wonderful finds his company had restored recently. Adam loved classic cars and would normally have been enthralled by what Franco was telling him. Today, he was distracted by Colleen.

He was delighted that she had taken him up on his offer of a job and had been looking forward to seeing her in the office ever since. She was dressed to look like a competent, capable secretary with her navy outfit and comfortable sandals. Smart, but chic—perfect.

Even more splendid was the fact that Doris liked her. They'd tried junior secretaries before and they had been either ambitious, changing things without asking Doris first, as they thought they knew best, or lazy, spending all day on their phones and taking hours to file a couple of sheets of A4.

Doris had declared that she was happy with Colleen so far. It was early days, and she had yet to prove herself, but Adam sensed that the two women would get on well and work together as a team.

Adam and Franco had been doing business for years, and Adam was planning another trip to Milan to visit the Italian company's headquarters. He would spend a couple of days doing business and buying a car or two, then spend the rest of the time relaxing and sightseeing. He loved Italy, it was a beautiful country, and he loved the people too. Maybe he'd take Colleen with him on the pretext of showing her the overseas part of their business.

'More coffee, Franco?' Adam asked when there was a lull in the conversation.

'*Si, grazie.*'

'I'll make it.' Straight away, Colleen stood up and hurried from the office.

'*Nuovo segretario?*' Franco asked.

'Yes, this is her first day. We think she'll fit in very well, don't we, Doris?'

'Early days, but she shows promise,' Doris said.

'*Lei è carina, vero?*'

'*Si, molto,*' said Adam. He needed to steer the conversation away from Colleen now that they had established that she was very pretty. He was glad that Doris didn't speak Italian.

Colleen came back into the meeting carrying a tray with a cafetiere of coffee and some biscuits, or *biscotti* as Franco called them.

'Thanks, Colleen,' said Adam.

He noticed Franco watching her with a smile on his face. Perhaps just Doris could attend the meetings in future, to give Colleen time to hold the fort on her own. And stop the lecherous looks that Franco was sending out in all directions as Colleen, oblivious to his reaction to her, leaned over the table to put his cup and saucer in front of him.

'Thanks, Colleen,' said Adam when she had poured coffee for them all.

'Biscotti?' Colleen asked Franco and he grinned and took one.

'*Grazie, signorina*.' Franco took a biscuit and munched on it.

As the meeting went on, Adam noticed that Colleen was glancing up at him periodically, from under her lashes, and scribbling in her notebook. Doris was taking the minutes, her hand moving like lightning over the page of her notebook, then stopping to let the conversation catch up with her speedy shorthand. Surely the two secretaries couldn't both be taking the minutes unless Colleen was practising. He'd get a look at her notebook later to find out.

Finally, the meeting ended, and Franco took his leave of them all, kissing Doris's hand and then Colleen's. Both ladies behaved graciously and smiled at him, which seemed to please him. When his taxi arrived, Adam escorted him to the ground floor and bid him goodbye, or *arrivederci*.

When he got back to the office, Adam smiled at his

secretaries. 'That went well. Thank you for your contribution, both of you.'

'You're welcome,' Doris said.

'I didn't do anything.' Colleen was smiling at him with her bedroom eyes, and he wanted to get her alone.

'Of course you did. You made coffee and charmed the old man.'

'He thinks you're very pretty,' said Doris, 'and, of course, you are.'

'I didn't know you spoke Italian,' said Adam trying hard to remember what else was discussed in Italian.

'Enough to get by, that's all. I love Tuscany and George and I are hoping for a holiday there this summer. We went there for our honeymoon, many years ago.'

'Oh, that sounds wonderful,' said Colleen, her eyes shining.

'Colleen? How about we have a quick visit to the showrooms and then I'll give you a lift home?'

'That sounds good. Is that alright with you, Doris?'

'Of course. Adam's the boss.'

Doris returned to her desk and Colleen nipped to the ladies. Here was his chance of looking at that notebook. He sidled up to Colleen's desk and flipped it open. There were no minutes of the meeting or anything else to do with work. What there was nearly took his breath away. Colleen had done a pencil sketch of him in profile. And it was good. More than good. It was excellent.

'Looking for something, Adam?' asked Doris.

'Have you seen this?' he asked lifting up the notebook.

'No. It's very good isn't it?'

'Yes. I bet she was bored in that meeting.'

'She obviously found you more interesting.' Doris

pierced him with her blue-eyed gaze, and he tried to look innocent.

'That's what this office lacks, you know—some decent artwork.'

'Umm,' said Doris watching him with a knowing look. He couldn't get anything past his PA. Never could.

Colleen came back from the Ladies with her hair combed and a hint of perfume.

'Right, let's go.' He opened the door for Colleen.

'See you tomorrow and thanks for all your help today, Doris.'

'Goodbye, dear, have a nice evening.'

Adam hustled Colleen out and into the lift.

'Must remember to sign the book,' Colleen said.

It was a timely reminder as he usually forgot, but luckily he had signed himself and Franco in today.

'Yes. Well remembered. Have you enjoyed your first day?'

'Oh yes, thank you again, Adam, for giving me this chance, I'm going to love it here.'

Adam couldn't resist palming her face and kissing her. She responded and the kiss deepened. If they hadn't reached the ground floor at that moment, they would have been screwing on the lift floor. Fortunately, they broke away before the doors opened as two of the accountants they shared their floor with were waiting patiently.

'Good afternoon,' said Adam cheerfully, hoping he didn't have lipstick all over his face.

'Good afternoon,' the accountants both responded. Colleen smiled but said nothing.

'That was close,' Colleen said.

'I like to live dangerously, don't you?'

'Don't know, never have.'

'If we're going to keep seeing each other, you'd better get used to it.'

'Then I will,' she said.

Chapter Nine

Adam loved the cars that Meredith Motors sold and enjoyed showing them off to anyone who was interested. And even those who were not. He didn't know which camp Colleen fell into; she might have been feigning interest for his sake, or she might be genuinely in love with them as he was.

He hoped it was the second but as she didn't own a car or a driving license, it was probably the first. Nevertheless, Adam conducted his tour as he would for anyone. Maybe she would become more interested in time if she stayed working for Meredith Motors.

'We have everything for the classic car enthusiast from Mercedes Benz, Jaguar—'

'What about that one,' said Colleen pointing to a metallic blue sports car.

'That's a Porsche, 2005 Boxster. Lovely car—'

'It's not classic in the true sense though. It looks really modern.'

'We sell all kinds of cars, not just classic. And you're right, it's too modern to be classic.'

'So, how old do they have to be?'

'It varies. Depends on the make as well as the age. About twenty-five to thirty years, but a lot of cars are older. We sold one of the old Volkswagen Beetles recently, a nineteen sixty-eight model. The car was expensive, but the insurance is surprisingly cheap. And, of course, if they're over forty years old then there's no road tax or MOT to pay.'

'Fancy,' said Colleen staring up at him. He looked into her eyes and she licked her bottom lip and caught it with her top teeth, a move that went straight to his groin and he realised the time to talk shop was over.

As soon as the door to the Chelsea apartment was closed, they fell on each other. Clothes came off as a breathless conversation took place in between kisses.

'Nora?' asked Adam.

'Still in hospital,' whispered Colleen.

'Good,' Adam said as he removed his trousers, then swept the almost naked Colleen up in his arms and carried her through to the bedroom and dropped her on the bed.

'Condoms?' asked Colleen.

'Pocket,' muttered Adam.

They kissed again as Adam pulled Colleen's bra off and started moving down her body, kissing her in all the places he had learned that she liked. It had taken them only a short time to get to know each other's bodies intimately and to learn what turned them on and sent them into orbit.

Adam took a nipple into his mouth and tongued it, eliciting a moan from Colleen that turned him on, so he did the same to the other nipple. He buried his tongue in her belly button and licked causing her to writhe up and cry out.

'Stop, that tickles,'

So he did it again, holding her down on the bed to stop her moving. Then he continued down to her pussy and buried his face in her damp curls. He opened her as she conveniently spread her legs for him.

She was wet and Adam marvelled at how responsive she was. A few kisses and a tickle and she was ready for him. He'd never had sex with a woman like her. Some he had turned on easily, some were hard work, though they got there in the end but no woman he had ever known had been as desperate for him as he was for her.

He ran his tongue over the lips of her sex, and she moaned and writhed on the bed.

'I love how you taste,' he murmured.

'What do I taste of?' she asked.

'Salty and sweet at the same time.'

'Like salted caramel?'

'Yes,' he said, knowing that he would never be able to eat salted caramel again without thinking of Colleen.

He stroked his tongue over her clitoris, and she bucked on the bed. He didn't want her to come yet, so he moved to the sides, circling around her inner lips in a slow, deliberate tease. She kicked with her heels and tried to raise her hips to manoeuvre herself into the correct place, but he held her down and spread her wider until she cried out.

'I want to come... I'm nearly there.'

'Patience, my darling, you will come when the time's right.'

'Now,' said Colleen revealing how desperate she was to orgasm.

If he'd been having sex with Rosamund he would have denied her the pleasure she so desperately sought, but Colleen was a different matter. He found it hard to deny her anything, so he gave her what she wanted, fucking her with his tongue until she yelled and wriggled as wave after wave of ecstasy rolled through her.

Adam was so turned on that precum glistened on the head of his cock. Shame he had to use a condom, he would have loved to have buried himself, balls deep, inside her. But he could have his way with one thing.

'Oh, that was wonderful. I don't know how you do it, Adam—you send me to the moon and back.'

'Let's try reaching further then. Turn around and kneel on the bed.'

Colleen grinned and obeyed instantly. She never questioned his demands.

Adam sheathed himself and entered her in one swift movement. He held her hips and they moved together as one. Part of him wanted to drive into her, sinking deeper until he possessed her completely then take his pleasure without a thought for her own. But the gentleman in him wanted her to feel as much joy as he did. Adam wanted them to be a couple, enjoying each other's bodies, mutual pleasure and orgasming together, reaching the moon and stars in each other's arms.

He withdrew slightly then slammed back into her, then again, until they were both panting, and their cries grew fiercer the nearer to their climax they moved.

'This is good,' said Colleen, 'fuck me harder.'

Adam was so surprised to hear Colleen utter a swear

word that he did as she asked. He grunted in time to every stroke as he used his body as a battering ram. He wondered if he was hurting her, but surely she would have said. Colleen was enjoying it as much as he was.

'Harder,' she shouted, and he obliged.

Adam plunged into her again and again until he was at the point of no return. He climaxed with a hoarse shout and Colleen squealed and orgasmed before collapsing onto the pillows.

After carefully disposing of the condom, Adam joined Colleen on the bed. They lay on top of the duvet side by side, their bodies pink and glistening with sweat.

'Wow,' said Adam as his heart rate slowly returned to normal.

'Triple wow,' Colleen replied as she lay with her eyes closed and her breathing slowing down.

It was quiet and peaceful, with just the muffled sound of early evening traffic, and their breathing returning to normal. Adam knew that, if he closed his eyes, he'd be asleep. He mustn't close his eyes as he had things to do. He was meeting Jeremy at his club for dinner so they could talk about arrangements for the wedding. He'd much rather stay with Colleen, cocooned in their own private little world.

'What are you thinking about?' asked Colleen.

'I'm thinking that I need to go, but my body hasn't got the memo yet.'

'Stay a bit longer. It'll be the last chance we'll get to have the flat to ourselves. They won't keep Nora in forever and then it'll be more difficult to be alone.'

'Tempting as that is, I really need to go. There will be other times like this, I promise.'

'Okay. Will I see you at work tomorrow?'

'Maybe, although I'll probably be at the showroom for most of the day. I'll see what I can do.'

'Right.'

Colleen sat up and rolled off the bed as if her body had lost all its bones. She laughed to show she was playing around, but Adam understood that feeling. When good sex had drained the body of all energy and your brain was crying out for sleep. He wished he could spend the night with her again. He'd have to find a way.

He got dressed as Colleen went into the kitchen for a drink of water.

She was waiting at the door. He took her in his arms and held her for a few seconds. She rested her head on his chest and he stroked her hair. It felt right, as if they were made to fit together so well. Colleen was becoming a habit; one it was getting harder to kick. He didn't want to stop but wondered if he should for her sake. There was so much going on in his life with his father-in-law at death's door and his wife being more high maintenance than usual. Perhaps it wasn't fair to let Colleen get mixed up in all that.

But when she kissed him goodbye and he held her in his arms, he knew for sure that he wasn't prepared to give her up. Not yet anyway.

When Adam had gone, Colleen had a shower, washed her hair, dried it, then sat in the living room in her beautifully clean and comfortable apartment and wondered what the heck to do with herself for the rest of the evening.

It was nearly June, and the days were growing steadily longer which meant she had more time in the evenings to do things before it got dark. She could go for a walk or visit

Nora in hospital and risk doing her head in like she had last time.

Colleen's life had improved so much recently with Adam and her new job and apartment. If only she could sort Nora's problem with the vicious drug dealers and get them out of her life forever, then everything would be perfect.

She was not naïve enough to think they'd leave Nora alone, even if they did manage to pay them everything she owed. They'd find some other way to keep her tied to them. They were bullies and cowards and Colleen hated them with a passion. How dare they terrorise her little sister like that?

The problem was, what could she do? She was tempted to go to the police but realised that she would have to implicate Nora who would probably be charged with possession, if not dealing. Who knew what the dealers would accuse her of. They'd put it all on her to take the heat off themselves. That was the kind of people they were.

And they weren't the bosses, just the bosses' henchmen. It was Big Man that the police needed to catch and get off the streets before he hurt more young people.

The ringing of the front doorbell jolted Colleen out of her reverie. She got up with a spring in her step. Maybe Adam had changed his mind about spending more time with her. In fact, it had to be Adam as he was one of only two people who knew this address.

'Hello,' she sang cheerily down the intercom, waiting to hear Adam's sexy voice.

'Colleen, it's me. I'm coming up.' The other person who knew.

'Nora? I thought you were still in hospital.'

'Well I'm obviously not, am I? Will you open the door.'

Colleen unlocked the front door for her, then the door

of the apartment. She waited until Nora had climbed the stairs and staggered inside, carrying a green bin liner, and wearing dark glasses and a baseball cap.

'You should have rung me, and I would have come to the hospital to collect you. When did they decide to discharge you?'

'*They* didn't. I discharged myself. I signed a disclaimer to say I wouldn't sue them if I dropped down dead.'

'Oh, Nora, why?' Colleen felt a twinge of exasperation. Nora had been safe in the hospital and would have received treatment. Maybe there would have been a social worker or some such who could have helped her.

'Why what?'

'Why did you discharge yourself, you were being looked after and getting help.'

'I can look after myself and I don't need any help.'

'What about the addiction?'

'I haven't got an addiction. I told you, I don't take heroin except when someone injects me with it against my will.'

'And what if they do that again?'

Colleen followed Nora around the apartment as she looked at everything, opening doors and peering in before shutting them again.

'They won't as long as they get their money and I do what they want.'

Colleen thought of the four thousand pounds which was locked in a safe in the bedroom. Adam had thought of everything for the rich and successful when he bought the apartment, including a safe for their important documents, money, and jewellery. All that Colleen had put in theirs was the envelope with Adam's cash.

'And what exactly will they want you to do?'

Nora stopped at her bedroom and looked in. 'I see you've got the bigger bed. I might be needing that myself soon.'

'The beds are the same size it's just that your room's a bit smaller.'

Nora glared at her. 'You've made yourself at home already, I see.'

'It's *our* home Nora, yours and mine. If you want the other room, that's fine, you take it.'

'No, it's okay. If the bed's a double, then it'll do.'

'For what?' Colleen didn't like the way Nora was talking. She remembered in the hospital Nora had said *"So now my high and mighty older sister is no better than me. She's come down to my level. Having sex for money."* At the time she'd let it go as she was so horrified by the things Nora was telling her, but now it had more significance.

'What d'you think?'

'Nora, do you have sex for money?'

'Yes. But so do you, so don't get on your high horse again. You haven't got the right to judge me.'

'I wasn't judging you, I'm just worried, that's all. Is it something to do with the dealers?'

Nora threw herself backwards and landed on the couch. She put her hands on her head over the baseball cap. She'd taken off the sunglasses.

'It's everything to do with them. If I can't pay what I owe, I work for them to pay it off. And by work, I mean have sex for money.'

'Here? No, Nora, you can't. This is Adam's flat, and you can't do that.'

'Why not? There's a perfectly good bed going to waste. He'll never know anyway as he'll be too busy screwing you for money.'

'No, he won't. It was just that one time and it was four thousand pounds. If you give that to the dealers, surely they'll leave you alone.'

'No chance. You don't know them, Colleen. I've got no choice. I either do what they say, or my body'll be found floating in the Thames.'

Chapter Ten

Adam met Jeremy at his club in London. It was called Bachelors and was one of the last London clubs that allowed women in by invite only. Adam had to be signed in by Jeremy as they were particular about the guests as well.

To become a member of this exclusive establishment, candidates must be proposed and seconded by two existing members. Application forms were submitted along with a letter explaining why the candidate wanted to join with letters of support from the proposer and seconder.

Jeremy had encouraged Adam to join many times, telling him how many influential people were members, and how every man needed a bolthole when things at home got too uncomfortable.

'We all need to escape from the little woman some-times,' he had said with a laugh.

They were in the restaurant tucking into roast beef and Yorkshire pudding, cooked to perfection. Jeremy only enjoyed British cuisine. The wine was one of the most expensive and tasted like heaven.

Adam was no connoisseur, but over time, and schooled by Rosamund in the early years of their marriage, he had learned a lot about fine dining and good wines. He still preferred a pint of real ale, although he kept that little nugget of information to himself.

'How are the wedding preparations getting on, Jeremy?'

'Splendid. Well, I presume so as Theo is arranging everything. She wouldn't trust me with the important things… or even the unimportant ones come to that. She told me that all I need to do is turn up. Not difficult seeing as the wedding is taking place in the old family pile.' Jeremy guffawed and a few heads turned, but then looked away again.

'How are you feeling about getting hitched?' Adam could have added "finally" as Jeremy had lost count of the number of times he had asked Theo to marry him. Jeremy had no idea why she'd been holding back on giving him the answer he wanted, but Adam suspected he knew.

Lady Theodora Blakely came from a family who, at one time, had been the richest in the whole of the country. But slowly, over the years, the money had leaked away due to gambling, poor land management and other reasons that he wasn't privy to. The family, reluctantly, had sold their family home to the National Trust, and Theo had found herself in a position of having a title but no money. Not the amount that she wanted to become accustomed to. Adam suspected she'd been holding out for a better deal that, sadly for her, wasn't forthcoming.

Jeremy had told her he'd wait as long as he had to for her. She was the only woman he wanted as a wife. So, seeing as he was her only suitor, she had—eventually—accepted his proposal.

Adam couldn't help wondering how much love the couple felt for each other.

'How am I feeling?' Jeremy took a thoughtful sip of his wine and frowned. 'I'm relieved she's said yes. I was beginning to feel like a complete prat being rejected by her so many times. And now I can plan for the future. An heir to keep the family name going and give the little lady something to do with her time.' Jeremy laughed again.

'What does Theo think of that?'

'Oh, she'll be fine. That's her role now, isn't it? To look after me and the children when they turn up.'

Adam said nothing. From what he knew of Theo, she would be the one wearing the trousers in the marriage and they'd have children if and when she wanted them.

'Pudding?' said Jeremy. 'I can recommend the rhubarb crumble.'

'Okay, go on.'

'Anyway, you're the one who's causing the gossip grapevine to vibrate. What about that stripper that you took home from the stag night? What happened to her?'

'She isn't a stripper. It's a long story, Jeremy, and I'd be grateful if you kept it to yourself.'

'If she isn't a stripper, what was she doing hiding in a box and wrapped up in ribbon?'

'Her sister is the stripper but she was ill so Colleen stepped in but had a panic attack when Rupert taped the box up and she couldn't get out.'

'Yes, that was a bad do. Rupert shouldn't have done that. But you took her home.'

The waiter brought the pudding and Jeremy thanked him graciously.

'Yes, I did because she needed help. I couldn't turn my back on her, now could I?'

Jeremy was tucking into his crumble and had finished before Adam had eaten half of his.

'She stayed the night, according to Rosamund. So you had sex with her. Did you pay her?'

If Rosamund had been talking, Jeremy probably knew everything she did. The woman couldn't keep her mouth shut.

'I did, but it's not what you think.'

'You had sex with her and paid her for the night. That makes her a prostitute.'

'Yes I paid her, but that doesn't make her a prostitute. She wouldn't have been paid for the stripping seeing as she hadn't done any, so I was just making up for that. She's not a prostitute, Jeremy, nor is she a stripper.'

'I think you'll find she is in most people's eyes. Mine included.'

Adam kept quiet. Jeremy was right to question him. He knew how it looked to outsiders, people who didn't understand the situation. Colleen was trying to help her sister. He hadn't believed her either until they found Nora in that hovel. But he wasn't about to tell Jeremy everything, even though they were friends.

'Shall we retire to the lounge and have a brandy and a coffee?'

'Good idea.' Adam just wanted to go home. He felt disloyal to Colleen just listening to the negative talk about her. But he had yet to tell Jeremy the best part.

When they were settled and sipping the brandy, lounging back in comfy leather armchairs, the talk turned to the wedding.

'We've put you and Rosamund in the best guest bedroom. Didn't know whether that was the done thing as you're estranged but still have sex. Hope that's okay.'

'I'm not accompanying Rosamund to the wedding. She's not my plus one.'

'Not your plus one? Well, who is?'

'Colleen. I haven't asked her yet but she's the one I want to bring.'

'Colleen? The prostitute?'

'She's not a prostitute, Jeremy, will you stop calling her that.' Adam was getting hot under the collar at Jeremy and felt like walking out. But he needed him on board with the idea of Colleen coming to his wedding as the opposition, once his wife's social circle found out, would be formidable. He needed his friend on his side.

'Well what is she then? Your mistress? Have you set her up in a nice little flat somewhere so you can visit her whenever you like?'

'I gave her a job and she lives with her sister.'

'You gave her a job? Doing what for goodness sake?'

'She's a secretary and she's assisting Doris and learning the ropes.'

Jeremy took a sip of his brandy and smiled. 'So, you pay her to spend the night with you, give her a job and set her up in an apartment. Which I bet is the luxury one in Chelsea. Nothing wrong with a man having a mistress, old bean, but the clever chap keeps her away from his real life. Why for God's sake do you want to be seen in public with her? You do realise, don't you, that over two hundred people are coming to the wedding and the whole of our social set is staying the night at Charmley Manor. Everyone who is anyone is going to be there. And probably some media people as well if Theo has anything to do with it. Are you sure it's fair to ask this pros... to ask Colleen to face all that?'

Adam had to admit that he hadn't thought about it like

that. He just knew he wanted Colleen to be there. As he was best man, he would have to leave her alone for a lot of the time and they wouldn't be able to sit together for the wedding breakfast. Maybe it wouldn't be such a good idea after all. Perhaps he'd be better off going alone. Or... ask Colleen what she would prefer. He'd be completely honest with her and give her the chance to go if she wanted to.

'I haven't even asked her yet.'

'There is another consideration of course and that's Hugo. If he found out about you and this filly he may not want to keep you on as CEO of Meredith Motors. You know how fanatical he is about appearing squeaky clean to the public.'

Adam was tempted to say to hell with the lot of them, Colleen was more important than their petty snobbery and double standards. None of them would stand up to scrutiny if their private lives were held up to the light. They all had their secrets, and a lot of them were murky.

'Thanks for lunch, Jeremy, and I'd be grateful if you could keep all this to yourself for now. Colleen is trying to help her sister and none of the things that have happened to her were her fault.'

'My lips are sealed. I won't say a word. Can't answer for Rosamund though. A woman scorned and all that. If trouble's on the way I would look for it in her direction.'

Colleen would normally have called out a hello when she arrived home after work, but something kept her silent. A sense that Nora wasn't alone in the flat. After the conversation they'd shared the day before, she was convinced Nora was "entertaining clients" in the double bed.

She let herself in quietly and stood listening at Nora's door. There was the distinct sound of sex going on; grunting and moaning which she was sure were coming from a man. She doubted Nora was enjoying it.

Colleen felt sick and saddened that her little sister had been reduced to this by a bunch of criminals. But Nora had been right when she'd said that Colleen had no right to judge, having engaged in sex for money herself, though Colleen couldn't reconcile what was going on in Nora's bedroom to the wonderful night she'd spent with Adam. Her first orgasm. That was something to celebrate, not to feel ashamed of.

Colleen went into the kitchen and made herself a cup of tea. She tried to keep as quiet as she could, but Nora would know she was home. It was impossible to hide the sound of a kettle boiling.

Fifteen minutes later, she heard the door of the apartment slam. There had been no conversation, no farewell, no sound at all since the grunting.

'Thought it was you,' Nora said as she wandered into the kitchen wearing an old housecoat and counting a wad of notes.

'Well, who else would it be? Nora, we need to talk.'

'Any tea going?' Nora slid onto a chair at the breakfast bar and stuffed the notes in her pocket.

Colleen made a fresh pot of tea and while it was brewing, she leant against the work surface and tried to get Nora to look at her.

'Nora?'

'What?' Nora was staring at the floor and yawning.

'You can't treat Adam's apartment as a brothel. It's not fair.'

'You are.'

'Me! I am not.'

'Don't tell me you've never had sex here 'cos I don't believe you.'

'That's different. He only paid me that first time. It's not the same now.'

'Yeah, only because he's using you. In exchange for accommodation and a job he has you exactly where he wants you.'

Colleen wished she could defend herself but everything Nora said was true. To an outsider, it looked exactly as she said. Adam had paid her for sex and wanted it to continue, so gave her a job and an apartment. But how many men would do that unless the woman was special?

Colleen had never really understood why Adam had paid four grand for one night with a woman he didn't know. Why had he done that? Why hadn't he driven her home and then washed his hands of any further involvement? He had a good job. A reputation to uphold. He had a lot to lose.

'Do you really think he's just using me, Nora?' Colleen hated that she had to ask her baby sister for advice about a man.

'Of course he's only using you. He's a man. They're all the bloody same. I wouldn't trust any of them. He's got sex on tap whenever he wants it. You do know that you can't meet anyone else, or you'll lose the job and this apartment. You'll be back to square one. He's got you exactly where he wants you.'

Colleen didn't want anyone else. Although she wouldn't say this to Nora, if Adam wanted sex every day, she'd be ecstatic. As it was, she didn't see him anywhere near as often as she'd like. He spent most of his time at the showrooms and only paid a visit to the registered offices when there was a meeting, or he needed to talk to Doris about something work related.

And now that Nora was here, she doubted that he'd visit their apartment either. When was she going to see him?

But she had bigger problems at the moment.

'Nora, I'm going home next weekend to see Mum. Will you come with me?' Nora shook her head but didn't speak. 'Nora! Did you hear what I said?'

'I can't. I don't want her to see me like this. She'll ask questions and what will I say? I've tried to give her the impression I was living it up, not that I was a drug addict and a prossie. I can't go home, Colleen.'

'But she's worried about you, as I am. What am I going to tell her when she starts asking questions?'

'Exactly!' Nora jumped up and backed away. 'That's my point. Don't go home, then you won't have to tell her anything. If you go home and try to keep things from her, she'll know you're lying and then you'll end up telling her everything.'

'But I want to see her. Make sure she's okay and whether she's got rid of Auntie May yet. Please come back with me. We won't tell her about the drugs, I promise.'

'You go back then. Tell her about your wonderful new job and shiny boyfriend but don't mention the way I'm living or so help me God I'll never speak to you again.'

Chapter Eleven

Each time Adam had visited Hugo, he looked worse than the time before. How much weight could the man lose before he was just skin and bones? The cancer was eating him alive, but still his father-in-law clung to the few shreds of life he had left.

There was a new development in his illness today; jaundice turning his wrinkled skin a strange shade of yellow. Even the whites of his eyes were no longer white.

Hugo sat in a large, comfy armchair propped up by pillows. A small table next to the chair contained an array of pills and a jug of water and a glass. His oxygen tank, which he was permanently connected to, sat on the other side of the chair.

'Hugo, good to see you again.'

'You too, Adam. Thanks for coming.' Hugo's voice was a rasp as if his vocal cords had dried up. He must be severely dehydrated.

'Would you like some water?' Adam moved towards the

table to pour some for him, but he shook his head and waved his hand for Adam to sit down. Perhaps the effort required to perform such a simple task as drinking was too much for him.

'How are things?' Hugo rasped.

Adam found it hard to look Hugo in the eyes as his face was beginning to resemble a skull with little flesh, his lips had almost disappeared, and his teeth were more prominent. The skin around his mouth looked cracked and sore and Adam wondered if he was impatient with his nurses, not letting them perform simple tasks like keeping his lips moist to avoid the cracking.

Hugo Meredith had always been an impatient and proud man. To be brought this low physically must be anathema to him. But mentally, Adam suspected that Hugo was as sharp as ever with a cunning and brilliant business mind. He wouldn't want platitudes or evasion of any kind, so Adam came straight to the point.

'I wanted to talk to you about Meredith Motors expanding into the Asian market. We've already got strong contacts in Italy. I had a productive meeting with Franco Alberto Bartolomeo the other day and things are progressing on that front. But China especially is showing interest in classic and vintage cars from Europe. They're looking at Germany and France, but I want to encourage them to start looking our way. It means spending a bit of money, but I think it would be well worth it.'

Hugo had listened to him without interrupting. Now he stared into the middle distance as if his thoughts had drifted off somewhere, but Adam knew he was thinking; mulling it over in his mind before passing comment. Adam waited without speaking.

'I'd need to see the figures. But it sounds promising.

Email me everything you've got and your thinking. I'll get back to you.'

'Sure. I'll do that as soon as I get home.'

It amazed Adam that even though Hugo was getting physically weaker by the day, he could still use his computer to read his emails and keep up-to-date with world affairs as well as anybody. Adam got the occasional message from him, full of typos but the gist of them as clear as ever.

Two nurses came into the room. One of them, the elder and probably the senior nurse, addressed Adam.

'Sorry to break up the meeting but he gets tired very easily.'

'Oh sure. We were finished anyway.'

Then she turned her attention to Hugo. 'Right, Mr Meredith, it's time for your afternoon nap.'

'Don't treat me like a child, woman,' Hugo said but he was helpless in their capable hands and they soon moved him expertly into a wheelchair.

Adam stood up and watched as Hugo was pushed out of the lounge by the two nurses. When they'd left he sat down again and stared into space. How much longer did Hugo have to live? He'd survived lung cancer for over a year now but was deteriorating fast. He guessed it would be weeks rather than months. How did he feel about that? Sad for the end of a life well lived. Hugo hadn't been an easy boss to work for, nor an easy father-in-law. He was abrasive, snapped at the slightest excuse but was honest, a man of principle and fair in all his dealings. Hugo had taught him all he knew about how to run a business.

Adam's father, Cyril Turner, had died of cancer ten years previously when Adam was twenty-two. Being with Hugo brought back memories of sitting with his father, hour upon hour, before he passed peacefully in his sleep.

Adam hoped Hugo's passing would be peaceful too. He owed the old man a lot.

Adam had been at university when his father died. He would have liked to have stayed to continue his studies, but he put his family first and got a job as a salesman at Meredith Motors and became the top salesman in record time, then promoted to higher posts in quick succession until he found himself in an executive position. It was at this point that he started courting Rosamund.

Hearing a noise in the hall, Adam stood up as Rosamund came into the lounge. Speak of the devil.

'Adam. I didn't know you were here.'

'Just keeping Hugo up to speed with a few things.'

'Right. So… how are you?' Rosamund stood behind the couch and ran her hands absentmindedly along the back while gazing at Adam in what she probably thought was a seductive manner.

'I'm fine, Rosamund. I'm just leaving as a matter of fact. So—'

'Oh, please don't go on my account. We should talk anyway. We need to discuss the wedding. You saw Jeremy I take it? He was going to fill you in on the details.'

'What details?'

'Ah.' Rosamund laughed. 'Obviously slipped his mind. Silly old fool. The details concerning our roles at the wedding. Best man and matron of honour. We have certain tasks to carry out. Not been to a big wedding like this one for years. It'll be fun, don't you think? In Jeremy's family pile. And I believe, according to Teddy, we're having the blue room which is one of the more superior guest bedrooms. What a laugh.'

Rosamund now sat on the couch and lounged back with one arm along the top. She had obviously just been out riding as she wore old jodhpurs and a riding jacket. There was a strong smell of horse in the room.

Rosamund had gone back home when Hugo started suffering with cancer, on the pretext of looking after him. The truth was that their marriage had been heading for the rocks when Adam found out about her affair with Max. Rosamund thought a bit of distance would do the trick and Adam would come crawling back to her. Except the opposite happened and Adam told her the marriage was over.

'Rosamund—'

'Why don't we meet up and discuss it. We can compare notes and make sure we're on the same page as it were. We want Teddy and Jeremy's wedding to be perfect with no hiccups or flaws which means careful planning. It's up to us to make sure everything is tickety boo.'

'Rosamund—'

'Whatever's the matter, Adam. You don't look very happy.'

'I'm taking someone else to the wedding.'

'What do you mean? I don't understand.'

'You're not my plus one. Someone else is.'

'We don't need plus ones, Adam, we've both got starring roles. Of course we're going to be together, we'll have to work as a team. I really don't know what you're talking about.'

Adam sighed. He'd known this conversation wasn't going to be easy but was Rosamund being deliberately obtuse?

'Rosamund, you need to listen to me. You and I are not together anymore. The fact that I am the best man, and you are the matron of honour is just coincidence. We will perform our tasks during the day, but at night, when we retire to our bedrooms, I will be with someone else, not you.'

Rosamund was now marching up and down the room. She'd removed her riding boots at the back door as was her custom after a ride, and her stockinged feet didn't make the same impact on the worn rug in the middle of the floor. She also looked shorter which put her at a disadvantage. Adam was preparing for Rosamund to lose it at any minute.

'Who is she? Do I know her? I didn't know you were seeing anyone, you could have had the decency to tell me.'

'Like you told me when you were seeing Max?' He hadn't meant to say that.

'Max isn't serious, you know that.' No, Max was her bit of rough.

'Do I know her? Have I met her? Is she one of our crowd?'

'She's not one of our crowd, and you don't know her.'

'Oh my God, Adam, why the big mystery? Just tell me who she is.'

'Her name's Colleen.'

'That name sounds familiar. Where have I heard that before?'

'She was the—'

'That slut! She was the stripper who was at Jeremy's stag night! You can't be serious. You're not taking her, I won't allow it. I'll talk to Teddy and she'll forbid it. What is the matter with you, Adam?'

'Rosamund, calm down.'

'Calm? Why should I be fucking calm when my husband is taking a prostitute to one of the most important weddings in years? Everyone will be there, Adam, you can't seriously think she'll be accepted can you?'

'I'm not prepared to argue with you about this. I'm going now. No need to see me out.'

'You're not going anywhere.' Rosamund ran to the door and stood with her back to it, so he couldn't leave.

'Rosamund, don't be stupid, just move away from the door.'

'No. Not until you promise me you'll forget this crazy idea. Dump her. She'll be the death of your career, your place in society. She'll bring you down, Adam, to her level. Is she really worth all that?'

'Yes, she is.' The moment he said it, he knew it was true. Colleen was worth fifty Rosamunds, Theos, and the rest.

'If you dare take that slut to the wedding, I'll make sure Daddy knows exactly what kind of a lowlife you really are. You will lose your job, you'll have to sell the penthouse and you'll be brought down so low that even the prostitute won't want you.'

Adam turned away but was ready for Rosamund's next move. He knew she was working herself up in readiness for the rough sex she wanted. But not this time. In fact, never again.

When Rosamund threw herself at Adam, he grabbed her wrists to stop her clawing his face. He was stronger than her, but it was still an effort to stop her attacking him. He held her off him, but seeing the lust in her eyes, knew he had to leave.

'I know what you want, but this time I'm not falling for it. I thought you'd keep your mouth shut after I'd given you what you wanted, but you didn't, did you? You blabbed to Theo and Jeremy about Colleen when it would have been so much more decent of you to keep quiet. As far as your *needs* are concerned, you won't get that from me anymore. I suggest you go to Max on bended knees and beg his forgiveness.'

Chapter Twelve

The London to Manchester train was full, but not as packed as it would be during the week with commuters squashed together like sardines. Colleen managed to grab a seat and gazed out of the window at the countryside flashing by, while her mind mulled over the story she would tell her mother of how Nora was getting on.

There was nothing about Nora's life that she could tell her mother. Nora had no job, and had sex for money to keep the thugs and criminals that she owed money to from beating her up, or worse.

Colleen sighed. She was tired to the bones and out of her depth. In contrast to her sister's life, she was riding high. She loved her job, got on well with Doris, she had Adam and a luxurious apartment. Life was good. How long would that last? It certainly wouldn't be forever, especially if something bad happened to Nora and she was powerless to help her.

Should she tell her mother the truth? Part of her wanted to come clean and be honest about everything. She needed help to deal with it as it was too much for her to solve on her own. But what could her mother do? She'd only fret and make herself ill. And Nora had threatened to never speak to her again if she told her. She had to keep quiet and sort it out herself.

The movement of the train and rhythmic sound of it eating up the miles soothed Colleen, who was tired to start with, and she felt her eyes closing.

The next thing she knew was the announcement that they had arrived at Piccadilly station and this was the end of the line.

Too tired and depressed to bother with buses or trams, Colleen decided to treat herself and jumped into a taxi at the rank just outside the main doors.

Manchester looked small compared to London and it felt as if she had been away for years, rather than a few weeks. So much had happened to her since she had left, that she felt like a different person. She had been so naïve then, expecting Nora to be living a life of luxury that she would be welcomed into with open arms. Stupid girl. But she was at home now and as the taxi sped towards South Manchester and her mum, she felt relief so great that she was almost in tears.

'Mum, it's so good to see you again.' Colleen threw her arms around her mum and held on tight. She wished she was five years old again and her mum could solve all her problems.

'Colleen, my love, why have you stayed away for so long and where's your sister? I thought you were bringing Nora with you.'

'She was busy, Mum, but she sends her love.'

'Busy doing what?' asked Auntie May from the depths of the armchair she had claimed for her own. Had she moved at all since she last saw her? She was still dressed in the same grungy tracksuit bottoms and oversized jumper which made her look even more enormous than she was. Still stuffing her face with crisps. Colleen swore she'd put on half a stone.

The house looked shabbier and far from the pristine, shiny home that she was used to. Her mother was dressed for cleaning with her hair tied back in a headscarf and a tatty overall over her blouse and trousers. The kitchen floor was wet, and a bucket and mop were on the doorstep, the backdoor open to help the floor to dry faster.

'I was hoping to finish all this before you came, but time got away from me. Would you like a cup of tea?'

'The floor's still wet, Mum.'

'Oh, don't worry about that, I can go over it again later.'

'I've got a better idea. Why don't the three of us tackle the lounge and the hall, then we can rest and have some tea and biscuits. What about that?'

'The three of us?' Her mum looked at her as if she'd gone mad.

'Yes, there are three of us in the house and we can get the housework done so much quicker if we work as a team.'

'Okay, dear, if you think that's best. I'll do the hallway and you and your Auntie May can share the lounge.'

'Great idea!' Colleen marched into the lounge armed with a bucket containing dusters, polish, cloths, and a powerful cleaning spray. She knew it was powerful as she always succeeded in soaking the place when she used it.

'Auntie May, you have a choice—do you want to dust or vacuum?'

'Me?' Auntie May fixed her with a penetrating look but Colleen wasn't intimidated. After the box fiasco at the stag night, she was ready to face anyone.

'Yes, you. We all need to do our bit, Auntie May. My poor mum's been run ragged with all the cleaning, cooking, and running about after you. You need to help her.'

'I do my bit. And I can't do housework with my arthritis.'

More like lazy-itis, muttered Colleen.

'What did you say?'

'I said you can dust then. That's not too strenuous. I'll vacuum.'

Colleen turned away and plugged the vacuum cleaner in, ignoring her Auntie May who was play-acting, struggling to get out of her chair, groaning and moaning all over the place. If she thought she was going to fall for that, she could think again. She'd seen her leap up at the sound of the ice cream van and she never bothered to ask if anyone else wanted an ice cream. Lazy bitch.

For the next half hour, Colleen and her mum cleaned the house, dusted, vacuumed, and changed the sheets on the beds. Her mum had been in a state because she hadn't had time to do them. Auntie May wafted the duster in the direction of the furniture but there was little to show for it. Colleen despaired of the woman and decided to ignore her.

When the kitchen floor had dried and the housework had been done downstairs, Colleen and her mother sat at the kitchen table with tea and biscuits. Auntie May was back in her armchair watching daytime TV.

'So, now you can tell me how she really is. What job has she got?'

Colleen had been dreading this moment. She'd decided that the best thing would be to tell her as much of the truth as she could and try to paint a positive picture of their lives.

'Look, Mum, I've taken some photos of our apartment to show you.' Colleen gave her the phone and she brightened up at the sight of the home her two girls were living in.

'Oh, that's lovely. What a gorgeous place. I'll have to come and visit and see it in person. You'll have to let me know when you're free to show me around.'

'Of course, we will, we'll let you know.'

'But what exactly does Nora do? She doesn't have any qualifications and I was so worried that she wouldn't be able to get a job.'

Colleen took a deep breath and prayed that her mum wouldn't see through the lies.

'She works for an agency, Mum, doing this and that. They ring her up when they need her.'

'But what kinds of things does she do?' Her mum obviously wasn't convinced. She'd have to try to be more specific without actually saying anything.

'It's a lot to do with the entertainment industry, you know, bars and clubs and the like.'

'Is she a waitress then?' Her mother had found something to latch onto that she understood.

'She does get jobs in the service industry.'

'Serving? Like a waitress? I do hope she can learn silver service, that's a good skill to have.'

'Kind of.' Colleen cringed as she lied to her mother. She longed to throw herself on her mother's mercy and beg her to help her younger daughter. She needed help. The situation was desperate. But what could her poor little mum do? Nothing but stress herself out and worry day and night. Colleen was already doing that, and it wasn't helping.

'Well, I know you'll look after her and help her, won't you?'

'I'll do my best, Mum.' Colleen needed to shift her mother's focus off Nora and onto herself as she, at least, had a good job. 'Have I told you about where I'm working, Mum?'

Colleen told her mother all about Adam, the boss, and Doris the personal assistant and all the lovely, shiny cars that they sold and how much she enjoyed working there.

'Well, I'm so glad my girls are happy and living in the big city. That's all I want, my girls to be happy.'

Colleen felt as if someone was sticking a knife in her heart and slowly turning it. Her poor mother. She hated lying to her, but what could she do? It was all on her to solve Nora's drug problem, but she had no idea where to start.

By Sunday night Colleen was back in London. It was strange that she felt just as much at home, arriving at Euston, and getting the tube back to the apartment. Leaving her mother had been hard, but she'd promised to phone more often and let her know a suitable date that she could visit and be shown the sights of the capital by her two daughters.

More guilt was heaped on Colleen when Auntie May piped up and said that talk was cheap, but actions spoke louder than words. Colleen thought she was trying to pay her back for the dusting. She ignored her at the time but later, thinking things over on the train, she realised that Auntie May was right. It was time for Colleen to act and rescue her little sister from her tormentors.

When she let herself into the apartment, she knew that

something had happened in the time she had been away. She could sense it even before she found Nora huddled in bed, sobbing.

'Oh, Nora, what is it? What's happened?'

Nora sat up and blew her nose. 'Sorry, just being a wimp.'

'You are not a wimp. What's happened? I knew I should never have left you alone. Why didn't you come with me?'

Nora shook her head and pulled her knees up, laying her head on them and shivering. She looked lost and more than a bit pathetic, huddled like a little girl who was afraid of the dark. But the monsters were real and Colleen had an awful feeling they'd paid Nora a visit over the weekend.

'Have they been here?' Nora nodded. 'How did they know you were here?'

'It was Big Man; he knows everything. There's nothing you can keep from him. Someone must have seen me—he's got spies everywhere. I tried to be careful, but perhaps I was followed.'

'What did he want?'

'His money. I gave him the four grand, but he says I still owe him two.'

'Two! That's ridiculous. You owed him five, paid him four, so you only owe him the one.'

'Interest. His rates are high.'

'That man is an evil bastard, he needs to be stopped.'

'I know.' Nora lay down again and stared at the ceiling. She looked pale and wan as if she was recovering from a serious illness.

'What's he like, this Big Man?' She spoke his name as if the very words were distasteful.

'Big. Big and scary.'

'What does he look like? Sound like?' Colleen had seen

enough programmes on the telly to recognise a baddy when she saw one. He would be dressed in black, have a face full of scars and missing teeth or sporting gold teeth. He would have two men with him who looked as if they lifted weights all day.

'He looks like an ordinary bloke. Upper-class accent. Nasty voice. Scary.'

'Upper class?' Colleen wasn't expecting that. Then she thought about the men at the stag night. They were upper class and had been like hounds baying for her blood. She shivered.

'Posh geezer. Looks as if he has a bad smell under his nose.'

'What did he say to you? Did he threaten you, hurt you? Nora, you need to start thinking of going to the police.'

'And spend the next ten years in jail. No way. Don't even think about it. He told me that if I cooperated and did what I was told, I didn't have to pay the two grand. If I didn't, I'd pay more as the interest was added daily.'

'And by doing as you're told, I presume he means having sex with men?'

'He told me he'd be sending more clients my way.'

'Oh, Nora.' Colleen felt sick but had no idea what to do. This wasn't the right time to tell Nora that their mother was threatening to come and stay.

Chapter Thirteen

The following Monday, Colleen went into work feeling as if she had the weight of the world on her shoulders. She couldn't help obsessing about Nora and the hold Big Man had on her and how in God's name they could break that hold without involving the police.

And it wasn't as if she could look forward to seeing Adam as he was away for a few days on business. She was becoming used to having him around, even though they didn't see each other often enough for Colleen's liking. She'd known from the beginning that they'd only have snatched moments and occasional nights in each other's company, and she was okay with that. She'd have been happy with anything after all the things Adam had done for her. But she wished theirs was a proper relationship where they could be seen in public and could hold hands and walk in a park or go shopping together. Even the food shopping would be exciting if Adam was with her to share it.

Colleen remembered to sign the book as she entered the building and got in the lift. She was early as she hadn't slept well the night before and decided she'd be more productive in the office, taking some of the weight off Doris, than sitting in the apartment staring into space. Nora had still been in bed when she left.

When she arrived at the office, Doris was already at her desk, typing furiously, and Colleen was pleased to see her. She admired the older woman so much, for her work ethic and her loyalty to Adam. She could learn a lot from Doris.

'Morning,' she sang brightly as she sat down and put her handbag in the drawer.

'Good morning, dear, you're early,' said Doris.

'So are you. Is there anything I can do to help?'

'Adam's away for a couple of days, as you know, so I'm taking advantage of that to go through all the correspondence that he lets me deal with without his approval. If I give you a copy of the standard letters—most of them are late payment letters to customers—you can type them up and send them out once I've cast my eye over them. You just need to change the details; name, address, date of purchase, and details of car, date of sale… well, it's self-explanatory. If you have any problems, just give me a shout. I'll email you the standard letter and list of customers.'

'Great, I'll just make a cup of tea and get started.' Colleen was pleased that Doris was entrusting her with more important work. It made her feel part of the company.

An hour later, the correspondence nearly completed, Colleen was beginning to feel more positive. She got up to collect the letters from the printer so Doris could check them over, before sending them off, when the intercom phone rang alerting them that someone was downstairs.

'Meredith Motors,' Doris spoke into the phone. 'Yes, of course, come on up.' She pressed the button that unlocked the front door. 'I wonder what she wants. She knows Adam isn't here.'

'Who's that?' asked Colleen.

'Rosamund Meredith. Adam's wife and Hugo Meredith's daughter. We're not often blessed with a visit from her.'

Colleen could tell that Doris wasn't pleased about this visit but Colleen was curious about Adam's wife. What kind of woman had he chosen to spend the rest of his life with? She was about to find out.

Rosamund Meredith swept into the office and stood in the centre of the room as if she was on show.

'Forgive this intrusion, Doris, but Adam asked me to look in his office for his signet ring. He appears to have mislaid it and you know how much it means to him as I bought it for him on our anniversary and he's simply devastated that it's gone missing.'

'A signet ring?' Doris asked.

'Yes, you remember the one with the garnet in the centre?'

'Do you know, I can't say I remember that ring. Would you like me to help you look for it?'

'Oh no, that's okay, I don't want to keep you from your work. You could pop out and get me a skinny latte from the corner shop if you don't mind, Doris. That would be lovely.'

'Right. Colleen—could you hold the fort? I'll be ten minutes.'

'Of course.' Colleen was intrigued by the pantomime playing out in front of her. It was obvious from Doris's expression that she didn't buy the story of the ring. Adam didn't wear rings and why would he care about one his estranged wife had bought for him? And sending Doris out on a wild goose chase. It was clear that Rosamund had a plan, and it included the two of them.

'Would you like me to help you look for the ring, Rosamund?' asked Colleen when she had made no move to go into Adam's office.

'It's Mrs Turner to you,' said Rosamund glaring at her from the centre of the room. She was dressed to impress with a cream skirt and jacket, a brown camisole and chocolate coloured shoes with an impressive heel. Her red hair was worn in an updo and her make-up was immaculate. The complete look was chic, stylish and expensive. Colleen was wearing a blouse and cardigan and felt a bit of a frump, but she hadn't planned on doing battle with Adam's ex.

'So… are you enjoying working here?'

'Yes, very much.' Colleen was determined to give nothing away until she knew what the woman was after.

'And where are you living?'

'Chelsea.'

'Oh yes, in Adam's apartment. Did you know he used to live there himself until he started working for my father when he could afford the penthouse apartment?'

'No, I didn't know that. It's a very nice apartment.'

Colleen could feel the tension in the air. This woman hated her, and she wasn't sure how to react.

'I'm here to give you a warning. If you want to keep your job and fine apartment stay away from my husband. I don't take kindly to sluts like you fawning all over him.'

'I am not a slut.' Colleen stood up and walked around the desk so she could stand in front of Rosamund. She was not going to be intimidated by her, so she stood tall and said nothing.

'I heard you were a stripper and a prostitute. In my book that makes you a slut. Having sex for money makes you a slut. Jumping out of a box dressed only in red ribbon in front of men to titillate them makes you a slut.'

Colleen said nothing but held Rosamund's gaze. Should she try to explain the circumstances of that night, or would that be a complete waste of time? Rosamund didn't want an explanation, she just wanted to bully Colleen. Well, she was sick of people pushing her and Nora around and this time she wouldn't be pushed.

'*I'm* going to the wedding with Adam, not you. He's my husband and he will be accompanying me. Do not go anywhere near the event that weekend or I'll have you arrested for trespassing.'

'What wedding?'

'Don't play the innocent with me. Adam told me he was intending to take you and I had to put him straight on a few points. So, if you know what's good for you, you'll take my advice and keep your dirty hands to yourself.'

'I really have no idea what you're talking about.'

'Now why don't I believe you?'

'You can believe whatever you like, it's nothing to me.' Colleen didn't know where she got the courage to say that to Rosamund. She never would have answered back before, but these people were no better than she was, just richer.

'Remember what I said. If you go anywhere need Charmley Manor then there'll be trouble.'

Colleen watched as Rosamund Turner, née Meredith, swept from the office, leaving only a waft of her heavy perfume.

The week dragged after that with Colleen fuming about the cheek of Rosamund trying to bully her and worried sick about Nora and the hold Big Man had over her. She wished there was someone she could confide in, but the only person she could tell was Adam and he had done enough for her without burdening him with her sister's problems. No, for now, she had to keep it to herself.

By lunchtime on Friday, Colleen was in the depths of despair and about to ring Adam just to hear his voice, when she got a text from him.

I'll pick you up at seven. Wear something posh.

'Is that Adam?' asked Doris who knew that they were seeing each other and approved.

'Yes. He says wear something posh, but I don't possess anything posh.'

'He'll be taking you to Citrus City, one of the new trendy places.'

'Is it posh?' Colleen was ecstatic to be taken out for a meal by Adam. They had never even been on a date, so this was a special occasion.

'Oh yes,' said Doris with a smile, 'the poshest of the posh.'

'What am I going to do? I don't want to let him down, but I can't wear my usual clothes. I'd better text him and tell him I can't go.'

'I wouldn't do that if I were you, Adam would be terribly hurt. Take the rest of the day off and use the company credit card. I've done that before now when I've been in a fix, Adam won't mind. Buy something that's a knockout.'

Doris handed over a Visa card and a sticky note with the PIN number.

'Are you sure, Doris?'

'Absolutely sure. Go on, off you go and I'll see you on Monday. Have a lovely evening.'

'Doris, you're an angel.' Colleen wanted to hug her but didn't think it'd be the done thing.

She hurried out of the office, remembering to sign the book, and made her way to Oxford Street to shop until she dropped.

'Will you stop your fidgeting, you're making me dizzy.' Nora was lounging on the couch watching the TV and Colleen was walking up and down in front of her. Her nerves were frayed, and she had questions running on a loop through her head. Would he like the dress? Would she know which knife and fork to use? Would she show him up and be a laughing stock?

'Are you sure this dress is okay?' she asked Nora for the umpteenth time.

'The dress is fine. You're fine. Now will you shut up and let me watch this programme?'

Colleen had agonised over the dress. She'd settled for an A-line scoop neck chiffon evening dress in a colour they were calling "pool" which was a shade of blue you didn't see very often but suited her colouring and her blonde hair. It had three-quarter sleeves and she'd bought big loop earrings, a cheap bracelet and a clutch bag to go with it.

She knew she looked okay but couldn't help comparing herself to Rosamund and how stylish she had looked in her suit. No matter how much money people paid for their clothes, some just looked good without even trying. Sadly, she wasn't one of them.

The intercom buzzed and Colleen jumped.

'Oh God, that's him.'

'Hallelujah,' said Nora.

'Right, I'm going. I might not be back tonight, so don't open the door to anyone, okay?'

'Have fun,' said Nora without taking her eyes off the TV. Colleen felt a twist of fear when she thought of all the things that could happen to Nora in her absence. 'Go!'

'Right, I'm going.'

She left the apartment and entered the lift, admiring herself in the shiny surfaces. A real date! With Adam. OMG. What did it mean? That he was thinking of her as more than a mistress? Men didn't take their mistresses for meals did they? Or did they? She didn't know, she'd never been anyone's mistress before.

Whatever happened, she was going to make the most of every second they spent together.

Chapter Fourteen

Adam wasn't sure why he was nervous as he waited for Colleen to emerge from the apartment building. When he had got the call from Doris to say that Rosamund had been in and making trouble, he knew he had to act, so he booked his favourite restaurant and was fortunate to get a table for Friday.

He'd wanted to take Colleen out somewhere special ever since that first night they'd spent together. He had longed to see her in her finery; dress, hair, and make-up, looking gorgeous as he knew she would.

This meal was really an opportunity for him to explain and apologise for Rosamund's visit. He needed to come clean about his relationship, or the absence of, with his estranged wife. And, of course, to invite her to accompany him to Jeremy's wedding. Nothing that Rosamund could say or do would stop him taking Colleen.

'Hi,' said Colleen as she skipped out of the building and strolled up to him.

'Wow, I mean hi,' Adam replied. She looked gorgeous in her blue dress, her hair shining and her eyes sparkling.

'Will I do? Doris told me to use the company credit card to buy a dress as I didn't have anything posh. Was that okay? I'll pay it back, of course. You can take it out of my wage—'

Adam kissed her and she linked her arms around his neck and the kiss deepened. He ran his hands over her back, enjoying the softness of the fabric and the warmth of her body underneath it. He wanted to take her back inside and show her how much he missed her, but she was expecting a meal and anyway, Nora was bound to be there.

When the kiss ended, he pulled away gently and smoothed her hair back from her face.

'You look spectacular. Gorgeous. I love the dress.'

'Thank you. You look good too.' Adam was wearing one of his Italian suits, the one he felt the most comfortable in. 'Right, let's go. I hope you like seafood as this place specialises in it. Although you could have chicken or steak if you prefer.'

'Seafood's fine. I love it, but don't get the chance to eat it often.'

'Right, well tonight we'll gorge on the stuff. Then back to my place?' He raised his eyebrows in a question. He didn't want to take anything for granted.

'I told Nora I'll be staying so, yes, back to your place.' The look she gave him was full of sexy promise and he felt his groin tightening in anticipation. But the waiting would make the mating all the sweeter.

'How is Nora?' He hadn't heard much about her sister lately, so hoped that meant her drug crisis had been resolved. Hopefully, she was in rehab and getting the help she needed.

'Nora's… she loves the apartment.'

'Good.' Colleen obviously didn't want to talk about it tonight. That was fine with him as he had lots to tell her, mainly about Jeremy and Theo's wedding and the truth of his relationship with Rosamund. He wanted it all out in the open so there could be no misunderstandings.

After a short ride in the Mercedes, with an instruction to Davis that he'd text when they were ready to go home, they arrived at Citrus City.

They entered on a wave of noise and a waft of different aromas of food that made Adam's stomach rumble. He hadn't eaten since breakfast and was ready to tuck in to a delicious meal.

When the waiter had seated them and handed them menus, Adam asked for a bottle of champagne. Not the most expensive, but a good one.

'Champagne? What are we celebrating?' asked Colleen.

'Our first real date,' said Adam grinning. He wished he could erase the way they had met and start again. They could always pretend and forget about the fiasco of the stag night. He wondered if he should suggest it to Colleen, but she might find it a bit weird, so he didn't.

'Of course.' She studied the menu with a frown.

'What are you going to have?'

'Well, most of the things I like are really expensive, so I'll just have—'

'Do you like lobster?'

'Oh I love lobster, but—'

'Right, that's easy.'

When the waiter returned with the champagne, he poured them a glass each and put the champagne bottle in the ice bucket. Adam gave them the order. Smoked salmon to start followed by half a lobster each.

When they were alone again, they clinked their glasses together and said "cheers".

'This is nice,' said Colleen, 'the two of us having a meal and champagne. I wasn't expecting all this.'

'Only the best for you.' She blushed and Adam thought how pretty she looked. 'I need to apologise for my estranged wife's behaviour. Doris told me she'd been in.'

'Yes, she was talking about a wedding and assumed I knew all about it.'

'Jeremy's and Theo's. I'm best man and Rosamund is matron of honour. I was going to ask you to accompany me. We'll be spending the night. Jeremy's family home. It's called Charmley Manor and is rather grand. Will you come with me?'

'Of course, I'd love to. Can I wear this dress do you think as no one there will have seen it? Except you of course.'

'If you want to do that, of course you can, but if you want to buy a new one, you can use the company card.'

'This is new. I like this dress.'

'Me too. Yes, wear that one, it suits you.'

'Great. Tell me more about Charmley Manor. It sounds intriguing.'

The waiter brought their salmon, and it was a while before Adam answered.

'It's a beautiful place in six acres of land. It's massive and has stables, tennis courts and an indoor swimming pool with hot tub and sauna.'

'Wow, that sounds amazing. Is Jeremy's family very rich then?'

'Yes, very. How's the salmon?'

'It's wonderful. Melts in the mouth.'

Colleen couldn't know the effect that image had on him.

He remembered the blow job she had given him and forced himself not to groan.

'It's going to be a big affair and we'll be there the whole weekend. The following day, there'll be riding if you're into equestrian activities, shooting, fishing, or just staying at the house and enjoying the pool and other facilities.'

'I think the last option will be more my thing.'

'Yes, me too. I don't ride. Or shoot. Or fish for that matter. But I like swimming.'

The waiter swapped their empty plates for the lobster and the aroma was heavenly.

Colleen's eyes nearly popped out of her head.

'This looks delish.'

'It certainly does.' Adam tucked in, enjoying the delicate flavour of the lobster.

'Can I ask you something, Adam?'

'Of course.'

'You're not like the others, are you?'

'What others?'

'Jeremy, Rupert… Rosamund and the one who was there on the stag night.'

'Lady Theodora Blakely.'

'That's the one. You're not like them. You don't talk like them. They're upper class aren't they, but you're not.'

'No, I'm not. I'm a working-class boy from London. I may have lost a bit of my accent, but at heart, I'm still just a cockney. When I got the executive job I made a concerted effort to lose the accent, I've never lost it completely. The problem is, you can't hear yourself as others do, so you don't always know when you're slipping back to the old ways.'

'But what's wrong with having an accent? I much prefer it to the toffee-nosed, stuck-up—'

'Hey, they're my friends you're talking about.'

Colleen put her hand over her mouth and gasped. 'Oh, goodness, I'm so sorry, I didn't mean to insult them.'

Adam reached over and took her hand. 'I'm joking, relax. I can't stand their voices half the time. Even Jeremy who's a close friend I can only tolerate in small doses.'

Adam took his hand away and sat back. He poured them another glass of champagne, surprised to see that they'd drunk nearly the whole bottle.

'So, when you married Rosamund, did you have to learn how to fit into their world?'

That was a bit of a sore point, but Adam was determined to be completely honest with Colleen.

'Yes, she even made me have elocution lessons. But I drew the line at riding.'

'That's awful. It's like saying you can marry me but only if you become a different person. Am I being rude again?'

'No, you've hit the nail on the head. Ours wasn't a marriage made in heaven, it was made in the boardroom. Hugo wanted me to be his CEO. Rosamund wanted the job but knew nothing about the business. So the next best thing for her was to marry me, then she could still have a say in the company. She sits in on board meetings.'

'So, she didn't really want you, just whoever was in control of Meredith Motors.'

'Exactly. And it worked for a while. Until she had an affair actually. Then I had the excuse I needed to end the marriage. The problem is, Hugo is obsessed with portraying Meredith Motors as a family concern, so we have to attend functions together to keep up the charade of still being happily married.'

'But what about the wedding? What will Hugo say when he finds out you're going with me?'

'That remains to be seen. But we're going together nonetheless and if Hugo and Rosamund don't like it, that's just tough.'

'I don't want to be the reason you lose your job. Maybe you *should* go with Rosamund.'

Adam remembered Rosamund's warning; that he could lose everything if he insisted on going to the wedding with Colleen. It was a risk he was willing to take.

'I'm going with you or I don't go at all. I'm not prepared to let Jeremy down. He's my friend and he deserves better than that. So, we're going—together. Now, do you want a dessert, or coffee?'

'No thanks.'

'Shall we go?'

'Yes, let's go.'

The meal had been fabulous, and Adam had loved her dress. It had been a perfect date and now they were back in Adam's penthouse suite and she should have been feeling on top of the world. But she wasn't. How could she when going to the wedding with her could lose Adam his job?

'Come here,' Adam said, and she moved into his arms. She held him and he wrapped his arms around her and kissed her head. They stayed like that until Adam broke away and looked her in the eyes. 'Okay, tell me what's wrong.'

'Nothing's wrong. It's been a lovely evening.'

'Something's on your mind. I know you well enough by now to recognise when you're brooding over something. Is it Nora?'

'No.' Although her sister was never far from her

thoughts. She still didn't know how to fix the drug dealers and get them off Nora's back. 'It's you and the wedding.'

'Don't you want to go?' Adam sounded disappointed.

'Yes, of course I do. Very much. But if I go with you, Rosamund will make trouble. She as good as said that to me. I don't want to be the cause of you losing your job.'

Adam kissed her gently and stroked her face. 'I won't lose my job because of you. Hugo will get to find out about it, that's certain. Rosamund will make sure he gets to hear all the details. But Hugo is a shrewd businessman who's dying of cancer and only has a short time to live. If he sacked me now, he'd be left without a CEO and would have to find a new one or appoint someone already in the company and there is no one who can do the job. His business means more to him than anything. He won't risk it.'

'Even for his daughter?'

'If it came to a showdown I think he'd choose his business.'

'Who do you think he'll leave it to?'

'That's a good question and one I can't answer, so let's stop all the shop talk and get down to the important business of fucking each other senseless.'

Adam took her hand and led her to the bedroom. He was such a gentleman that it shocked and delighted her when he talked dirty. It turned her on. That had come as a surprise as she'd never liked uncouth people before. But Adam had class. He was suave and, for all his protestations of being a working-class boy, he was quite sophisticated.

When they reached his bedroom, Adam went straight to his wardrobe and removed a hanger, handing it to her.

'For that lovely dress. I don't want to rip it no matter how much I long to see you naked.'

'Thanks.' Colleen took the hanger and slowly and carefully removed her dress. She put it on the hanger and gave it back to Adam who hung it in the wardrobe. He then removed his jacket and trousers, hanging them carefully and putting them in the wardrobe too. Then he loosened his tie and pulled it off as Colleen stood in her bra and panties watching him.

'Your turn,' he said.

Colleen removed her bra and threw it on a chair. 'Now you.'

Adam unbuttoned his shirt slowly, removing his cufflinks carefully and putting them on the dressing table. He then shrugged out of his shirt and pulled his socks off, throwing them on top of Colleen's bra. He stood watching her with a smile on his face, dressed only in his boxers. He was aroused and so was she. Her nipples were standing to attention and she wanted Adam's hands on them.

Without breaking eye contact, Colleen slipped out of her panties. She discarded them and stood proudly, naked and waiting for Adam to remove his boxers. He did, slowly and leisurely as if they had all the time in the world. This was different to the frenzied sex they usually engaged in. It was good, as if they were building up the anticipation, like gazing at an ice cream sundae before plunging the spoon in and scooping up the sweetness.

Colleen's mouth was watering at the thought, but it wasn't ice cream she craved.

They slowly started walking towards each other, their gazes locked and when their bodies came together, Colleen breathed a deep sigh of relief.

Colleen's nipples brushed up against the hair on Adam's chest, the friction causing them to tingle. She ran her hands over his back and down to his buttocks, grasping them tightly. She loved his bum, it was firm and tight, and she squeezed them before running her hands up his sides. She buried her face in his neck and breathed in his spicy aftershave. Then their mouths found each other, and they kissed long and sensually, exploring, teasing and hot.

Then Colleen broke the kiss as Adam's erection pressed into her. She knelt down and took him in her mouth. Of all the things they did together, this was her favourite. She loved the feel of him, the taste of his cum and the way she could bring him to his knees with her mouth and tongue.

She took her time, teasing him, licking around the head, then tonguing his urethra, before taking him deep into her mouth again. Adam was moaning softly, and his fingers were in her hair. She could tell by the amount of pressure he exerted on her scalp and the little moaning sounds he made, that he was growing ever nearer to his climax.

Colleen knew she had to control Adam, by gently squeezing his balls, and tightening her grip on the shaft as she licked and played with him. She kept him on the edge as long as she could, until she could feel him reach the point of no return.

Then he came in an explosion in her mouth, crying out as waves of pleasure rendered him helpless and his knees buckled. He knelt in front of Colleen and they hugged.

'You do that so well,' said Adam, stroking her hair and kissing her face.

'I love doing that to you, I could do it all day.'

Adam laughed, 'What a pleasant prospect that would be.'

Adam stood up and Colleen followed. He led her to the bed, and they lay face to face, gazing into each other's eyes.

Colleen stroked Adam's face and he did the same to her.

'What are you thinking?' she asked, even though she

knew it was a question most men hated to have to answer, insisting they weren't thinking about anything.

'Actually, I was thinking about the wedding. You're not nervous about going are you?'

'A bit. Especially if the men who were at Jeremy's stag night are going to be there.'

'They were all quite drunk and I doubt any of them will recognise you unless you intend to go wrapped up in red ribbon again?'

'God don't remind me. If I never see another red ribbon as long as I live, it'll be too soon.'

'Sorry, shouldn't have brought it up.'

'But I'm glad I did, or I would never have met you and that would have been a tragedy.' She kissed him on the end of his nose, and he laughed.

'Right, time for me to show you how much I appreciate red ribbon as a fashion statement. You did look incredibly sexy in it.'

Colleen was ready for Adam, and he spread her legs wide and kissed her all the way down her body then licked and kissed and fondled her until she had no coherent thoughts left and all the worries that were playing at the back of her mind disappeared with the first mind-blowing orgasm.

Chapter Fifteen

Saturday, the day of Jeremy and Theo's wedding. Another chance to wear her blue dress and, more importantly, the chance to spend all day with Adam. Although, with him being Jeremy's best man, he would have duties to perform which would take him away from her for a lot of the time and she would need to be able to entertain herself for large chunks of the day.

The ceremony itself for instance, when Adam would be standing next to his friend as they awaited the entrance of the bride. Who would doubtless look stunning. And the wedding breakfast when Adam would be sitting at the head table and she would have to fit in where she could.

At the last minute, when she was packing her suitcase, she slipped in her sketch pad and pencils. There may be time over the weekend when she could do some drawings of Charmley Manor and the gardens. Maybe even the guests if she was allowed to. It would help pass the time.

Now that the day had arrived, Colleen's stomach was churning and she was starting to wish she'd insisted Adam and Rosamund go together, it would have been easier all round. And—a little voice in her head chastised her—the coward's way out. And Adam wasn't a coward, so she needed to step up and support him. She was only there as a guest for goodness' sake, she didn't have to do anything. If she could survive being taped into a cardboard box wearing nothing but ribbon, she could survive anything.

She did a twirl in front of the mirror and went to find Nora.

'How do I look?'

'You look amazing. He doesn't deserve you.'

Nora was lying on the couch in her pyjamas, looking pale and subdued.

'Why do you say that?'

'He's one of them. The rich, important people. The ones with more money than sense.'

'No, you've got him all wrong. Adam is from a working-class background, he just married into money. He's not like them at all.'

Nora looked at her and again, Colleen felt the sharp stab of concern when she thought of all the obstacles her sister was facing.

'If you say so.' Nora turned her head away and stared fixedly at the television.

'Nora, what's wrong? Are you worried about Big Man? I don't have to go to this wedding, I can stay here with you.'

'I'm okay, I'm just tired. You go off with the posh knob-heads and leave me here to sleep. I'll be fine.'

'Are you sure?'

'Of course I'm sure. Go.'

'Okay.'

At that moment, the intercom buzzed, and she went to answer it. It was Adam and she got goosebumps in a thrill of anticipation at the thought of seeing him in his wedding finery. She grabbed the suitcase on wheels that she had bought especially for the occasion. It had been quite expensive, but Colleen hadn't wanted to show Adam up by dragging along a cheap looking thing.

When she got outside, Davis was waiting patiently to put her suitcase in the car.

'Thank you,' she said breathlessly.

'You're welcome, madam.' Davis was elderly and immaculately dressed with impeccable manners. She smiled at him to show that she appreciated him treating her with respect. She had a fleeting thought that she might not be treated so well by some of the wedding guests. But sod them, she was going to enjoy herself, starting with seeing Adam in his best man's suit.

Colleen wasn't disappointed. Adam looked scrumptious in a dark grey morning suit, with a silver, double-breasted waistcoat, dusky pink tie, and a white shirt. Colleen was amused to see the top hat sitting next to him on the seat of the car and longed to see him wearing it.

'I've got a hat too,' she said as she put her white floppy affair next to his top hat.

'You look beautiful and the hat's a winner.'

'We'll have to get a photo taken of the two of us in our hats.'

'Sure. We'll get lots of photos. And the sun's shining. What more could we want?'

For it to be their wedding. Now, where had that thought come from? Adam couldn't marry her as he was already married. And she wouldn't be the kind of woman he chose to marry anyway. Okay for a mistress, but not a bride.

'You okay?' asked Adam as Davis moved the car through the London traffic, heading for Berkshire. 'You're not still worrying, are you? It'll be fine you know. I bet you have a great time. Wait 'til you see Charmley Manor. It's quite an experience.'

'I'm fine. I am a bit nervous, but I've given myself a stern telling off this morning and I'll be okay on my own for some of the day.'

'I'll have my phone on me all the time, so if anything does happen—which it won't—give me a ring or send a text. Okay? And you look a knockout. You really do.'

'Thanks, Adam, I appreciate that.'

Colleen had a picture in her head of what Charmley Manor would look like. But when the car turned down the long driveway and emerged at the turning point in front of the house, she realised she had been wrong on all counts.

The house itself must have been quite modest when it was originally built and then, over the years as the home of many generations of Baxters, it had been built on in all directions to include a conservatory and the indoor swimming pool, and two separate cottages, no doubt for the servants.

Davis got out of the car and opened the doors for them to alight. He took her suitcase and a larger one that must be Adam's out of the boot, before making his way to the front door of the house.

'Davis will make sure our cases get to the right room. It's the blue room if you need a moment to freshen up.'

'Oh, okay.' Colleen hadn't thought any further than the ceremony, but she had a whole night with Adam to look forward to.

'Right, I'm going to find Jeremy. Have a wander round,

but don't get lost, and be in the ballroom in time for the wedding.' He kissed her quickly, then marched off to perform his best man duties.

Colleen felt a pang of loss, watching him stride into the house and decided to have a look around the grounds first before she braved the other guests. Nerves were kicking in again.

After looking at the tennis courts and the stables she moved on. She could hear the animals inside. Colleen was a bit nervous of horses, they were so big, and she'd never been interested in riding and hadn't even read *Black Beauty* like a lot of her friends had done. She also didn't want anybody to catch her loitering and tell her she was trespassing.

It was a beautiful July day; the sun was shining, birds were singing in the trees and the sky was a deep blue with small white fluffy clouds, that reminded Colleen of candy floss, only white. She stopped on a wooden bridge over a pond to watch the fish swimming about in the water.

Colleen was procrastinating and just putting off the evil hour when she had to go into the house and risk bumping into someone who didn't want her there. The bride and her matron of honour for example.

After exhausting all the places she could think of to investigate, she meandered slowly back to the house.

As she walked around the side of the house, she stopped in her tracks. A peacock stood in her path, his tail feathers in a fan behind him. The colours of blue, green, red, and gold were iridescent in their brilliance, making the "eye" patterns shimmer. The bird stared at Colleen who stared back. She was wary of making any quick movements, in case the bird went for her, so she stayed as still as possible.

'Shoo, you stupid bird,' a man behind her said, waving

his hands. The peacock shook his feathers and stalked off in disgust. 'Don't worry, dear, it's a testy creature the peacock, but you weren't in any danger.'

'Oh, thank you,' said Colleen.

'I'm Lord Bebbage, on the bride's side. And you are?'

'Colleen O'Shea, I'm here as a guest of the best man.'

'Ah, yes, the chappie that sells those wonderful cars. Well, very pleased to meet you, my dear. Would you like me to escort you inside?'

More people were arriving, the cars dropping them off at the door, some with luggage and some without. They all looked rich and well-to-do, making Colleen freeze a little inside. To enter on the arm of a lord, even if they had only just met, would be preferable to going it alone.

'That would be very kind, thanks.'

Lord Bebbage offered her his arm and she took it gratefully. She felt, for a second, like a heroine in a historical novel, rescued from a killer peacock by a member of the aristocracy.

When they arrived at the front door of the manor, Lord Bebbage made a show of helping her up the steps. Did she come across as a helpless female? Not the image she wanted to present to these people.

'Thank you, Lord Bebbage, I'll be fine now.'

'Splendid. Right, I'll go and find Lady Bebbage. Lovely to meet you, my dear.'

'And you too.' She watched him wander off to the back of the house so, alone again, she continued her admiring study of Charmley Manor. The hallway was magnificent.

Two flights of stairs, one on the left and one on the right of the hall, curved upwards to form a half circle that joined on the landing. The banisters were black wrought iron, with a pattern of ferns and leaves that was intricately made and contrasted with the white stair carpet to produce an image that Colleen found breathtaking. She didn't know much about interior design, but whoever had designed the staircase knew what they were doing.

Colleen ignored the sound of voices echoing in the hallway. Some were talking quietly, but others had loud, entitled tones, used to staff jumping to do their bidding. She hoped she'd find someone pleasant to talk to otherwise it was going to be a painfully long day.

She passed the room which must be the great hall, decked out for the wedding breakfast. A rectangular table at the top of the room would be the head table where Adam would sit with Rosamund and the bride and groom and their parents. There were round tables in the rest of the hall and Colleen wondered if she should look for the seating plan. Forewarned was forearmed after all.

All the tables were adorned with white cloths and red chiffon placed as runners across the tables and tied into huge bows over the backs of the chairs. But why red? A strange choice for a wedding.

Colleen moved on, after failing to find the seating plan, and decided to have a look upstairs. She ascended the sweeping staircase, marvelling at the beauty of the house. How the other half lived. Did she envy them? Not really. She'd be happy living in a modest house with the right man. She didn't need fancy décor and posh food. She was happy living in the Chelsea apartment and having take-out now and again. Although the penthouse that Adam lived in was beautiful.

Colleen was lost in a daydream of living with Adam, and she didn't notice a woman standing in front of her until she was up close.

'I think there's been some mistake. This is a respectable

high society wedding, and we haven't ordered a stripper or a prostitute, so if I were you, I'd crawl back to the gutter where you belong.' Rosamund stood with one hand on her hip, the other clutching a glass of champagne. She was wearing a ballgown in dark green. Colleen looked her up and down, deciding that the colour was too dark for a wedding and didn't suit her.

'I'm here as Adam's guest, so you have no right to insult me.'

'I have every right. This is the wedding of one of my closest and dearest friends, and nothing is going to stop it being a roaring success. Certainly not a woman like you. You're not fit to be seen in this house and I should have you escorted off the premises.'

'Is everything alright?' A smartly dressed elderly woman arrived out of nowhere and looked from one to the other. Colleen had no idea how much she had heard or who she was.

'I don't think we've been introduced. I'm Delilah Baxter, the mother of the groom.' She put her hand out to Colleen who wondered if she should curtsy.

'Colleen O'Shea, I'm here with Adam,' she said, shaking her hand.

'Oh yes, dear Adam. We haven't seen him for ages, the poor boy is always so busy. How do you know Adam?'

Colleen looked at Rosamund expecting her to step in and tell her about the stag night, but she was quiet, glaring at Colleen.

'I work at Meredith Motors.'

'Oh, splendid. Well done.' She turned to Rosamund. 'And how's your poor father, Rosamund? It must be such a worry for you. Give him my regards, won't you?'

'Of course,' said Rosamund.

Another elderly woman was passing and grabbed Jeremy's mother's attention. They wandered off, arm in arm.

A child came up to them, dressed in a red bridesmaid's dress. 'Lady Theodora wants you to help her,' the little girl said to Rosamund.

'Fine. Tell her I'll be there presently.'

'She said I was to bring you back with me.'

Rosamund sighed theatrically and Colleen thought the girl was brave standing up to her. She turned her back and hurried off with the child running to keep up.

Colleen found herself alone again. Having just dodged a bullet, she badly needed a drink, so wandered back downstairs to find a waiter with a tray of champagne.

'Give me a hand with this wretched buttonhole, there's a good chap.'

Jeremy was starting to exhibit signs of nerves and it was Adam's duty, as his best man, to calm him down and reassure him.

Adam pinned the dark red rose on Jeremy's lapel.

'There, sorted. How are you feeling?'

'I feel like a drink. You wouldn't go and fetch me one, would you? Anything will do. Have one yourself.'

'You know what Theo would do to you if you turned up at the altar drunk. And me, for letting you get drunk. There's not long to go now and you'll see your blushing bride and it'll all have been worth it.'

'Blushing... ha!' Jeremy gave his famous donkey bray laugh, 'I don't think Theo's ever blushed in her life. She's not the type.'

Adam knew what type of person she was, and he didn't

envy Jeremy one bit. But this was his friend's wedding day, and he was charged with making sure it all went smoothly.

'Right. Let's get on with it, shall we?'

'Have you got the rings?'

'Of course, safe and sound,' said Adam patting his coat pocket.

Adam and Jeremy made their way down the stairs to the ballroom to wait for Theo to arrive. As they went, he searched the groups of people clustered together in the hall, on the stairs and hovering around the entrance to the ballroom, but he couldn't spot Colleen.

Jeremy's mood had lifted now they were in the thick of it. He shook hands with some people, waved to others, and seemed to be having the time of his life. He was naturally a people person, effusive, and loved being the centre of attention.

Knowing how easily Jeremy got distracted, he steered him down the centre of the room to the front row of chairs and encouraged him to sit down and take some deep breaths.

A string quartet at the back of the hall played something that sounded like Vivaldi. He wasn't knowledgeable about classical music.

The wedding planner was scurrying around, checking last-minute details, and talking to people.

The civil celebrant stood patiently behind the table, gazing benignly out at the assembled group. She was probably used to all this and had her practised expression that she kept in place at all times. A cross between "I've seen all this hundreds of times before" to "how wonderful, another couple getting married".

Time seemed to stretch as everyone waited for the bride. He did hope Theo would do the right thing and not be deliberately late. It was bad enough that the great hall would be packed, and he had yet to make a speech—his nerves were frayed just thinking about it—but he wanted the ceremony and breakfast to be over so he could enjoy being with Colleen for the rest of the weekend.

Then the string quartet started playing "Here comes the bride" which was his and Jeremy's cue to stand up. The civil celebrant smiled which Adam took as a good sign. Perhaps it was "thank goodness now we can get on".

Neither man risked looking over their shoulders at Theo, but when she arrived next to them, and Adam stepped away leaving Jeremy and Theo standing together, Adam was surprised by the feeling of emotion that washed over him. She did look stunning. Lady Theodora was a beautiful woman in the classical sense. Fine cheekbones, a retrousse nose, large eyes, and a full mouth. She wasn't Adam's type, but Jeremy was beaming at the sight of her.

Adam wished he could turn around and find Colleen. She'd been on her own now for a few hours and he needed confirmation that she was okay. But the service had started, so he had to sit tight and wait for the ceremony to be over before he could go and look for her.

Chapter Sixteen

Colleen had followed the crowd streaming into the ballroom. She didn't know anyone that she could sit next to so chose a seat right at the back. She took her hat off and put it on her knee.

The décor in the ballroom mirrored that in the great hall. Chairs wrapped in white with dark red bows, a red carpet sprinkled with rose petals and at the top, where the ceremony would take place, an arch made of greenery of some kind, white lights dotted around it, and red roses everywhere.

It looked amazing and Colleen drank in the atmosphere. People smiled at her and she returned the smiles, trying to convey that she was fine with being on her own.

When the musicians started playing, Adam and Jeremy stood up and Colleen craned to get a look at him. Adam looked gorgeous in his morning suit and even Jeremy looked okay. She had only seen him once, at his stag do, and he had made very little impression on her. But that was probably because she was having a meltdown and was scared out of her wits.

Colleen turned, as everyone else did, as Lady Theodora Blakely floated down the aisle on the arm of her father. She looked amazing in a wedding dress with a sweetheart neckline, off-the-shoulder long sleeves, and sequined embroidered lace. The dress had a long train, carried by four little bridesmaids looking cute in their red dresses with red headbands.

Theo carried a bouquet of red roses and looked beautiful and sophisticated, even though she also looked serious, staring straight ahead without smiling or acknowledging anyone.

Then the ceremony started, and Colleen struggled to follow it. She could hardly hear what they were saying and wished she'd sat nearer the front. To amuse herself she gazed around at the people watching the couple get married, although not everyone was paying attention. She spotted at least three people on their mobile phones, their heads bent as their thumbs flew over the screens. She had turned hers off as that was the right thing to do and there was a sign in the doorway asking people to respect the sanctity of the wedding ceremony and turn off all devices.

The ceremony seemed to go on for ages and Colleen felt her eyelids growing heavy. Perhaps she shouldn't have drunk that second glass of champagne.

Then it was over, and she heard the words, 'You may kiss the bride.'

Jeremy kissed Theo who looked as if she wanted to wipe her mouth. Not a love match then.

The happy couple and the rest of the wedding party went outside to have the photos taken. Adam had told her that this could take anything up to an hour. She had a choice: watch from a distance or amuse herself inside until the wedding breakfast started. Adam had explained that this was cocktail hour, and she could talk to people and get to know them, if there was anyone there she wanted to know, that was.

Colleen decided that she'd like some time alone, so she made her way upstairs to find the blue room.

As she reached the next floor, a man was standing in her way, smirking at her. With a start, she recognised him as Rupert, the man who had taped her into the cardboard box at the stag night. He was big and beefy looking with a red face and a thick neck. Even dressed in a morning suit, he looked more like a bouncer than a guest at a posh wedding.

'Well, if it isn't the stripper. When I saw all the red ribbon, I wondered if you would be leaping out of the wedding cake in the nude. I'd definitely pay to see that.'

Colleen was shaking in front of him but was determined that she wouldn't let him see how frightened she was. She was alone, without Adam, or even Lord Bebbage to help her.

'It's chiffon, not ribbon.'

'Oh, I beg your pardon, how silly of me.' His voice dripped sarcasm and his upper-class accent was exaggerated, making Colleen think he was putting it on for effect. 'Although even better as it's transparent.'

'Would you let me pass, please?' Colleen tried not to look him in the eye, but his gaze was compelling. She just wanted to get away from him and take refuge in the bedroom.

'No need to be hasty. This is a social occasion, and you're not being very sociable, are you? And if we stay up here talking, we're missing cocktail hour. You wouldn't want to miss that now would you?'

'I don't care,' Colleen said. Her mouth had gone dry, and she felt queasy.

'Oh dear, has Adam gone off and left you? That's what happens to tarts. Oh, sorry… no, you're a high-class prostitute, aren't you? Adam's paying a lot for you.'

'I'm not a prostitute, or a tart—or even a stripper, now please let me pass.'

'Cut the bullshit, we all know what you are. I was there, remember. Anyway, we could be good for each other. If you ever need work—if Adam gets fed up with you, which he will in time, men having such short attention spans—I could put some business your way. Rich clients. Richer than Adam. Men looking for a superior experience if you get my meaning. And if you ever need a pick-me-up to get you through the long hours on your back, I can supply that as well.'

'I don't need—'

'Here—my card. It's got my mobile number. Don't use it for any other purpose, okay? No names. If someone else answers, just ask for Big Man.'

Colleen took the card but couldn't speak. She was slowly turning to stone. Big Man. It couldn't be the same one. Could it?

Colleen hurried along the corridor until she got to the blue room, unlocked the door, and sat on the bed, shaking. Rupert was Big Man. Big, menacing, upper-class accent, nasty, beastly… Oh God, it must be him. The man who had Nora in his clutches and wasn't about to let go. What could she do?

Colleen took her shoes off and lay on the bed, clutching a pillow for comfort. She felt like crying but what good would that do? She had to get through the rest of the wedding for Adam's sake, she owed him that much. It was important to keep it together. Rupert, aka Big Man, wouldn't make the connection between Nora and herself. He had never seen her at Nora's flat and there were no photos of her anywhere. Likewise, he wouldn't have any reason to think she was Nora's sister. When he'd ordered a stripper for Jeremy's stag night, he wouldn't have cared who they sent and wouldn't have asked for a name.

So, she must make sure that Rupert never made the connection, or he would make Nora suffer for sure. That was the only thing she had over him and she had to think of a way to use it to her advantage. But so far, her mind was blank.

The biggest question before all else was—should she tell Adam? If she did, would he think she wasn't worth the effort and end their relationship? After all, Rupert was part of his social circle. A friend of Jeremy's. Did they all know that he was a drug dealer and a pimp? Was this something that went on freely in their society? Were they all at it and that was why they were all so rich? Did Adam know about Rupert?

At that last thought, Colleen stood up and started pacing up and down. Could she trust Adam? Yes, of course. He'd sat at Nora's bedside in the accident and emergency department and watched over her. Adam was kind, sweet, caring, generous and loveable. Everything that Big Man who had such a high opinion of himself wasn't. Yes, she could trust Adam. She had no choice.

Colleen made her way down to the wedding breakfast in the great hall praying she didn't bump into Rupert. She was seething inside at the knowledge that the man who had caused her sister so much pain and grief was here at a wedding, stuffing himself with good food and wine with not a care in the world. She wondered how many more girls and young men were being made to prostitute themselves just so they could hand over all the money to him to continue his lavish lifestyle.

Colleen could have wept with the anger that was churning her stomach and the hatred that shook her to the core. If she had a gun and she met that bastard again, she'd shoot him without a moment's hesitation. He didn't deserve to live.

'Hello again, are you enjoying the wedding, my dear?' Lord Bebbage, her knight in shining armour and tamer of peacocks was standing next to her with a smile on his kindly face.

'Yes, thank you, very much, Lord Bebbage. Are you?'

'Good, good. Me? Oh yes, I'm an old romantic at heart you know. Enjoy the breakfast.' He moved away to find his table and Colleen could hardly control the tears that threatened to fall.

She wished she could throw herself at the feet of the kindly old man and beg for his help to save her sister from the nasties. But they'd probably carry her off in a white van if she did, so she kept a social smile on her face—one she'd been perfecting throughout the day—and got on with the business of being with people she didn't know, would probably never see again, and didn't give two hoots about—except Lord Bebbage who she was becoming quite fond of—when all the time she wanted to see Adam and tell him all about Nora and the drug dealers.

Colleen found her table and sat down, surrounded by cousins of Jeremy's and their wives, who all had the same braying laugh, and two maiden aunts who could have belonged to anyone, she didn't really care at that point. Their table was as far from the head table as it was possible to get which sent her a message that she wasn't remotely important as a guest. No doubt the Lady Theodora had worked on the seating plan herself, egged on by her bestie Rosamund.

Perhaps she should go home and leave a message on Adam's phone that she wasn't feeling well. But she'd miss out on spending the night with him and they rarely got to enjoy each other's company for more than a stolen hour or so. She wasn't going to let that obnoxious… her phone vibrated, and she pulled it out of her clutch bag. It was Adam asking if she was alright and saying he couldn't wait until she was in his arms. She replied, feeling stronger.

The food was fine dining and Colleen found, surprisingly, she was ravenous and ate everything on her plate. The trouble with posh food was that there was never enough. But she felt considerably better after eating.

Then the speeches, which went on too long. The only speech she listened to was Adam's. He was articulate, amusing and everyone laughed at his jokes. Jeremy, who Colleen was sure was drunk, stumbled his way through his speech and the Lady Theodora Baxter née Blakely had to take over and finish it for him. Another sign of how their marriage was going to go moving forward. What a joke.

Colleen stifled a yawn, as another boring speech threatened to send everyone to sleep. Big Man was sitting at a table nearer the front and off to the right side. His face was in full view of Colleen and she took her phone from her clutch bag and, under cover of pretending to photograph the happy couple, she snapped a couple of photos of him. Then she moved her chair slightly, so he was no longer in her eyeline. Hopefully, he hadn't noticed her.

After the speeches and toasts, they all trooped back into the ballroom which had been cleared of the chairs and now had a live band in one corner of the room for the dancing.

Colleen felt an arm around her waist and turned to see Adam smiling at her.

'Hi, sorry you've been on your own so much. Are you okay?'

'I am now.' It was such a relief to see Adam, that she nearly threw her arms around his neck and sobbed on his morning suit.

'It's nearly over. The happy couple has the first dance, then we all join them. The bouquet is tossed to some poor unfortunate and then they cut the cake, provided Jeremy doesn't get any more inebriated or he'll be in danger of cutting his hand off.'

'Then we can go? To the blue room?'

'Wild horses wouldn't keep me away.'

They held hands as Theo tried to keep Jeremy upright for the first dance. It didn't help that the man couldn't dance to begin with but being drunk as a skunk wasn't conducive to being graceful on the dance floor.

'Thank God for that,' said Adam as the rest of the bridal party piled onto the dance floor. 'Right. Come and dance with me.'

Colleen didn't need asking twice. She'd waited all day to be in Adam's arms and the pleasure of being close to him was like water to a parched throat. Despite the fact that they were in the middle of a dance floor surrounded by people shuffling around aimlessly, Colleen felt that there was no one else in that room but them.

She was disappointed when the dancing was interrupted for the bouquet tossing. She couldn't give a toss who caught it and wished she and Adam could continue their dancing alone.

'Right, ladies and gentleman, can all the single ladies, and men, gather together for the bouquet tossing. Come on now, don't be shy.'

'Can we leave yet?' asked Colleen thinking that if she didn't get Adam alone soon she was going to explode with frustration.

'After the cake cutting.'

Colleen sighed and turned around to watch. At least she wasn't involved in all this stupid bouquet throwing…

'Catch it!' someone screamed as the bouquet flew through the air in Colleen's direction. She didn't even need to put her hands out, the bouquet of red roses landed in her arms and Adam was laughing so much he was nearly doubled over.

'Is this you? Did you arrange for them to throw it at me?'

'Of course not,' said Adam wiping his eyes. 'Why would I do that?'

Yes, thought Colleen whyever would he? He's married and I'm just his squeeze. She felt a second of sadness that she'd never be any more to him than a mistress, but then shrugged off any thought of feeling sorry for herself. There were more important things for her to worry about. Later. For now, she wanted Adam all to herself.

'Right. I've waited long enough. I don't care about the cake or seeing them driving off in the nineteen-thirties Rolls Royce, all I want is to be naked and in bed with you.'

'Well,' Adam said, his gaze burning into hers, 'when you put it like that, let's go.'

Chapter Seventeen

It had been a long day and Adam was thankful that it was over. His best man's duties had been performed to the best of his ability and Jeremy and Theo were now on their own.

Colleen had been so good about the day. A lot of women would have complained bitterly about being invited to a wedding and then being left to fend for themselves, even though he'd had no choice as best man. But Colleen had been so sweet about it.

When he studied her closely, her eyes were a bit red. From weeping—a lot of women cried at weddings even when they didn't know the people getting married—or tiredness, or perhaps hay fever. There were flowers everywhere and it was a place of nightmares for a hay fever sufferer.

'Let's shower together,' she said as she stepped out of her dress.

'Now that's the best suggestion I've heard all day.'

Adam quickly removed his clothes and hung the

morning suit up in the wardrobe. He'd hired it rather than bought it and he wanted to get his deposit back and return it to the shop in a good condition.

Colleen got in the shower first, so the water would probably be scalding hot. Adam joined her and turned the temperature down a bit.

They stood together under the gushing water. Colleen had her eyes shut and Adam studied her face closely. Was she crying? Difficult to tell in the shower.

'Are you alright?' Adam asked.

She nodded and held him tightly with her face buried in his chest. He stroked her back, then reached for the shampoo and washed her hair, slowly and sensually.

'That feels wonderful,' she said, moaning softly at his touch.

When he'd rinsed the shampoo off and massaged some conditioner into her hair, he took a face cloth and lathered it with bath gel that smelled like woodsmoke and brandy and proceeded to wash her all over. She stood still and let him, helping him by lifting up an arm, turning around. Then he discarded the cloth and used his hands to caress her stomach and then lower. Colleen opened herself to him, linked one leg around him and her arms snaked around his neck.

He lifted her so he could reach the place that he bet was aching to be stroked. After inserting two fingers, he played with her clit with his thumb, and she came almost straight away. So he kept his fingers inside her and kept stroking her as her orgasms kept coming and she cried out with the intensity as she spasmed around his fingers.

When the storm had abated and they had soaped each other between kisses, Adam took a bath sheet and wrapped

Colleen in it. He dried himself quickly with a bath towel, then picked her up and carried her to the bedroom, gently laying her in the centre of the bed.

Adam sat at the bottom of the bed and took one of Colleen's feet. He gently massaged it, starting at the heel and working his way up to her toes. It had been a long day in a strange house with even stranger people and she'd been alone. He thought she'd done marvellously but didn't want to be patronising by telling her that.

He changed to her other foot and gave it the same treatment. Deliberately not speaking so as not to disturb the mood, he listened to her breathing becoming deeper and watched her body relaxing. He stopped the massage when he was convinced Colleen had fallen asleep then lay beside her and dozed.

Colleen awoke and wondered where she was. Oh yes, the wedding. She sat up and Adam opened his eyes.

'When I said naked in bed, I meant both of us.' She discarded the damp bath sheet and lay on top of him. 'How long have I been asleep?'

'Not long. I think you were just dozing. It hasn't been easy for you being here today, has it?'

'I've met some interesting people. Jeremy's mum, Delilah, and Lord Bebbage.'

'You have been socialising. I'm glad there were some nice people for you to talk to. Did you have any run-ins with Rosamund?'

'Only one, nothing I couldn't handle.'

'Good for you.'

Colleen kissed him and he responded eagerly. She sat up still straddling him and he caressed her from the hips upwards, stroking her stomach and cupping her breasts, his thumb lightly teasing her nipples until they stood erect, making her tingle and squirm under his fingers.

'The condoms are in the bedside cabinet,' he whispered, and she took one out and sheathed him. She was getting quite expert at putting condoms on Adam but wished they didn't have to use one. She wanted to feel him inside her with nothing separating their bodies. She was on the pill but understood that Adam was being careful for both their sakes.

Colleen carefully lowered herself onto him, marvelling at how easily and neatly they fitted together. He filled her in such a satisfying way, how could they not be made for each other?

Adam was still fondling her breasts and she could feel the heat rising in her as each careful thrust took her to a higher level. She closed her eyes and gave herself up to the feelings surging through her. No matter how much she wanted to slow things down and make it last, her body betrayed her by crying out for release.

Then Adam quickly and expertly flipped her on her back, and she hooked her legs around his waist as he thrust deeply into her.

'Yes, more...'

Adam withdrew and then thrust into her again, and she rose to meet him, each thrust bringing her closer to her climax.

'Fuck me, fuck me,' she whispered. Adam loved it when she talked dirty.

It was over too quickly, as they orgasmed together, and Adam collapsed next to her. He disposed of the condom and then returned to the bed to hold her in his arms again. Colleen loved these times, when they were weak with the after-effects of good sex, floating and peaceful, locked together with their arms around each other. She never wanted those moments to end. But they always did as they slipped over into sleep.

Colleen woke again, as the light was just beginning to fill the bedroom. Adam was sound asleep, lying on his back with his arm over his head and the duvet just covering his hips.

Colleen felt an overwhelming urge to draw him as he lay in the bed, relaxed and untroubled, his hair ruffled and his face soft in repose. She wondered if she should try to pull the duvet further down so she could draw him in all his naked magnificence, but didn't want to risk waking him up, so didn't.

When she drew, Colleen got lost in another world. She forgot where she was, as she became absorbed in creating the scene or person in front of her. She wanted to do justice to Adam as he looked so sexy lying in the bed in complete abandon.

Colleen hadn't drawn a nude before as the last time she'd done any real art was at school and the nuns wouldn't have approved of all that flesh on show.

Eager to get as much done as she could, she sketched loosely with the intention of coming back to it when she had more time to concentrate on the finer details. She took a quick photo of Adam to remind herself and to help her draw an accurate representation of him.

When she had done all she could, she looked at her drawing from a distance and realised she had made the right decision in not moving the duvet as the tantalizing hint of him was sexier than a full nude would have been.

Happy with her work, she shaded the light and dark, and accentuated the contours of his body, loving the way the light played across his chest and abs.

The peace was shattered when Adam's mobile phone buzzed, annoyingly loudly. Colleen wondered if she should answer it, so as not to wake him, but it was too late, as he opened his eyes and fumbled on the bedside table for the phone.

'Hello.'

Colleen listened to his half of the conversation trying to work out who he was speaking to.

Adam sat up straight, awake suddenly. He pushed his hand through his hair and frowned.

'Right. I'll be there as soon as I can. Has Rosamund been told?'

'Okay, I'll see if I can track her down. Thanks.'

'We need to go. That was Hugo's nurse. She wants us there as soon as we can as Hugo is fading fast, and she doesn't think he'll live for much longer.'

Colleen put her hand over her mouth. 'Oh God, that's awful. Poor Hugo. Yes, you must go.'

'Will you come with me? Please.'

'Yes, of course. What about Rosamund?'

'I'll see if I can find her.'

They packed quickly, throwing toiletries in the cases, and placing their clothes on top. Adam wore jeans, a T-shirt and a jacket and Colleen had a simple summer dress and sandals. Their wedding finery was packed away, the celebrations over. They were back to reality with all the problems that brought.

Adam texted Davis and asked for the car to be brought

around. It was still the early hours of the morning and no one was up except for a few members of staff.

Colleen hung around in the hallway, wondering what to do to be useful. Her stomach rumbled and she wandered into the kitchen where a cook was preparing breakfast. Colleen told her that they had to leave urgently but they would be grateful if there was something they could take with them to eat on the journey.

The cook sprang into action and made them coffee to go, warmed up some pain au chocolat and included some fresh fruit for them to take.

'Thank you so much, I really appreciate this,' said Colleen.

'You're welcome, madam,' said the cook.

Colleen wondered what life would be like with staff at your beck and call twenty-four seven. She decided she wouldn't like it. She felt guilty asking someone to do something that she was perfectly capable of doing for herself. Although she wouldn't mind having a driver like Davis. He was a sweetheart.

Adam came running down the stairs towards her.

'It's hopeless, I have no idea what room Rosamund's in and there's no one around to ask. I've sent her a text, but she hasn't answered. Come on, I want to go. I'd never forgive myself if I was too late to say goodbye to Hugo.'

'Right. I've got us a bit of breakfast. We can eat in the car.'

'Excellent. Let's go then.'

Davis was waiting outside, dressed in his chauffeur's uniform, looking fresh as a daisy. Did that man ever sleep? He had loaded the car with the cases and bags and held the door open for them to climb in the back.

'Thank you,' said Colleen.

'Sorry about this, Davis,' said Adam.

'Not a problem, sir.'

As Davis drove away from Charmley Manor, Colleen sighed in relief. It had been a strange weekend. A glimpse of how the other half lived. She'd been on the receiving end of insults and kindness. She'd spent the night with Adam and caught the bouquet at the poshest wedding she was ever likely to go to. Despite the sadness of the occasion, she was glad that she was leaving it all behind her.

As they ate their breakfasts and drank the coffee, they were silent. There wasn't much to say, and Adam would be grateful for the chance to think and mentally prepare himself for Hugo's death.

Colleen remembered her own father's death and how sad they had all felt. But her family were there to say goodbye and that meant a lot at the time. She shouldn't really be with Adam to witness Hugo's death. Rosamund hated her and Colleen didn't want to make her pain worse.

Adam sighed.

'Are you okay?' Colleen asked him.

He nodded. 'I was there when my father died. We all were. It was the strangest experience I've ever had. One minute they're with you, still breathing. You hold their hands and they're warm, alive, just as they've always been. And then the next...'

Colleen grabbed his hand and kissed it. 'It's okay, you don't have to explain.'

'I need to. I have to make sense of things. You don't mind, do you, Colleen, but you're the most grounded person I've ever met. I need your strength today.'

Grounded? She'd never thought of herself in that way.

'I'll be with you for as long as you need me. I promise.'

'Thanks. I appreciate that.'

Colleen wanted to tell him that she'd be there for him forever, in whatever way he needed. For Colleen knew that she was in love with Adam. She was sure he didn't love her back, but somehow she could live with that. She had enough love for both of them.

Chapter Eighteen

Adam had long thought that death illuminated life. When his father died, he'd been aware of his surroundings in a way he'd never been before. Every colour seemed brighter, the sky was bluer, sounds were clearer and more distinct. He felt this way now, as he stood next to Colleen waiting for the nurse to open the front door and let them in.

After the grandeur of Charmley Manor, Hugo's house seemed small and insignificant, even though it was a grade two listed building and there were stables and paddocks as well as tennis courts.

The building itself was in need of repair. Ivy grew out of control around the front porch. The stucco on the outside walls needed replacing. There were large areas where it had come away completely leaving grey patches that looked unsightly. But the gardens were well tended, and the lawn was a vivid green.

The front door opened, and Hugo's private nurse stood in the doorway.

'Is he…?' Adam couldn't finish the sentence.

'He's hanging on. Come in.'

The nurse glanced at Colleen but didn't say anything. Adam could have introduced them but was in too much of a hurry to get into the house to bother with social niceties.

'Did you manage to reach Rosamund?'

'No, I left a voicemail. I'll try her again in a bit.'

'Right. If you want anything, I'll be nearby. He's comfortable but not conscious.'

'Okay.' Adam went into the house which smelled stale as if the windows hadn't been opened for a long time.

'Adam? I'll stay down here. It's not appropriate for me to be in his bedroom. If Rosamund found me…'

Colleen was right, of course. Rosamund would go apeshit and he needed to consider her feelings. Hugo was her father, and, in her own way, she loved him and would be devastated at his death. Still, he felt better knowing that Colleen was nearby.

He crept in and approached the bed slowly. There was a chair at the side of the bed, and he sat on it.

He stared at the man on the bed. Adam could see little resemblance to the Hugo he had known before the cancer struck. Then he'd been active, busy, impatient, and always wanting everything done five minutes ago. He'd had a quick mind and could be ruthless but was a great businessman. Now, he was a little shrivelled man with skin that was so thin Adam could almost see through it. His hands were curled into claws and his nails looked transparent.

Adam didn't want to talk to him as he had no idea what to say. But the theory was the hearing was the last sense to go, so it was possible that Hugo could hear him. Theirs had been a business relationship. Even when he'd married

Rosamund, Hugo had shown no emotion at all. He had done his duty by his daughter but had shown no love, or pride in her. Hugo had told Adam his daughter had made the right choice for a husband as he was the best candidate to inherit the business. He was relieved he was leaving it in safe hands. He didn't care whose hands he was leaving his daughter in, just Meredith Motors.

'Hugo. I'm here. Rosamund's on her way.'

After almost an hour of just sitting and staring at Hugo, feeling inadequate and useless, Adam got up and stretched his legs by wandering around the bedroom. The nurse came in periodically to check her patient, wet his lips, check the syringe driver that supplied him with painkillers and other medication, then left again without speaking.

Adam needed a break, so went downstairs to find Colleen. She was in the library, reading David Copperfield. Adam remembered reading it when he was at school.

'Hi, how is he?' Colleen asked.

'Still holding on. He's not conscious and not in any pain.'

'Well, that's something.'

'I've been thinking,' he said, 'it's not really fair to expect you to stay here. You don't know him and who knows how long it'll be before…'

'It's okay, Adam, I said I'd stay with you and I will.'

'Well, if you're sure. Thanks.'

A noise in the hallway made them look towards the door as it was flung open. Rosamund strode in. Without attempting to lower her voice, she started on Adam.

'You could have waited for me. I got the voicemail message you left hours afterwards. He could have died in that time. You are such a selfish…' Rosamund caught sight of Colleen sitting in an armchair with a book open on her knee and her voice got even louder. 'What the hell is she doing here? My father is dying, and you bring that tart with you to gloat. Have you got no sense of decency at all?'

Adam moved quickly to stand in front of Colleen who cowered behind him.

'Rosamund, keep your voice down for God's sake. What's the matter with you?'

'What's the matter with me? There's nothing the matter except for the fact that my poor father is lying on his deathbed—'

'Rosamund, keep your voice down. Hugo's unconscious but that doesn't mean he can't still hear—'

'What were you thinking, bringing that little tart here? Isn't it bad enough that my poor father is lying—'

'Rosamund, just shut up and listen for a minute. The only thing that matters now is that we all keep calm and let Hugo die in peace. Shouting isn't helping. Colleen came with me because I asked her to. I would have woken you up, but I didn't know which room you were in and there was no one around to ask. That's why I left the voicemail. Now, can I suggest we go and sit with Hugo and think about him just for once?' And for the last time, Adam could have added but he didn't want to inflame Rosamund further.

'Send her home. She is not welcome in my house.'

Adam sighed, a sound that seemed to come from his boots. He was tired out after the weekend and weary of all the fighting and bickering that surrounded Rosamund. But he had to think about her feelings as he knew how heart-breaking it was to lose a father.

Adam turned to Colleen who was standing by this time, holding her clutch bag, obviously ready to leave.

'Colleen, I'm sorry but can you go home with Davis? Thanks for staying.'

'Yes, of course. Ring me later,' she whispered and walked out of the library without looking at Rosamund who glared at her.

'I should think so as well.'

'Right, she's gone. No more trouble?'

'I'm not the one causing trouble, Adam.'

Together, they climbed the stairs to Hugo's bedroom. Now he had to be strong for Rosamund.

It was going to be a long night.

As soon as Rosamund had come charging into the library, Colleen had known that it was time for her to leave.

Now, in the peace and comparative tranquillity of Adam's Mercedes, with Davis driving her home, she put her head back on the seat and closed her eyes.

She said a prayer for Hugo, asking that his death when it came, would be painless and quick. She could have gone through a list of people she needed help for, but the main one, the one that kept her up all night, was her sister, Nora. She needed help and Colleen was sure it was beyond her powers to provide that help.

When she got home, Nora was sitting in the living room, watching TV.

'Hi, how was the wedding?'

'Eventful. I met a lord.'

'Bully for you. Were they all posh knobheads?'

'Not all. But most of them were.'

'Yep,' said Nora stretching her arms above her head and yawning. 'I thought they would be.'

'I need to show you something,' said Colleen. 'A photo of a man. I want you to tell me if you've ever seen him before.'

'Why? Who is it?'

'I need you to look first, then I'll tell you.'

Colleen showed Nora the photo of Rupert on her phone. Nora jumped up looking frantic.

'Shit! That's him. Big Man. Where the hell did you get that photo? He wasn't at the wedding, was he? Please tell me he wasn't.'

'Oh God, Rupert is Big Man.'

'Rupert? What kind of a stupid name is that? I thought it was a bear.'

'Big Man's name and don't for pity's sake tell him you think he's got a stupid name.'

'He was a guest at the wedding?'

'Do you remember me telling you that a nasty man taped the lid of the box so I couldn't get out? That was him. He's a friend of Jeremy's, the groom.'

Nora was staring at her as if she was talking another language. She'd gone pale and said nothing, just stared with her mouth open.

'Nora. You're in a trance, will you snap out of it. We need to do something.'

'What? What are we going to do?'

'I don't know. He doesn't know we're sisters so he mustn't see us together whatever happens. He gave me his card and said he could send rich clients my way. Men who are looking for a superior experience, whatever that means.'

Nora looked at her in amazement. 'You don't know what that means?'

'No of course not. Why should I? I'm not a… anyway, no I don't know.'

'It means BDSM. You know what that is?'

'Like bondage you mean?'

'Exactly like that.'

Colleen felt sick all of a sudden. This was worse than she had first thought, and her first thoughts had been bad enough.

'We have to go to the police. We've got no choice.'

'I'll end up in gaol, is that what you want?'

'Nora, we can't fight this on our own. We need help.'

'I'm not going to be arrested. I'll run if you go to the police.'

'Okay, okay, no police.' Nora relaxed but still looked at her warily. 'There's nothing else for it then. There's only one person who can help us.'

'Adam?'

'Adam.'

In the early hours of the following day, Colleen received a text from Adam to say that Hugo had died, and he was going to stay for a few days to help Rosamund arrange the funeral.

On the way to work, Colleen made a detour to the nearest Catholic church and lit two candles and said a prayer for Hugo's soul, and her father's. Sitting in church made her aware of how long it had been since she'd been to confession. In fact, she hadn't been to church once since she arrived in London. But there were more practical problems to deal with first.

When she got to work, Colleen gave Doris a brief description of the wedding; the cake, the dress, and a few other details she thought Doris might find interesting including the incident of Lord Bebbage and the peacock which made her laugh.

'I spoke to Adam on the phone this morning,' Doris said. 'He's helping Rosamund with the funeral. Although from what he says, it sounds as if he is doing all the practical stuff and Rosamund is receiving visitors and sitting around looking mournful.'

'Well, she has just lost her father. I remember how I felt when my dad died. It's a terrible feeling knowing that you'll never see them again, never be able to speak to them…' Colleen stopped as she felt the tears in her eyes.

'How long ago did your father die?'

'A year ago.'

'I'm sorry,' said Doris and Colleen knew she was sincere.

'Thanks. Would you like a cup of tea? I think I'm going to have one.'

'Yes, thank you, Colleen. There's some biscuits knocking around too.'

'Right.'

As Colleen made the tea she thought of the plan she had come up with in the early hours when she couldn't sleep as she felt stressed out worrying about Nora. She needed a long lunch hour but hated to ask as she didn't want Doris to think she was taking advantage of her kind nature.

When they were drinking the tea and munching on biscuits, Colleen took a deep breath.

'Is it okay if I take a longer lunch break today? I have an appointment at the bank. I'll make the time up if necessary.'

'You don't need to do that. With Adam away for the rest of the week, there won't be as much work for us to do. Take as long as you want.'

Colleen returned from lunch with a sandwich she hadn't had time to eat and a wallet full of papers to fill in and sign.

Once again, however, she had to throw herself on the mercy of Doris as she didn't know anyone else to ask.

'Doris?'

'Yes, dear. Did your meeting at the bank go okay?'

'Well… that's what I wanted to speak to you about. I need to apply for a loan but because I have no credit rating, as I've never needed credit cards or loans before, it needs to be a guaranteed loan. I wouldn't ask this if I wasn't desperate, but… would you consider being my guarantor? If you think I'm being cheeky, just tell me. I know I am, I'm sorry, Doris, I shouldn't ask, forget I said anything.' Colleen was creased up with embarrassment. Why the hell had she asked the poor woman something like that? They hardly knew each other.

'How much did you want to borrow?'

'Two thousand pounds.' Colleen looked away, too ashamed to look at Doris.

'You say you're desperate. I need to ask what the money is for? Are you in trouble?'

'No. Well, not me, my sister. She has a debt that we need to clear before she can get on with her life. I'd rather owe it to the bank where I can pay it off in instalments. I can't really tell you any more than that, I'm afraid.'

'Well, I wouldn't normally do this for someone I hardly know, but… I've come to be very fond of you, Colleen, in the short time I've known you and you have a steady job, so… okay, I'll do it.'

'Oh, thank you so much! I really mean that I can't thank

you enough. And… could we just keep it between ourselves do you think?'

'Of course. It's your personal business and I won't breathe a word.'

You're an angel.'

'Oh, I'm no angel, dear, just ask my husband.'

Chapter Nineteen

The money was in Colleen's bank account by the end of the week. She went out in her lunch break and took the cash out, thinking that Big Man wouldn't be too keen on a bank transfer.

As she was walking back to the office her mobile rang.

'Hi, Mum, how're you doing?'

'I'm fine, Colleen, how's yourself?'

'I'm okay but I have to get back to work, so can't talk for long.'

'Okay, and how is the job going?'

'It's fine, Mum.'

'Great. So, when am I coming to stay with you? I can't wait to see my girls together in their new swanky place in London and you can show me the sights. Buckingham Palace and all those shops. Is it going to be soon?'

'Well, I'm not sure. We're both really busy so maybe next month?'

'Can't it be this month? August is when all the tourists

will be there, and it'll be crowded. I'd rather come when it's quieter.'

'Well, I'll see——'

'And how's your sister? She never rings me. Has she fallen out with me?'

'No, Mum, of course not. She works in the evenings and sometimes has to catch up with sleep during the day. She doesn't mean to ignore you.'

'Well, tell her to ring me, okay?'

'I will, Mum. Listen I've got to go. Love you, Mum, speak soon.'

Colleen rang off before her mother could ask her any more questions. She'd have to try and put her off coming to stay at least until the drug problem was sorted out.

The last thing Colleen needed was the complication of their mum asking questions and criticising the way Nora was living. She hardly ever left the apartment and was still "entertaining" men at night. Colleen was desperate for her to pay her debt and stop the sex and get herself a job. Or, even better, go to college so she could get herself some qualifications and look to the future. Nora was bright and if she could just get rid of all the bad things in her life, she could start living as a young person her age should live.

When Colleen got home from work on the Friday, Nora was asleep on the sofa. She looked ill and probably needed the rest, so Colleen decided to wash the bedding and get some other chores done before Nora woke up. Maybe they'd have take-out and enjoy a sisterly night in watching Netflix.

She had only spoken to Adam once. He'd sounded flustered and said he was going to stay with Rosamund until after the funeral as she was distraught by the death of her father and needed support. Colleen couldn't help wondering why someone like Rosamund didn't have other people to support her, but then she had to admit that Rosamund didn't act as if she was estranged from Adam. This would be the perfect chance for her to try to get back with him and patch things up.

That thought made her feel shaky inside. What would Adam do if Rosamund wanted to try again? Would he agree? She wished she could speak to him but didn't want to disturb him. He'd contact her when he was ready. Probably after the funeral. She'd just have to be patient and concentrate instead on helping Nora.

'Hi, you're awake. How are you feeling?'

'Okay. Didn't know you were back.'

'I've not been home long. I thought I'd do some housework and then we can have a quiet evening together.' Nora said nothing but sat on the couch and yawned. 'So, what do you think of that idea?'

'Yeah. Sounds good.' Colleen didn't think Nora had listened to a word she'd said.

'Mum phoned. She wants you to ring her. You should, you know, she's worried about you. If she doesn't hear from you she'll worry even more. And she still wants to come and visit us. I tried to put her off 'til August but she wants to come this month.'

'Right.' Nora was lying down again, and her eyes were shut.

'Anyway, I've got something that might cheer you up.' But from Nora's lack of response, she doubted it would. 'We've won the jackpot on the lottery —ten million pounds. What d'you think of that?'

'Great, yeah.'

'You haven't heard a word I've said, have you?'

Nora had fallen asleep again, so Colleen continued to clean and tidy the apartment. She went into Nora's room and started to strip the bed, aware that this was where she had sex with strangers. She bundled the sheets and pillow-cases up, then noticed that the bedside cabinet door was open. She opened it wider and peeked in. There were needles and syringes in there. A tourniquet as well, one of the old fashioned types made of rubber.

It was obvious Nora was still using.

By the time Colleen had washed and dried the sheets, then tidied up, Nora was starting to wake up.

'We need to talk.' Colleen would have to be firm with her sister. She had taken out a loan to stop the drug taking, not so Nora could buy more.

'What? Is there any tea going?'

'I'll make you some in a bit. I've got the two thousand pounds for Big Man.' Colleen refused to call him Rupert, even to herself. 'You need to give it to him and tell him that he's getting no more money from you as you've paid your debts for the last time.'

'I'm going to make some tea,' said Nora shuffling out of the living room in the direction of the kitchen. Colleen followed her.

'Sit down, I'll make it. You need to listen to me, Nora, this is important.'

Colleen filled the kettle and took two mugs from the cupboard.

'I did listen. You've got the money and I'm to tell the Big Man that he's not getting any more. Correct?'

'Exactly. When will you see him next?'

'Today probably. He usually collects on a Friday.'

'Collects what?'

'Scalps of course, what d'you think? Money.'

'Will he come here?'

'Of course.' That was bad. He mustn't see her when he came. Nora would have to be alone when she paid him. He couldn't find out they were sisters.

'Why does he collect the money himself? Doesn't he have henchmen or something to do that for him?'

'He doesn't trust anyone else. And... he'll be convinced I can't pay, so he'll be waiting for me to offer payment in other ways.'

'What do you mean?' Colleen was starting to realise that leaving Nora alone with this evil man wasn't a good idea after all.

'Use your imagination, Colleen.'

'But you've got his money, so he can't expect you to offer anything else. By which, I take it you mean sex?'

'How did my big sister get to be so innocent? I can't blame everything on the nuns. You've lived a sheltered life.'

Colleen was speechless as she poured the tea. She sat at the breakfast bar next to Nora and sipped the hot brew. The more she heard about Big Man, the more frightened she got for Nora and herself for, if he ever found out they were sisters, well it didn't bear thinking about. She remembered his reference to "superior experience" and shuddered.

'I'm not leaving you alone. I'll wait in the bedroom and hide in the wardrobe if necessary. If you pay him everything you owe, what more can he do?'

'Tell me the interest rate's gone up and I owe more. That's what he always does. You see, Colleen, he doesn't want me to pay him everything I owe. He wants me to owe him permanently, then he can control me, send me clients, keep me close so I become dependent on him. That's how he works. I appreciate the offer of the money, but if I give it to him, he'll just come back for more.'

'So what happens if you don't pay him back?'

'I'll have to work harder.'

'Nora, what are we going to do?' Colleen had never felt so helpless in her life.

'I could give him half of it and tell him he'll get the rest later. It might buy me some time. Keep him away for a while. He knows then he's still got me under his control.'

'I'm scared for you, Nora.'

'Me too. Don't worry.'

Don't worry she says. Probably the most stupid thing anyone had ever said to her. Because she was frantic with worry. She was sick with it.

'I love you, Nora,' she said.

'Straight back at you, sis.'

Nora had been right. Big Man visited her that evening. Colleen had managed to climb into the wardrobe and shut the door before Nora let the man in.

In her hideaway, deep in the wardrobe, she couldn't hear much of what was said, as the bedroom door was also closed. Voices were muffled; Nora's high and Big Man's low and rumbling.

Colleen had given a thousand pounds to Nora and put the rest in the safe. The safe was in her bedroom, behind a painting.

If what Nora had said was true, that Big Man would never let Nora go, they had to think of something else. A plan B. She had no idea what that could be but knew that they needed to think of it quickly as she had no wish to get herself in deeper debt with the bank. She couldn't keep borrowing money.

Colleen's blood froze as she heard shouting. Big Man's voice. Wanting to leap out of the wardrobe and run to Nora's defence but knowing that if she did, they were both doomed, she prayed, harder than she had ever prayed in her life. And she listened but she couldn't hear any more shouting. Her senses were heightened, and she heard her heart beating, thrumming with the blood flowing through her body.

Then the door of the wardrobe opened, and Nora stood there, looking shaken but unhurt.

'Nora, thank God you're okay. I was all for leaping out and beating him off with an umbrella.'

'You're mad, you know that?' Nora wandered back to the living room and collapsed on the couch with her arm over her eyes.

'What did he say? Did you give him the money?'

'I gave him the money and he said he'd be back for the rest later. Meanwhile, he was sending me some clients.'

'Did he say you owed him more?'

'No, just the other thousand.' Nora sat up and held a cushion to her chest for comfort. She looked so little and pathetic that Colleen's heart was breaking for her.

'So, if we pay the other thousand we could be free of him?' Colleen felt a faint hope, like a green shoot in spring, but then some clumsy oaf trod on it when Colleen remembered Nora's addiction.

'No. Like I told you before, he'll keep me dependent on him. I'll never be free of the man.'

'Nora, I need to ask you something.'

'Fire away.'

'Are you still taking heroin?' Nora looked down and shook her head, but she wouldn't look Colleen in the face. 'Swear on our mother's life that you're not taking it.'

'I can't. Yes, I'm still taking it. I try to stop, I really do, honestly, you've got to believe me, Colleen but then I get the cravings and the pain and there he is taunting me and telling me I can have all the dope I want, if I do what he says.'

'Oh, Nora, why didn't you tell me?'

'I kind of thought you knew. Anyway, you've been doing so much for me, and I feel bad about still needing the stuff. I don't want to be an addict. I hate that feeling that I get when I know I'm going to need more and more of it just to survive. And I need him to supply me with it. I could never afford it alone.'

'Let me get this straight. He sends Maggot or someone like him to befriend a person, then the Maggot character gets them taking drugs. Then when they're well and truly hooked, Big Man steps in and tells them they belong to him now and he sends them people to have sex with in exchange for drugs. They can't keep any of the money, it all goes to Big Man. I wish we could call him something else, there's nothing big about him in my opinion.'

Nora smiled. 'We could try calling him Fat Bastard. That works for me.'

'But at the hospital, you were going to get help to quit the drugs. What happened with that?'

'You were alone in the big city and I couldn't leave you to cope with it all while I was in rehab. You needed me as much as I needed you.'

Colleen thought of the truth of that. She'd been a naïve innocent when she'd arrived in London. Before stripping and Adam, drugs, and weddings. She'd lived

more in the last few months than all the years before put
together.

'What are we going to do, Nora?'

'We could do what you always suggest we do in a crisis.'

'And what's that?'

'Put the kettle on.'

Chapter Twenty

Finally, the day of Hugo's funeral had arrived. It was a beautiful summer day, in contrast to the sombre mood of the people, all dressed in black, streaming into the Anglican church where the service was to take place.

Adam was glad the day had finally arrived. He had been going stir crazy staying in the house alone with Rosamund. Once the nurses had left and Hugo's body had been moved to the chapel of rest, there had just been the two of them alone in the house, making arrangements for the funeral.

Hugo, being the control freak that he had been, had arranged his funeral when he had first been given the diagnosis of terminal cancer. He had specified everything be done as per his instructions, right down to the readings and hymns. As far as Adam knew, Hugo had never been a churchgoer, so this was all for show as all his friends and foes would be at the funeral. Not to mention some people from the media. Hugo had been well known amongst the classic and vintage car fraternity.

Rosamund had been flaky in the extreme. She burst into tears at the slightest wrong word, or expression and sobbed on Adam's chest whenever she could. His sympathy for her was starting to run out. Rosamund had shown little love or interest in her father all the time he had lain in bed waiting to die. She had left all the caring up to Hugo's private nurses and spent most of her days riding and visiting friends.

Adam was trying to be supportive but all he wanted was to be with Colleen. He had texted her a couple of times but, fearful that Rosamund would hear, he hadn't phoned her once. He hoped she would forgive his neglect of her and understand that he had no choice, it was his duty to make sure Rosamund got through this distressing time in her life.

The car that had been hired to take them to the church was a Rolls Royce Silver Cloud from Hugo's personal collection. It was a beautiful car and Adam silently thanked Hugo for his kindness. They felt like royalty as they rode in the back to the church, people stopping to stare as they passed.

The church was packed, and Adam nodded to people he knew and shook hands with others who expressed their sorrow at Hugo's passing. Rosamund was playing the bereaved daughter for all she was worth, holding a lace hankie to her eyes periodically and keeping her head down as if in prayer. But she kept close to Adam as if she wanted the world to see them as a couple still.

The vicar gave a good sermon, emphasising all the splendid work Hugo had done for the community, and all the charities he supported. Several of Hugo's close friends spoke of him as a family man and a pillar of the community who would be sorely missed. He'd faced his illness with dignity and was an example to them all.

Adam had stopped listening after the first five minutes. These people had known only what Hugo had wanted them to know. Adam would remember him as a ruthless businessman who had taught him all he knew about being the best in his field.

They sang the usual hymns: Abide with Me and Guide Me Oh Thou Great Redeemer, and the reading was from the Old Testament, although Adam didn't recognise it and wasn't really listening anyway. He was thinking of Colleen and how beautiful she was, how sexy but innocent at the same time. He had missed her desperately over the last week and wanted this circus to be over so that he could be with her again.

Then they were standing around the grave and there were more Bible readings and Rosamund was playing to the gallery, weeping on Adam's chest and he held her and tried to comfort her. He noticed a couple of camera flashes going off and hoped they wouldn't make the front page.

Rosamund threw soil on the coffin and the vicar said the final words and then the mourners wandered off back to their cars which would take them to the house for the wake. Rosamund and Adam had decided between them that caterers could do the lot. Let people in, pour drinks and serve food. It was the least they could do to give the people who had come to pay their respects a good feed.

'Thank God that's over,' said Rosamund.

Adam looked around, but they were alone. It was time for Rosamund to drop the pretence of the grieving daughter and, separately, they could get on with their lives. Rosamund, however, had other ideas.

'How are you feeling now?' Adam asked.

'Just glad it's all over. Except, of course, that it isn't. Not quite. We have the will reading to go. Who do you think will benefit?'

Adam shrugged. 'I don't know. Hugo never discussed it with me.'

'No, I don't suppose he did.'

'Did he discuss it with you?'

Rosamund laughed. 'He didn't need to. I'm his only child. Of course, he'd leave it all to me.'

'You sound very sure.'

'I am.' So that was it. Rosamund would inherit and he would be out of a job. But Adam didn't think that was the end of it. Hugo thought too highly of Meredith Motors to leave it to someone who had no idea of how to run a business.

'We'll have to wait and see.'

'Adam. I know things haven't been amicable between us recently, but I just want you to know that I am willing to forgive and forget. We should be presenting a united front to the world at this time. It's what Daddy would have wanted. He believed that couples should solve their difficulties and stay together rather than throwing in the towel at the first sign of trouble. So, what do you say? Shall we give it another go for the sake of Daddy and everything he worked so hard to build up?'

Adam was speechless. Did she really think that he still wanted her after all that they'd been through?

'Rosamund, I understand the spirit in which you are saying these things, but our marriage is over. It was over a long time ago. You had an affair, and I met Colleen—'

'Yes, about that. You'll have to ditch the slut I'm afraid as I won't stand for you seeing her behind my back. I understand that men need to have their fun and someone like her... well, it's sex on tap and—'

'Don't, Rosamund, just don't insult Colleen or I'll walk away, and you'll never see me again.'

'Oh don't be so dramatic, Adam, you have no intention of walking away from Meredith Motors. That business is your life. You were the one that kept it going when Daddy got sick. You're the only one who knows how to keep it going, so don't pretend you can just walk away as I know you can't.'

Adam wondered if Rosamund was right. Could he walk away so easily? It was true, he did love the company and he was the only one who knew everything about how to run it. But no one was indispensable and if the worst happened, he had transferrable skills. Thanks to Hugo he knew he could run a company in his sleep. Any company, not just Meredith Motors.

'We should go. They'll be waiting for us.' Adam started to walk away without waiting for Rosamund who ran after him.

'Don't forget what I said. We're good together, Adam, and I'm sure our small disagreements could be ironed out. You don't need to answer me straight away. Take a day or so to think about it. But don't leave it too long, or you could miss out.'

On Friday, Colleen wanted to go home early and prepare for Big Man's visit. She didn't want Nora to have to face him alone again. He was dangerous and Colleen needed to be on hand in case he turned nasty and tried to hurt Nora. She would hide in the wardrobe again and be ready to spring out to defend her sister, if necessary. But if he accepted the other thousand pounds and agreed to leave

Nora alone, then she could be encouraged to go into rehab, and all would be well.

Who did she think she was kidding? He wasn't going to leave her alone, was he?

But they had to try, they had nothing else.

Things didn't go to plan from the start. Doris had given her more work to do and she left the office half an hour later than usual.

She hurried into the flat, saying, 'Hi, Nora, only me…' and then stopped dead when she went into the living room. Big Man was already there, sitting in an armchair, smirking at her.

Colleen nearly wet herself at the sight of him and she stood in the centre of the room, with her hand on her heart as if she was keeping it beating by sheer force of will.

'Well, well, well, what a surprise. You must introduce me to your friend, Nora. I am disappointed that you haven't mentioned her before.'

'Big Man—Colleen. Colleen—Big Man.' Nora, who was sitting on the edge of the couch, stared at Colleen as she spoke, and her eyes pleaded with her. What for? To not let on that they were sisters?

'Colleen, the stripper. Now things are starting to make sense. It was Nora's job to jump out of that box, wasn't it? So why were you doing it?' Colleen was speechless. She didn't know what to say. She shook her head. 'Cat got your tongue?'

'Nora wasn't well.' Her voice was trembling as was every muscle in her body.

'So you did the job in her place. How loyal. You're not lesbians, are you? Not that it would matter if you were. Men pay a lot of money to see woman on woman action. You two could earn me big bucks.'

'We're not. Lesbians that is.' Nora sounded calm but the expression on her face showed the fear underlying it.

'Pity. Still, you could pretend couldn't you? So what are you then—friends, sisters…?'

At the word "sisters" Colleen jumped and gave them away.

'Sisters. Of course, I can see it now. The family resemblance. Pity you're not twins. I know some men who'd mortgage their houses to watch twins together. Dirty bastards.'

'We're not prostituting ourselves for you. You've got your money.' Colleen looked at Nora for confirmation and she gave a small nod. 'So get out because you'll not get another penny from us. And Nora won't sleep with men and give you the money anymore.'

Colleen didn't know what gave her the strength to say those things. She expected Big Man to explode with rage and tear the flat apart like the Incredible Hulk, but he kept the infuriating smirk on his face as if Colleen was telling him a joke.

Nora was looking frantic, and Colleen felt defeated suddenly. Her brief burst of bravado hadn't impressed anyone, and she felt about half an inch tall.

Suddenly Big Man leapt out of the chair and stood over her menacingly. He was light on his feet for such a big man and Colleen suddenly felt fear the like of which she had never experienced before.

'You listen to me. You'll do as I say. I'll excuse that defiance this time as you don't know how we work yet. Nora will tell you. Do as you're told, don't answer back, pay on time. It's easy, even for someone as simple as you.'

'And what if I won't do as you say?'

It came out of nowhere like a bolt of lightning. He slapped her so hard that she fell and landed with her face hitting the edge of the coffee table. Nora screamed and cowered in the corner of the couch sobbing.

'Okay. Let's call that your first lesson. For the next lesson, you'll get the same thing Nora had. Let's just hope, for your sake, that you'll have learned by then, for lesson three is something you don't want to have to face, trust me.'

Colleen lay on the floor, crying softly. She couldn't move as the pain in her face was excruciating. She could hear Nora crying but the sound was quiet. She was on the point of fainting.

Then there was silence. Colleen slowly and carefully lifted her head off the carpet, whimpering as she did so.

'Oh my God, Colleen, your face!'

There was no sign of Big Man.

She couldn't speak and was too weak to stand, so she sat on the floor with her back against the couch and Nora went into the kitchen, coming back five minutes later with ice cubes wrapped in a cloth.

'Here, put this on your face or it'll blow up like a balloon.'

'Arrghh,' Colleen couldn't help crying out loud at the feel of the cloth on her cheek.

'Two inches higher and you would have lost your eye.' Nora sat next to her, her knees drawn up and her head on her knees.

Colleen sat with her eyes closed, fighting off the pain of the bruise that would be sure to come, even if the ice kept the worse of it at bay.

'Nora? Could you get me some paracetamol and a glass of water please?'

'Of course.' Nora got up and went into the kitchen again. She came back with the pills and water.

'Thanks.' Colleen could hardly open her mouth with the pain of her cheek, and she slid the paracetamols in and slurped enough water to swallow them.

'Is it broken? Do you need to go to hospital?'

'I don't know. Maybe. It's agony, Nora.'

'Oh my God, I'm so sorry. This is all my fault. All of it. The whole sorry stinking thing is all my fault because I let Maggot talk me into trying weed.'

'You weren't to know. Don't blame yourself.'

'I can't help blaming myself. I'm so sorry, Colleen.'

'Tell me something. He said for the next lesson I'd get the same thing you did. What did he mean?'

Nora stared at the floor. 'He just meant that they'd give you heroin and you'd be hooked too.'

'Oh. And what is the third lesson that I wouldn't want to face, do you know?'

Nora sighed. 'No. But whatever it is, it'll be bad. This is why I keep telling you we have to do as he says.'

'Are you absolutely sure you won't go to the police and demand protection?'

'I can't. I'm so scared of being locked up.'

'What scares you the most, Big Man or going to gaol?'

'Both. I'd rather end it all than face either of them.'

'Don't talk like that, please. I couldn't bear it if you did something stupid. Promise me you won't.'

'Alright, I promise. But don't keep asking me about the police, okay?'

Colleen didn't reply. Things were getting too serious to keep the police out of it. She realised now that there was nothing she could do against the fat bastard. They needed help.

'I'm going to bed, I don't feel very well.'

'Okay. Night.'

It was only when she was in bed, in the darkness that she gave in to the pain she was feeling and sobbed into her pillow. Eventually, when the paracetamols started to kick in, she fell asleep.

Chapter Twenty-One

Adam was thankful to be back home in his penthouse apartment. He'd played his part of supportive husband as well as he could but now he just wanted to get on with his life.

The solicitors were dragging their heels with regards to the will reading and wouldn't give Rosamund and himself a definite date. More waiting around, but this time, on his terms and the only person he wanted to be with was Colleen.

As it was Saturday and he had no plans for the weekend, he wondered whether to ring her and arrange a day out. They could just take off and drive and see where they ended up. Stay in a hotel or a bed and breakfast. Spend quality time together. Make up for his neglect of the last couple of weeks. He would drive his Mercedes and give Davis the weekend off.

Stopping on the way to buy a huge bouquet of flowers and a bottle of wine, he parked the car outside the apartment and pressed the intercom. It took ages to be answered and when it was, it wasn't Colleen's voice.

'Hello?'

'Hi, it's Adam—Adam Turner. Is Colleen there?' There was silence on the other end of the line and Adam said, 'Hello, who is that?'

'Nora.'

'Oh, hi, Nora, I didn't recognise your voice. Is everything okay? Where's Colleen?'

'She isn't feeling well at the moment. She's still asleep.'

'What's wrong? Listen, just let me come up will you please?'

'I don't think she wants to be disturbed.'

Adam felt the hairs on the back of his neck tingle. Nora was trying to hide something.

'Let me in, Nora, please. I just want to see her, okay? Just five minutes.'

There was a further prolonged silence and Adam felt like battering the door down. Something was wrong. Why would Colleen refuse to see him, even if she wasn't feeling well? Then he heard the click of the door unlocking. He pushed the door and got in the lift, his heart racing and his mind filled with all the things that could have gone wrong.

The door was open when he arrived, and Nora was waiting.

'Now don't freak out, okay?'

'Freak out about what? Nora, I don't know what you're talking about.'

'She's in there.' Nora pointed at the living room.

Adam went straight in still carrying the flowers and wine.

At the sight of Colleen's face, he dropped down in front

of her, dropping the flowers and wine on the carpet, and stroked the hair off her face.

'Oh my God, Colleen, what happened?'

Adam was shocked at the extent of the bruising on Colleen's face. The whole of the left side looked red, purple, and blue. So this probably happened yesterday or the day before. Adam knew bruises changed colour over time.

Colleen was crying and incapable of speech, so he sat next to her on the couch and held her. Nora came in and sat watching Adam. She looked wary and there was an atmosphere of tension that made him suspicious that there was more to this than simply a fall or something similar.

'What happened?'

'She knocked her face on the edge of the coffee table. Shall I put the flowers in water and the wine in the fridge?'

'Okay. Then come back and tell me what the fuck is going on.'

'I'll tell you… in a minute,' said Colleen, trying to breathe deeply to control her sobs.

'Do you need to go to hospital?'

'No, it's not broken.'

'Are you sure? How do you know?'

'It looks worse than it is. When Nora gets back, I'll tell you everything.'

Adam held Colleen, kissing her forehead, and stroking her hair.

'Did somebody hit you?'

'I need to tell you from the beginning, and I want Nora here as it involves her.'

'Is it something to do with her addiction? Is that it? Were you defending her?'

'Yes, but I need to tell you everything, or it won't make any sense.'

Nora came back into the room and stood uncertainly looking from Adam to Colleen.

'If this is going to take ages, shall I make us some tea first? Colleen thinks it'll solve all problems and I'm parched.'

'No, I don't want fucking tea—'

'Yes, Nora, please do that. I want one, then come back and help me tell this story.'

Nora went back into the kitchen and Adam had no choice but to wait. He had a bad feeling about this. Consorting with drug addicts could never end well.

When Nora was back and they all had cups of tea, Colleen started talking.

'Now, Adam, I want you to promise me you won't interrupt until I've finished. At the end, you can ask anything you like, but I need to be able to tell this in my own way.'

'Okay. But please hurry and put me out of my misery. I'm imagining all kinds of things at the moment.'

That was their cue to laugh and tell him that he was thinking the worst and it wasn't that bad. They didn't. Nora sat in the armchair biting her nails and Colleen sipped her tea before putting the mug down.

'When I arrived in London Nora was spending time with a man called Maggot. He was the one who got her hooked on heroin.'

'So, this scumbag Maggot hit you?'

'No, Adam, will you please just listen.'

'Sorry.'

'Nora had the stripping job, but she wasn't well enough to do it, so I was going to do it for her. The stag night when Rupert taped the box shut.'

'I remember. The night we met.'

Adam wanted to hold Colleen's hand or put his arm

around her, but she had moved up the couch away from him, so they sat separately at either end.

'And the night Nora nearly died from a drug overdose. She hadn't taken it herself, it had been forced on her.'

'Yes, I remember.' Adam wished Colleen would get to the point. She was just going over old ground.

'Well, the man who taped me in that box and the man who injected Nora is the same man—your friend Rupert who calls himself Big Man.'

'What?! Rupert. No, it can't be, you must have got it wrong. He would never do that.'

'And he was the man who hit me so hard that my face collided with the coffee table.'

Adam stood up and went to the window. He needed to think. Rupert wasn't a friend of his, but he was part of Jeremy's social circle. And Jeremy was a friend of his, who had once confessed that he didn't have many close friends and Adam was his closest. The rest were people who inhabited the same world: private and boarding schools, Eton, universities, clubs, hunts, and major events on the social calendar. Jeremy had rarely spoken of Rupert, so he had no idea what Jeremy's thoughts were about him.

'Are you both absolutely sure it was him?'

'A hundred per cent,' said Colleen.

'Why didn't you tell me this before?'

'I only found out that Rupert was Big Man who is terrorising Nora at the wedding. But when he came to collect his money yesterday, I came home from work and he was already here. I was just trying to protect Nora.'

'But you knew that Nora was using and must have been getting it from somewhere?'

'I naively thought that, if we paid the money back, Big Man would leave her alone. But he forces people to become addicts so they will work for him in exchange for drugs, but they have to give him everything they earn. Nora is already addicted and I'm next.'

'Over my dead body. He won't get away with this.'

'He's dangerous, Adam, and now he's made the connection between me and Nora, he'll know that I will have told you.'

'I need to talk to Jeremy. He knows him better than anyone. Will you two be okay on your own. Don't answer the door to anyone, especially him, okay?'

'Okay,' said Colleen.

Adam looked at Nora. 'You're being quiet. Haven't you got anything to say for yourself? It was you who started all this.'

'Adam, that's not fair…'

'No,' Nora said, 'Adam's right. It's my fault. I was stupid and I never wanted you to get involved, Colleen, believe me.'

'I know.'

'Right. I'll be back soon. Go to bed, Colleen, you look as if you're about to collapse.'

'I will. Thanks, Adam.'

'So, how's married life treating you?'

'Well, it has its ups and downs you know.'

Jeremy and Theo had only just got back from their honeymoon and already there was trouble in paradise. When Adam told Jeremy that he had something serious and urgent to talk to him about, he jumped at the chance of spending an evening in his private club, despite Theo's protestations.

Adam couldn't help noticing that Jeremy relaxed and seemed more like his normal self after a couple of drinks and a good roast dinner.

'Yes, I do know. Anyway, about the thing I want to talk to you about.'

'Oh, so there really is something. I had wondered if you were using that as an excuse to spirit me away from the little woman. I was going to give you a hearty handshake for thinking outside the box. Or outside the marital home, anyway.' Jeremy laughed, or brayed, and Adam couldn't help smiling.

'It's about Rupert.'

'What—Rupert Graveson? What's the old bugger gone and done now?'

'How well do you know him?' Jeremy looked perplexed by the question. 'I mean, is he a close friend? Have you known him long?'

'No to all three. I don't really know him at all. He's a friend of a friend and just seems to tag along to all our dos. Whenever there's a party or a weekend in the country, he just seems to turn up.'

'So, whose friend is he? How was he introduced to you all?'

'Do you know, I haven't the foggiest idea. Like I say, he just seemed to turn up.'

'Right.' Adam had hoped that Jeremy could give him some information about Rupert that would help him think of a way to stop him dealing drugs and terrorising young women. But he seemed to know very little.

'What's this all about?'

'Well, it turns out he's a drug dealer and a pimp. He gets people addicted to heroin and then makes them work as prostitutes so they can pay him back for the drugs he supplies them.'

'Not your little woman, that girl that was tied up in ribbon?'

'No, her sister.'

'Oh good Lord, that's awful. So, he's up to his old tricks.'

'What do you mean?' Adam leaned forward and listened intently. This could be what he was looking for.

'There was a bit of a hoo-ha a while back. Rupert had been accused of beating up a girl who ended up in intensive care. He got off with the help of a good lawyer. It turns out the girl was a drug addict and Rupert did a good job of besmirching her name and claiming his innocence. Most people bought it, after hearing that she took drugs.'

'Drugs that the bastard gave her himself.'

'No one forces a person to take drugs though, surely.'

'Two or three strong men against one young woman could easily inject her with heroin. She wouldn't stand a chance.'

'Is that what happened to…'

'Nora. Yes and now he knows that Colleen is Nora's sister, he is threatening to do the same to her.'

'Good God, man, he needs to be stopped. What are you going to do?'

'I'm going to the police once I've got evidence. That's where he's clever. He visits his victims in their own homes to collect money. He hit Colleen and she fell and has a badly bruised face. It could have been worse, but I think it proves that he has no scruples. I need to think this through and not go in all guns blazing.'

'Yes, quite. I know what you need. Surveillance equipment. I know a chappie who sells state of the art cameras.

High-resolution pictures, night vision, low-light capabilities, and even infrared light. They can even work through your Wi-Fi. And, of course, audio surveillance so you can catch him threatening the girls.'

'I knew it was a good idea coming to you, Jeremy.'

'Absolutely, just leave it with me.'

Chapter Twenty-Two

Two days later, Jeremy texted to say he'd got the merchandise. His friend was willing to fit it and show Adam how to use it. The text looked as if it had been written in code, to throw anyone who saw it off the scent. Adam smiled when he thought of Jeremy's enthusiasm and willingness to help. It was just the distraction he needed to help him forget the "little woman" waiting at home for him with a metaphorical rolling pin.

Adam arranged to meet Jeremy and his friend—no names, no pack drill—at the apartment and he arrived first to brief Colleen and Nora.

'When that bastard comes back, we'll catch everything he does and says on audio and video. Then I'll take it to the police.'

'I thought we were keeping the police out of this,' said Nora who was huddled on the couch, biting her nails.

'We can't I'm afraid. This man is rich and powerful. He's been taken to court before for beating someone up but got off. This time, we'll have enough evidence to send him down for a long time.'

'Can we keep Nora's name out of it?' Colleen asked. Her face was less swollen, and the bruises had faded to yellow and purplish brown.

'I'll try but can't promise anything.'

'Okay. It'll be strange knowing that there are cameras all over the house.'

'They'll only be in this room. He never goes in the bedroom does he?'

'Not so far.' Colleen looked at Nora who shook her head.

'When is he next due to collect his money?'

'Friday.' Nora looked petrified and Adam felt pity for her. She was a young woman who had accidentally got herself mixed up with criminals. But he wanted to keep Colleen safe, and he realised that what they were doing was risky. They were dealing with a highly dangerous man who had no scruples and wouldn't hesitate to hurt someone to achieve his goals.

'Right. I'll be here, in the bedroom, when he arrives. You'll have to try to act naturally and not look at the cameras or give the game away. Do you think you can do that?'

Nora gazed at him with big eyes in a pale face. 'Yes,' she said finally.

He looked at Colleen, who looked scared but determined. 'Of course. We want him out of our lives and off the streets.'

'Good.'

The intercom announced the arrival of Jeremy and friend. Adam let them in and introduced the sisters briefly.

'Pleased to meet you,' said Jeremy smiling. Adam

wondered if he was saving Colleen any embarrassment by pretending he didn't know her. Or maybe he just didn't recognise her.

The friend said very little but worked swiftly to set up the hidden cameras and microphones. The first one he put on top of the curtain rail. It was so small that it was hardly noticeable. The next one, he fixed near to the television. Then there were other places such as the bookcase, where the camera itself was book-shaped and didn't stand out at all. Other ingenious places included a table lamp, a coffee mug, and a potted plant.

Next, he took Adam into the bedroom and showed him how to access the pictures and sound on his laptop. He had to remember to use his headphones if he didn't want to give the game away and alert the person to his presence.

Then Jeremy and his friend left, Jeremy wishing them good luck and Adam thanking him profusely for setting it up.

'Shall we try it?' asked Adam.

'I suppose we should,' said Colleen.

'You're going to need to get used to those cameras being there, so let's have a trial run.'

Colleen and Nora went into the living room and talked about nothing in particular. Trying different places in the room. Colleen was good, but Nora kept looking at the cameras. He'd have to warn her about that. Adam watched them on the screen, getting used to how everything worked. It was state of the art and the sound quality was superb.

'Right,' said Adam when they were once more drinking tea and sitting comfortably in the living room. 'Now we wait for Friday.'

'What if he doesn't come on Friday or decides to come on another day?' asked Colleen.

'I've been thinking about that. I think we should leave the security system running all the time. I could link it to my laptop at home and if I can't be here with you, then at least I'll know what's going on.'

'You can watch us being beaten to death from the comfort of your own home,' said Nora sarcastically.

'So what do you suggest—that I stay here twenty-four seven?'

Adam was beginning to feel irritated by Nora. She had started this whole mess but was doing nothing to get herself out of it and now she'd dragged Colleen into the middle of it as well.

'Well… you could. If you didn't mind,' said Colleen.

'You're right. I should stay. It would be foolish to leave you two alone. He could turn up at any time.' Adam took Colleen's hand and brought it to his cheek. She was cold and the bruises stood out against her pale skin. If something happened to her and he wasn't here to step in, he'd never forgive himself.

'What about Colleen? Doesn't she need to go to work?' Nora asked.

'No. I'll tell Doris not to expect her in this week.'

'What about…?' Colleen looked at Nora who stared back at her. She blushed and looked away.

'Oh, you mean…' Nora nodded. 'Yes, good point.'

'What the hell are you two talking about?' Adam was growing increasingly irritable. He wanted to be alone with Colleen, but now he was stuck in the apartment with both of them, waiting for God knew what to happen. And these two had started talking in code.

'Colleen's referring to the clients that Big Man sends me. Do I still…?'

They were both silent and Adam had no idea how to respond.

'No,' said Colleen suddenly animated. 'You don't answer the intercom to anyone. Then, when they report to Big Man that they couldn't get a response, he'll come round to see what's wrong.'

'And we'll be ready,' said Nora.

'Yes. That sounds like a plan. Listen, you two, you do know that we're playing a dangerous game. This man is a hardened criminal and will stop at nothing to protect himself from arrest. You're going to have to get him to talk and say something that will implicate himself. We need hard evidence. We might not get it on the first attempt.'

Colleen frowned. 'So what are you saying? We have to entice him to admit that he's a pimp and a dealer?'

'More or less. I wish I could give you some advice but, I think you'll just have to assess how the meeting goes.'

Colleen fell silent and Nora was biting her nails again. It all fell on them to get the evidence they needed. It was a big ask.

———

Big Man surprised them again and turned up the following day. After Nora had told him to come up, Adam secreted himself in the bedroom and Colleen and Nora waited in the living room, huddled together on the couch.

Colleen's heart was beating so fast that she feared she'd have a heart attack before the evening was through. She wasn't meant for espionage.

'Good evening, ladies,' he said.

Neither of them spoke, not wanting to appear too friendly on the tape.

'Well, that's not very welcoming I must say. I go to all the trouble of coming around to see you and this is the response I get.'

Colleen was trying not to appear too frightened, but at the same time, she was trying to analyse how the conversation would come across to the police when they heard it. So far, it appeared that he was just being pleasant. But she needn't have worried as things soon changed.

'Nora, have you got my money?'

'Yes.' Nora stood up and handed him some cash. He made a production of counting it and then looked at her with his hands out as if in supplication.

'Is this it? What the hell have you been doing all week? How much are you charging these guys?'

'Just the usual amount. What you told me to charge.'

'Well it's not enough. You either charge them more or get more punters. This isn't going to keep you in dope, get it?'

'Yes,' said Nora.

'Right, now down to the serious business, the reason for my visit.' He smiled as if he expected them to be simply thrilled to get a surprise visit from him. 'And it concerns you.' He smiled at Colleen who felt as if snakes were wriggling in her stomach. He was one slimy bastard.

'What?' asked Colleen. She didn't need to act scared as she was frightened to bits. Everything about the man was repulsive and she knew if he came near her she'd throw up.

'I think it's about time you started earning like your sister. Although not like her as she's as much use as a chocolate teapot. You, however, have the looks, the blonde hair and you look good in costume. You're exactly what men want.'

'I can't….' Colleen touched her face where the pain hadn't entirely gone away. 'I have a job…'

'Your *job* is to work for me. You'll do as you're told, or you'll get what Nora got. In fact, I might let you have a taste of that anyway, just as a reminder of what will happen if you continue to defy me.'

'Okay.' Colleen was shaking and her voice was in danger of giving out altogether.

'I'll send you someone tomorrow. Be nice to him. Be accommodating. I'll be checking. Unless you want to end up an addict like your sister, you'll do as you're told.'

'What will you do if Nora's too sick to work?'

Big Man stared at her for ages and Colleen wondered if she'd blown it. By asking him leading questions, she'd given them away.

'I only let her have enough to keep her happy, but not enough that she can't work. I'm not stupid, I know what I'm doing. If she's too lazy to get off her arse and get on her back, that's down to her and she'll pay for it. Do you understand?'

'Yes, I understand.'

'Good. Now we're getting somewhere. I'm expecting good things of you, Colleen. I may be round one night to sample the goods so I can assure my clients of top quality merchandise.'

Colleen was just about to ask what he meant by that, but it was obvious, and she was terrified of putting her foot in it, so she said nothing.

'If you both behave yourselves, I might make you my top girls. You could take part in the special parties I have for close friends and business associates. You could work together if you know what I mean. Men would pay a lot for the novelty of screwing two sisters at the same time.

And if there's any more like you at home, they can join as well.'

'There aren't,' said Colleen quickly. Surely they'd got enough evidence by now. She wanted him out of her home before she was sick, or screamed, or both.

'Pity. Still, I've got you two. You'll be seeing me again. Very soon.'

Then he left, shutting the door quietly after him. Neither Colleen nor her sister moved or spoke. In fact, they barely breathed. He was listening on the other side of the door. Once they heard footsteps running down the stairs, they breathed a sigh of relief. Then Adam came out of the bedroom.

'Please tell me we've got enough evidence. I couldn't go through that again, my heart was in my mouth.' Colleen put her head back and closed her eyes.

'I think so,' said Adam sitting next to her. 'I swear I'll hang the evil bastard up by his bollocks if he ever comes anywhere near you two again.'

'Nora, are you okay?'

Nora was sobbing and Colleen put her arms around her. They hugged and Nora held on to her as if she was a lifeline.

'I hate him,' she sobbed.

'I know, darling, but at least we've made the first step to getting him locked up.'

'Nora?' Adam asked. 'What did he mean when he said Colleen would get what you got? And that comment about sampling the goods?'

'He means sex.'

'Did he rape you?'

Colleen couldn't believe she hadn't thought of it before. Nora nodded and her sobs increased in intensity.

'The rotten bastard. You never said.'

'I'm sorry. I couldn't talk about it, it was too awful.'

'Oh, you poor darling, I'm so sorry. Come here to me.' Colleen and Nora hugged even tighter, and Nora sobbed as if her heart was breaking.

Colleen knew that Nora's hard talk and bravado was just a front. Inside she was a frightened little girl who was in way over her head. Colleen was desperate for her sister to be spared any more abuse and was so grateful to Adam for helping them. She realised that she should have asked him before, and she could have spared them both a lot of grief.

'Right, you two,' said Adam. 'Pack a bag, you're both coming back to my place. Tomorrow, we'll go to the police. Okay? Is that okay with you, Nora? You're the victim in all this, the police won't charge you, I'm sure of it.'

'Yes, Adam's right,' said Colleen. 'We've done all we can, and the police need to take over now.'

'Okay,' said Nora.

'Wait 'til you see Adam's penthouse, you'll love it.'

Nora smiled, but it was a poor thing and Colleen's heart went out to her little sister. She hadn't deserved any of this. Maybe now she could turn her life around.

Chapter Twenty-Three

The following day, the three of them took the tapes to the local police station. Colleen kept Nora close to her, not because she thought she'd do a runner, but because the poor girl was shaking with fear.

'Don't worry, you're the victim in all this.'

'But I'm an addict,' said Nora through clenched teeth.

'Exactly, you need medical assistance, not a prison sentence.'

The officer in charge took them into a small room and they watched the tape together.

'Rupert Graveson, aka Big Man. We've been watching him for a while. This will help us with our investigations. You'll each have to write a statement, okay?'

The man didn't look anything like the investigating officers on the police procedurals Colleen watched on television. He seemed more like a kindly uncle who put them all at ease.

'There's something else.' She looked at her sister, 'Go on, tell him, Nora.'

'He raped me, and I had to have sex with men and give him the money.'

'When did he rape you? Was it recently?'

'No, a few months ago.'

'Would you prefer to speak to a woman?'

'No, it's okay.' Nora was trying her best to be brave and Colleen was proud of her.

When they'd written their statements, the officer witnessed their signatures and then they were free to go.

'We'll want to speak to you again, especially about the rape. We'll appoint a dedicated officer to provide you with the help and support that you need. She will be your single point of contact during the investigation. She'll take a more detailed account from you and keep you updated on how the investigation is going.'

'Right.' Nora seemed stunned by everything that was happening and held Colleen's hand tightly.

'How soon do you think you'll arrest him?'

'I'm afraid I can't answer that at the moment, Mr Turner, but we will keep you updated and will want to speak to you all again.'

'Right.'

'Have you got somewhere to stay seeing as he knows where you live?'

'They'll be staying with me,' Adam said.

'Good. Well, we'll be in touch.'

They were escorted out and the three of them stood on the pavement. Colleen had mixed feelings. They'd done everything they could do and now it was up to the police, but she felt as if it was all an anti-climax. What if they couldn't make the charges stick? What if they let him out on bail? He'd come after them again. Maybe they'd never be free of him.

When they arrived back at the penthouse apartment, Nora said she didn't feel well and was going for a lie down.

Adam was looking at her in that special way he had when he wanted her. Colleen wanted him, but although her body would be as willing as it ever was, her mind couldn't think of anything but Nora, Big Man and how long it would be before she felt safe again.

'What's on your mind? I can tell when something's bothering you. Or is that a stupid question in light of everything that's going on?'

Adam lounged back on the cushions on the couch with his hands behind his head.

'I feel it's all a bit of an anti-climax. I think I was pinning my hopes on the police doing something straight away, instead of taking statements and saying they'll be in touch.'

'What did you expect them to do?'

'Arrest him.'

'It's not how they work. The officer did say that they've been watching him, so they know everything already. We haven't told them anything new. But at least they took Nora's claim of rape seriously.'

Colleen moved to sit next to Adam, and he held her tenderly and kissed her forehead.

'I'm worried about Nora. She needs to get help for her addiction.'

'Yes, she should be in rehab.'

'She would have been if it wasn't for me. When the doctor referred her, she didn't go as she thought I'd be alone and at risk.'

'Which you would have been. Why didn't you tell me earlier? I could have helped.'

Colleen sat up and stroked his face. 'You have helped. We couldn't have got all the surveillance equipment if it wasn't for your friendship with Jeremy.'

They kissed, a gentle loving kiss, rather than a passionate lust filled one. Neither of them was in the mood for sex. Not yet anyway. But tonight, Colleen intended to make up for the time they'd been apart.

'I need to check on Nora.'

Colleen went into the spare bedroom which would be Nora's room for the foreseeable future. She was asleep, but not in a natural way. She was lying on her back, her mouth open and a syringe was next to her on the bed.

Colleen couldn't blame her. It wasn't her fault she'd become addicted to heroin and now that she was, she needed help to come off it, she couldn't do it alone.

Colleen searched the bedroom until she found Nora's purse. In it was the card that the doctors at the hospital had given her with the contact details for the Drug and Alcohol Liaison Team. She took it back into the lounge and dialled the number.

Adam enjoyed a malt whisky while gazing out at the view of London at night. Nora was out for the count and probably wouldn't wake until the morning. Colleen had phoned the Drug Team and asked if Nora's referral could be reinstated.

Adam felt as if they were all in limbo, just waiting for news from the police. He wanted to make love to Colleen but didn't think she'd be in the right headspace for that. No matter, he'd wait. He would wait forever for her. His job now was to be supportive and help her in practical ways, like the surveillance equipment. Good old Jeremy, he owed him one.

The next big thing, apart from the, hopefully, imminent arrest of that evil bastard Rupert, was the will reading. He had received a formal letter in the old fashioned way – by post. Solicitors always did things the correct way. An email would have sufficed in Adam's view as the letter merely gave the date and time of the will reading and inviting him to attend. It was in a week's time. Not long to go before he knew his fate. To keep his role as CEO of Meredith Motors or to move on. Rosamund hadn't contacted him recently, but Adam bet she was feeling confident enough to wait until it was official. She was convinced she'd get everything, and Adam had a sneaking suspicion that she was right. Hugo had been such an advocate for the family, that he would leave everything to his only child.

Colleen came up behind him and put her arms around his waist.

'Hi,' she said. She wore a bathrobe and smelt like freesias in spring.

'Hi,' Adam replied. He knocked back the rest of the liquor then he turned and kissed her.

'Umm, you taste of whisky.'

'Do you want one?'

'No thanks. I want you though.'

They kissed again and Adam undid the belt on her robe and slipped it off her shoulders. She had just had a shower and her skin was pink from the water being hot. Adam smiled.

Then Colleen undid the buttons on his shirt, and he took his cufflinks off and put them in his trouser pocket. She ran her hands over his chest and stomach, causing waves of lust to wash over him. It was amazing how quickly he could go from zero to fully erect in such a short time. Colleen's hands were magical, playing his body like an instrument.

Colleen undid the belt on his trousers, running her hand over his hardness, making him moan softly. She slipped his trousers down, followed by his boxers and he kicked them out of the way. He took his socks off, using Colleen's shoulders to balance, which made her giggle like a little girl.

He wanted her. Her touch, her taste, the sounds she made when she came, the light that danced in her eyes when she looked at him…

'Let's go to bed.'

'Your wish is my command.'

Both naked, they held hands as they moved towards the bedroom. Then he picked her up and lay her on the bed, then moved over her to kiss her breasts and fondle them until she squirmed and moaned. He took a nipple in his mouth and gently tongued it. He cupped her other breast and did the same.

He licked her body, and kissed, and stroked her until she was panting. Then he spread her legs and she cried out as his mouth touched her sweet spot. She was wet and hot and ready for him.

'Yes, oh yes…'

'Do you like that?'

'Yes. Make me come.'

He didn't need any persuasion and licked her clit marvelling at how little she needed to climax. They were in perfect accord, in sync, together in everything their bodies were expressing.

Adam wanted to be inside her. Suddenly his need was urgent. He couldn't wait. Taking a condom from the bedside cabinet, he sheathed himself and entered her. She wrapped her legs around him and he thrust deeper into her.

'I want more,' she cried.

'What do you want me to do?'

'Fuck me…'

'How?'

'Hard.' Colleen was thrusting her hips up to meet him, and he thrust harder and faster.

'Is that hard enough?' he gasped.

'No, more.' Colleen's eyes were shut and her mouth open as she strained to reach her climax. Unlike Rosamund who could only orgasm when she'd been dominated with her partner taking total control, Colleen was an equal, with him all the way. She knew what she wanted and wasn't afraid to ask him for it. She was no longer the mistress, attending to his every need. She was his equal and they faced life together.

And to prove it, they orgasmed together, then lay side by side, replete.

A week later, Adam was sitting next to Rosamund in Hugo's solicitor's office, on one side of a huge oak desk. On the other side sat Hugo's solicitor, Clive Brandreth. They were the only two people he had asked to be present, and Adam knew this was Hugo's last chance to control events, even from the grave.

'Thank you for coming today,' said Clive. 'I'll keep it as short as possible. Hugo's instructions were simple and concise.'

'Good,' said Rosamund, who fidgeted by Adam's side. So she wasn't as confident as she tried to make out.

'The instructions are these: as long as Adam and Rosamund stay together as man and wife, they jointly inherit everything, chiefly the house and the business, Meredith Motors. If, in the event that they separate or divorce, everything reverts to Rosamund.'

Adam could hear Rosamund sigh as if she had been holding her breath.

'That seems clear enough to me, does it to you, Adam?' She turned to him with a dazzling smile.

'Yes,' he said quietly, 'couldn't be clearer.' Hugo had given him an impossible choice. If he stayed married to Rosamund he would be joint owner of Meredith Motors and the Meredith family home. But if he followed his heart, he'd lose everything.

'There are just a few smaller items to report. Hugo has bequeathed the Rolls Royce Silver Cloud motor car to Adam. All the other cars in his collection, vintage or modern, will be part of the estate that Rosamund and Adam will share.'

'You got the Roller then,' Rosamund said to Adam, 'Daddy knew it was your favourite. Good for you.'

Adam nodded but said nothing. It was true he did love that car. Hugo had bought it as a status symbol as it wasn't a practical car to own in London. Adam loved it for its appearance, the sleek lines and luxurious interior. But it would only be used for special occasions. His Mercedes would suffice for daily use.

'Thank you for coming,' said Clive Brandreth, standing up and shaking their hands.

'Now I've read the will, as per Hugo's instructions, I'll post a copy to each of you.'

'Thank you, Clive,' said Rosamund. 'I'm just glad this

whole business is over now, and we can get back to our normal lives. What say you, Adam?'

'Agreed.' Adam had nothing to say, he just wanted to get home as he had a lot to think about and he needed to be alone. Rosamund had other ideas.

'Let's go somewhere to celebrate, shall we? This is the result we wanted isn't it?'

'No, Rosamund, it isn't the result I wanted.'

'But surely you didn't think Daddy was going to let you inherit everything and me nothing? That isn't what you thought at all is it?'

'To be honest, I wasn't sure what Hugo was going to do. But he's made his wishes clear, and I have to think about the next steps. I'm going home now, I'll let you know what I've decided in due course.'

Adam walked out of the solicitor's office and found Davis waiting outside for him. He got in the car and told Davis to head for home.

Chapter Twenty-Four

It had all happened so fast. Nora was offered a place on a twenty-eight-day residential course at a London drug rehab clinic. She would be given specialist treatment for her addiction, exactly what she needed. And then, when it was over, she could come home and start to live the life of every other twenty-five-year-old. Maybe Colleen could persuade her to go to university or college and become the person she was always meant to be. It wasn't too late.

The next major event was the phone call from the police. They had Rupert, aka Big Man, in custody. He'd been charged with raping Nora, dealing drugs and actual bodily harm, and was refused bail. Colleen had taken photos of her bruises to show to the police. There was a long way to go, as he was facing so many charges it would take months for the officers responsible to collect all the data. But at least the evil man would be behind bars and couldn't hurt Nora anymore.

Colleen did wonder about people who worked for him taking over where he left off and Adam suggested leaving the surveillance equipment running just in case. But, as the only person who had visited the apartment was Rupert, she felt fairly secure about moving back in.

Colleen wished she could stay with Adam at the penthouse apartment but, as he hadn't suggested it and because of everything he had done for her already, she couldn't really complain and moved back to the Chelsea apartment. He had said nothing about the will reading, and she hadn't liked to ask. He would tell her when he was ready.

Colleen was relieved to get back to work the following Monday and hoped that Adam would stop by at some point that day.

'Good morning, Doris,' she said as she entered the office.

'Good morning, Colleen, are you better now? I was so sorry to hear you were unwell. How's your face? Bruises gone?'

'Yes, thanks for asking, they're quite gone. It was just a stupid accident, totally my own fault, but I'm better now. I'm so sorry I had to leave you in the lurch with all that work, but I'll work extra hours to make it up if you like?'

Doris was looking smart in a pristine white blouse, a pale blue cardigan and minimal make-up. She had lovely skin for an older woman and her light blue eyes twinkled as if she was always ready for a bit of fun.

'Oh, that's not necessary. Now that you're back, we'll get through the work together, no trouble.'

'Did you have a nice weekend?' asked Colleen.

'It was our anniversary, and we had the whole weekend away in a bed and breakfast in the Cotswolds. It was sheer bliss.'

'That sounds divine. Was it a special one? I mean the numbers thing.'

'No, the big one is a few years away, but we always cele-brate whatever, it helps us to remember why we fell in love. Keeps romance alive.'

Why couldn't she have a relationship like that? Adam had been quiet recently and, when she had tried to talk to him, he had clammed up and said he had a lot on his mind. Since she'd moved out of the penthouse, he hadn't contacted her or called round to see her. If only she knew what Hugo's will had said.

Just before lunchtime, they had a visitor and Colleen found out everything she needed to know.

The intercom buzzed and Doris answered it, telling the caller to come up.

Rosamund swept in and stood in the middle of the room like last time. Unlike last time, she wasn't dressed to kill, having chosen to wear blue jeans, a white T-shirt, and a checked jacket. She wore little make-up but had a smug, satisfied look on her face and Colleen's heart sank. What-ever she was about to say wasn't going to be good news.

'Good morning, ladies, good to see you hard at work, just as I like my staff to be.'

Doris and Colleen exchanged a look. Doris's sparkle appeared a little dimmer at Rosamund's words.

'Doris, would you be a pet and run to the corner shop for me? A skinny latte would be just the ticket.'

Doris raised her eyes to heaven and, with a last pitying glance at Colleen, she grabbed her purse and left the office.

Colleen said nothing, but she could feel her cheeks burn with rage. Once again, Doris had been dismissed by this wretched woman, so they could be alone. She wouldn't speak, just listen, until she had said whatever it was she was bursting to tell her. For Rosamund looked like a cat who had found the most delectable cream.

'I imagine you are dying to know the contents of Daddy's will?'

Despite telling herself not to answer, the temptation was too great.

'Not particularly. Why should I? It doesn't concern me.'

'*Au contraire*, I think you'll find it does. In fact, I'd go so far as to say it changes everything for you.'

'In what way?' Colleen thought she may as well get it over with. Rosamund was going to take great delight in telling her no matter what Colleen said.

'Daddy has left everything to me and Adam as long as we stay together. In the event we separate, it all reverts to me. So you see, your sordid little liaison with my husband is now over. There is no way Adam would jeopardise his part ownership of Meredith Motors by carrying on with a tramp like you. He doesn't have feelings for you, other than the obvious and, as I'm sure you'll agree, when men are led by what's in their trousers, common sense flies out of the window.'

Colleen wanted to object, scream at her that Adam did have feelings for her, but she knew it was useless. She had to hear it from Adam himself and so far, since she'd moved out of his penthouse, he'd been silent.

'Congratulations,' Colleen said with as much dignity as she could dredge up.

'Of course, your time working at Meredith Motors is also at an end. Adam and I will be running the company together and I have appointed myself in charge of staffing. You may as well finish at the end of the day as I don't want to leave poor Doris without an assistant for too long. Although I'm sure you'll be easy to replace.'

'Does Adam know?' Colleen was stunned by the thought that she'd lose her job so quickly and thoughts of taking them to a tribunal for unfair dismissal crossed her mind. But it left just as quickly. How could she face the court case against Big Man as well as an employment tribunal? It was more than she could bear.

'Of course Adam knows. We're working together now. Didn't you hear anything I just said?'

'Yes, I heard you,' Colleen whispered.

'Oh, and you need to vacate the apartment as well. Adam and I have plans for it. You don't need to go today, you can have until the end of the week.'

The apartment was Adam's. Colleen was sure about that. She was going nowhere until she had spoken to him.

Doris came in and plonked the cardboard carton of coffee on the edge of her desk. Rosamund ignored it.

'Right, I think that's everything. Back to work, ladies. Time's money you know.'

Then she swept from the room with her head high and her nose in the air.

Doris sat back at her desk and took the lid off the carton.

'She never pays you for all the coffee she orders. Neither of us drinks skinny latte.'

'Don't worry, my dear,' said Doris, 'I never buy what she asks for. I buy myself a caramel macchiato and charge it to expenses.'

'Good for you.'

'Anyway, what did the bitch want this time?'

Colleen was startled, She'd never heard Doris use any swear words. She was going to miss her. She'd grown really fond of the older woman in the short time she'd worked at Meredith Motors and thought they could have been good friends in time.

'She came to gloat. Hugo's will stated that, as long as

Rosamund and Adam stay married, they get everything between them. If they separate it all reverts to Rosamund. So she's won, whatever happens.'

Doris sipped the coffee and stared into space. 'I'm not surprised by that. Hugo thought that Adam was good for his daughter. Sadly, he didn't care that Rosamund was poison to Adam. I wonder what he'll do.'

'He'll stay with her. Adam loves this company and couldn't bear to part with it. And then there's the house and Hugo's private vintage car collection. He'll get a half share in all of it.'

'It's a lot to give up.'

'It is.' Colleen felt like crying. Why had she been so stupid as to fall in love with a man like Adam? Despite being born to an ordinary working-class family, he had moved up in the world. What could she possibly offer him that would match up to what he already had? Nothing, that was what.

'So where does that leave you, Colleen?' Doris sipped her coffee. It smelled delicious.

'Out of a job. She wants me to finish tonight.'

'No! She can't do that. I'd ring Adam if I were you and clarify the situation.'

'She said that Adam already knows. She's appointed herself in charge of staffing.' Colleen reached for a tissue from the box that sat on her desk. She wiped her eyes.

'I'm so sorry, Colleen, that's awful. And just when we were beginning to gel as a team.'

'Don't worry, she thinks I'll be easy to replace.'

'Well, take it from me, you won't be. We had a stream of temps doing that job and none of them could hold a candle to you, Colleen. You'll be sorely missed, I promise you that.'

'Thanks, Doris. I'll miss you as well.'

'Well, if she thinks she's going to get any work out of us

today, she can think again. How about we have a long lunch? My treat. Do you like Italian food? There's a nice place a ten-minute walk away. They do lovely pizza and pasta. We could have a bottle of wine too.'

'What about the phones?' asked Colleen taking her handbag out of the drawer.

'What about them? The way you've been treated, we owe them no loyalty. If she's in charge, the place will go down the drain anyway.'

When they arrived at the restaurant, Doris greeted the waiter like an old friend.

'Marco and I go way back. He's a nice boy,' she whispered.

'What can you recommend?' Colleen asked Marco.

'I recommend the *Fettuccine Carbonara.*'

'Sounds good. We'll both have that then and a glass of white wine each.'

When Marco had gone, Doris put her hand over Colleen's.

'I know it's none of my business, but I've known Adam for quite a few years now and I would be surprised if he stays with Rosamund, even for the sake of the business. Especially as he's got you. He confided to me how much he feels for you. His marriage to Rosamund was over a long time ago. Give him a chance, Colleen. He's a good man. Don't give up on him yet.'

A week later, Colleen returned to the office of Meredith Motors. Adam hadn't phoned, nor had he returned her calls or texts. She'd left several messages on voicemail, but he hadn't replied to any.

Rosamund had won, that much was obvious. Despite Doris telling her not to give up on him, she was beginning to realise that he had given up on her. The temptation of owning Meredith Motors had obviously proved too much for him. When she'd met him, that infamous night of Jeremy's stag do, he had been kind to her and Nora. He had helped in a way that no one else would have bothered to do. The job, the apartment, the surveillance equipment, had all made such a difference to her life. He had cared about her, she knew he had. However, his love for the business and his way of life had proved more important in the end.

Doris was on her own and looked harassed.

'Hi, Doris, how're you doing?'

'Colleen—please tell me you've come back to work, I'm snowed under here.'

'No, I'm afraid not. I've come to ask you a favour.'

'Okay. Whatever I can do.'

'When you see Adam, could you give him this?' She handed over a brown envelope.

'Yes, of course, and I won't even ask what's in it.'

'Thanks. I'm going back to Manchester to see Mum. Nora is safe and I've notified the police of Mum's address if they need to get in touch with me.'

'When are you coming back?'

'Not sure. Maybe never. There's nothing for me in London. When Nora's better she'll come home to be looked after by Mum until she's back on her feet again.'

'And Adam?' Doris asked quietly. Doris looked sad and Colleen felt the same way. She'd found a friend in Doris and now she had to say goodbye.

'I haven't heard from him. He hasn't answered my calls, so I've stopped making them. I can take a hint as well as anyone. We were never meant to be forever. It was good while it lasted, but now it's over.'

'I'm sorry, Colleen. I hope you'll be happier back home with your Mum. You've been a great friend as well as a co-worker and I wish you well.'

'Thanks. I'd better go.' Colleen wanted to get out before she broke down and cried.

'Goodbye then.'

'Goodbye, Doris, and thanks for everything.'

Chapter Twenty-Five

The sound of the train on the tracks and the view of the passing countryside lulled Colleen into a doze. She daydreamed of Adam riding a white stallion and keeping pace with the train. He was dressed in medieval garb like a knight of old and shouted "I love you" at her.

'I love you too,' she replied, then jerked awake as a man opposite her coughed loudly. Whether he'd heard her and was trying to wake her up before she embarrassed herself further, or whether he was just coughing, she didn't know. He was hiding behind a newspaper so she couldn't see his face.

Despite Big Man being in custody, Colleen hadn't been able to relax, thinking that people who worked for him would be watching her and waiting for a good time to threaten her, or worse attack her. She couldn't get out of her mind how easily Nora had been injected with heroin by him and his henchmen. She'd feel much safer when she was living in Manchester again.

Her next problem was how to tell her mother about

Nora and the drugs. None of it was her fault, she had gone to London and fallen in with the wrong people. A common story for youngsters. But now, Nora was getting the help she needed and would be home soon too.

The man opposite got out at Stockport. He was an ordinary businessman and didn't look at Colleen once. She must stop taking fright at everything around her. That was no way to live.

Colleen had thought she'd feel better when she arrived at Piccadilly, Manchester, but seeing a couple greet each other off the train, hugging, kissing and crying with joy, she realised how much she had lost.

Would she ever find a man she loved as much as Adam? He'd been such a gentleman, kind, considerate and a wonderful lover. But he'd chosen money and a wife he didn't love over her and she could never understand that.

As she took a taxi home, she concentrated on her mother and how she would explain the drugs to her. It would be one of the hardest conversations she would ever have.

———

'Mum.' Colleen hugged her mother on the doorstep and fought to stop herself from crying.

'Colleen, that's an emotional greeting, come in, come in.' Her mother took her arm and pulled her into the house. 'We don't want the neighbours nosing at us. Come in now.'

It felt good to be back home, but why did everything look smaller when you've been away? Adam's apartment was large and spacious, and she must have grown used to that way of living. Well, she'd just have to relearn living in a three bedroomed semi in South Manchester. After all, it was her family home, the place she'd grown up in and she had fond memories of her childhood.

But somehow, all she could think about was the apartment and making love with Adam in the double bed.

'It's lovely to see you but you worried me with that message that you had something to tell me. You're not pregnant are you?'

'No, Mum, I'm not. It concerns Nora.' Colleen had phoned her mother to tell her she was coming to visit but then decided to send her a text saying she had something to tell her. With hindsight, she shouldn't have done that as she should have known her mother would only worry.

'Nora? Is she in trouble? I knew it. I knew going to London was a mistake. What is there for you in that place that you can't get here at home?'

'Mum, now listen to me, okay. I have something to tell you and it's a long story, so you need to listen without interrupting—'

'What are you saying? I never interrupt.'

'Good. Let's have a nice cup of tea and make ourselves comfy and I'll tell you all about it.'

'I'll put the kettle on.'

As her Mum busied herself with making a pot of tea, Colleen rehearsed in her mind how she would break the news that her younger daughter was a heroin addict. She'd be gentle and hope that her mother didn't freak out.

When they were settled in the living room with tea and biscuits, Colleen realised something, or rather *someone* was missing.

'Where's Auntie May?'

'Gone,' said her mother before stuffing a biscuit that she had dunked in her tea into her mouth.

'Gone back home?'

Her mother nodded as she had a mouthful of soggy biscuit and couldn't answer. She swallowed it quickly and took a swig of tea.

'We had a falling out, you might say.'

'Oh, tell me.'

'Well, she's my sister and blood's thicker than water. Family is important, Colleen, I want you to understand that.'

'Oh I do, Mum,' she said thinking of Nora.

'But...' Her mother took another gulp of tea. 'She was starting to get on my nerves. She said she'd come to help but there was no help forthcoming if you understand my meaning.'

'She was lazy and had you running around after her.'

'Now you said that not me. I would never think badly of her but you're right. I was exhausted with it all. Anyway, she wanted me to go home with her and clean her house as well.'

'She what!'

'She said she couldn't do housework on account of her bad back and her house was in a state and would I go back with her and clean it. She said I was so good at the cleaning and she knew I wouldn't want her to be living in a dirty house, not when I was so particular.'

'The cheeky bitch.'

'Colleen, there's no need for that kind of language.'

'But she is. How dare she expect you to do her cleaning. I'm glad you said no.'

'Well that's the thing. I didn't. I went to clean the house, top to bottom. But then, instead of thanking me and staying in her own place, she came back here and carried on as if I was her unpaid skivvy.'

'That's not on. I can't believe you fell for it and cleaned her house for her. So when did you fall out?'

'Last week. I'd cleaned and polished and dusted as Father Moss was coming round to see me. I'd not been to Mass for a while, and he was concerned. Wonderful man, Father Moss.'

'Why haven't you been to Mass?' That wasn't like her mother who never missed Mass if she could help it.

'Because I've been so worn out with cleaning, that's why.'

'Oh, Mum, that's awful. Tell me the rest.'

'Well...' Her mother stood up and poured them both a second cup of tea. 'I expected May to at least understand why it was so important to me, but when I came back from the shops, the place was a mess. Clothes everywhere, the sink full of dishes, and Father Moss walking up the drive-way... I lost it, Colleen, I had a breakdown and couldn't stop crying.'

'Oh, Mum, you poor thing. What did Father Moss say?'

'He said I was working too hard and to forget the cleaning. Come to Mass, he said and receive solace and comfort in the House of the Lord. So I did, and I told May that she'd have to do her own cleaning from now on as I was too busy talking to God.'

'I bet that went down like a lead balloon.' Colleen loved her little Mum so much, that her heart was breaking at what she was about to tell her.

'Well, let's just say it had the desired effect. She'd packed her bags and was away the next day.'

'Good. She'll have to learn to clean her own house. And

I'm glad you're going to Mass again, I know how much you love it.'

'I do. Now, we've prevaricated long enough. I want to hear the story with Nora. All of it, and I promise I won't interrupt.'

'Before I went to London I thought Nora was living a good life, with a job, friends, a nice place to live—'

'So did I, Colleen, so did I. But you're saying she wasn't?'

'That's what I'm saying. The flat was dirty, cold, empty of any comfort.'

'Oh my goodness, why was she living like that, do you know?'

Colleen realised that expecting her Mum not to interrupt was like expecting a donkey to win the Grand National.

'I do. She was taking drugs.'

'No!' Her mother was speechless for the first time since Colleen had come home.

'It wasn't her fault, you mustn't blame her. Young people going to London and knowing no one can easily fall in with the wrong crowd. They're easy prey for the drug dealers who befriend them and then get them to take drugs.'

'But… Nora's a good girl, she's smart. Why in the name of all that's holy did that happen to her?'

Colleen went and sat next to her mum on the couch and held her hand.

'They start off with things like weed—'

'You mean like marijuana?'

'Yes, Mum, exactly like that.' Colleen wished that she had told her mum the worst, but she hadn't, and she knew she couldn't tell her half a story. She deserved the truth.

'Oh dear. Poor Nora.'

'Then they give them stronger drugs. But these drugs are expensive, so they have to earn money to pay for them.'

'But you said Nora didn't have a job. How could she afford them? And why couldn't she have just told these people to leave her alone?'

'It's not that easy. When they're addicted, they get cravings and have to have the drugs to get through the day. The dealers have got total control over their lives and there's nothing they can do.'

'You're talking about heroin aren't you? I'm not stupid, Colleen, I know what goes on in the world. She's hooked on heroin.'

Colleen squeezed her mother's hand to try to impart some comfort to her. To learn that one of your children is a drug addict must be horrific.

'Mum, it's okay, Nora is in a residential rehabilitation unit getting the care she needs. They're looking after her round the clock and getting her off the drugs. And the man who controlled it all is in prison, awaiting further investigations.'

Colleen wanted to avoid telling her mother about the prostitution and the fact Nora was raped by the Big Man. If these facts came out in subsequent conversations she wouldn't lie to her, but for now, her mother had heard enough bad news. She looked as if someone had pulled the floor out from underneath her and she was floundering, trying to find solid ground.

'And you did all this for your sister on your own? In a strange place and knowing nobody, you rescued her. You're an angel, Colleen, that's what you are.'

'I didn't do it all myself. I met a man called Adam who gave me a job and let Nora and me stay in his apartment. He helped me... with everything.'

Colleen didn't want to tell her mother about the surveillance equipment as she'd have to tell her everything else as well.

'And who is this man?'

'He's just someone I met. But he's married and... he was just being a friend.'

'Well, he's a good man whoever he is. I'll say a prayer for him tonight. Jesus must have sent him to you to help you girls so much.'

Colleen couldn't disagree. Adam had done so much but now he was gone. She didn't know how she could bear to keep on living thinking of what might have been. Or was that just her stupid imagination again? Always wanting what she couldn't have. But then she realised that if she hadn't met Adam, Nora wouldn't have got the help she needed. She'd have become more entrenched in the drug world, having sex with strangers, and perhaps becoming a Maggot character herself, enticing innocent people to become addicts. There might have been no hope for her at all if it wasn't for Adam. She owed him so much, but he was lost to her now and she had to forget him.

Chapter Twenty-Six

Adam had been busy but was still aware of the number of calls from Colleen he'd missed. He wanted to phone her and explain. He'd stared at his phone several times, his thumb hovering near her number. But it wasn't the right time. He had too much to do beforehand.

Rosamund was also busy. She had hired an up-market firm of interior designers to completely change the look of Hugo's house, which was now Rosamund and Adam's. All the old furniture had gone and the whole of the house had been redecorated and refurnished. It must have cost a bomb and she'd done it all herself without telling Adam what she was doing or consulting him on colour schemes and the like. Not that he would have been interested if she had.

She had been to the office hassling Doris and Colleen, as she had appointed herself the new staffing manager. It was a laugh as the salesmen and mechanics were specialised members of staff who Adam interviewed and employed. Rosamund had never had the slightest bit of interest in cars and didn't know a vintage car from a taxi. Her new title purely gave her control of the admin staff and an excuse to boss them around.

Rosamund was having the time of her life, thinking she'd won.

One of the jobs on Adam's to-do list was to talk to Doris and Colleen and tell them that, as far as he was concerned, nothing had changed, and they only took their instructions from him. In effect, to ignore Rosamund altogether. But he hadn't been near the office in weeks, as he'd been too busy.

Jeremy had invited him to Bachelors for a Friday night roast dinner and a catch-up. Adam responded willingly.

'So, I hear they've got the blighter banged to rights. Jolly good work,' said Jeremy tucking into roast pork and apple sauce.

'Yes, thanks to you. And thanks for the loan of the equipment. You can have it back whenever you like.'

'Right. I'll make the necessary arrangements to collect it. So what are your plans now? You'll be staying with Rosamund presumably, but what about the stripper? Are you keeping her on in a private residence or letting go? I wouldn't advise the flat in Chelsea as everyone and his dog knows about that place.'

'Colleen's not a stripper, that was all a misunderstanding. And as far as the apartment is concerned, I'm putting it on the market…'

'Good idea.'

'…as well as the penthouse.'

'What!? Not the penthouse. It's a wonderful little bolthole. You're going to need somewhere like that. Marriage isn't all smooth sailing, you know. Take it from one who knows.'

'Yes, Jeremy, I know. Rosamund and I have been married for a long time, but it's over now.'

'I don't understand... oh, yes, I think I do. You're going to have a modern arrangement. Stay married, but live separately and have partners so long as they're not made public. I must say, Adam, I never thought you of all people would go down that road.'

Adam sipped his wine and watched Jeremy hoover up his roast potatoes. He didn't know anyone else who could demolish a large plate of food as quickly. He was lucky he never put on any weight.

'What do you mean, me of all people?'

'Well, you've always appeared to be a man who took the righteous path, if you know what I mean. In fact, until the strip... Colleen, I'd never heard any rumours of affairs and the like connected to you.'

'That's because I've never had an affair, until Colleen. But can you call it an affair if you're estranged from your wife? Rosamund and I were living separate lives when I met Colleen otherwise... well, things would have been different.'

'I think that's a moot point, Adam, you were appearing as man and wife in public at Hugo's instigation, so people can be forgiven for thinking that you *were* man and wife.'

'Yes, I suppose so. But we're not anymore, despite what Rosamund would like to believe.'

The waiter removed their plates and replaced them with ginger sponge and custard. Jeremy nearly salivated over his.

'It's sad that the poor girl can't accept the truth. But if you did separate, who would run Meredith Motors?'

'Rosamund. Although she obviously couldn't take charge herself, she'd have to hire a CEO to do it for her.'

'And how do you feel about that?'

'They're cars, Jeremy, and they can sit quite happily on any forecourt.'

'That's cryptic. This sponge is delicious.'

Adam tried some and agreed it was.

'I've got plans that I can't really talk about at present, but once they're finalised, you'll be the first to know.'

'Jolly good. Do you think we could be cheeky and ask for seconds?'

The following day, Adam visited the office and was amazed and enraged to find that Colleen had left.

'What the hell's been going on?' he asked Doris.

'Your wife paid a visit and sacked her. She had to leave the same day.'

'Oh, did she now. Well, Colleen will be reinstated, and you have my permission to ignore everything that woman says. I'm still the CEO and I'm responsible for hiring and firing, not Rosamund.'

'I doubt she'll come back now, she's gone home to Manchester.'

'What! Why didn't she tell me she was leaving?'

'She did say you weren't answering her calls,' Doris said tentatively.

Adam was guilty as charged. He had ignored the flurry of texts that Colleen had sent after the will reading, some asking what was happening, as he wanted to talk to her properly, face to face. He'd foolishly assumed she'd wait until she heard from him, not up sticks and run back to her mother. But that was unfair, Colleen had been through a lot recently and he should have put her first and told her everything.

'I should have rung her, it's my fault.'

'She did give me this envelope to pass on to you.'

Adam took the envelope and studied it. A Dear John letter perhaps? Well, if it was, he wouldn't accept it. If he was to lose Meredith Motors, he certainly wasn't going to lose Colleen as well.

'I'll be in my office, Doris, and I don't want to be disturbed. By anyone.'

'Okay.'

Adam sat in his comfy leather office chair but didn't bother to turn his computer on. He hadn't come here to work, but to see Colleen. It was his fault that she'd got tired of waiting to hear from him and who knows what lies Rosamund had told her when she sacked her.

He stared at the envelope for ages, wanting, but not wanting, to know what was in it. In his mind he had seen it all clearly, but why the hell hadn't he confided in Colleen from the beginning. Then he might not have lost her.

He carefully opened the envelope and fished out a letter and a drawing. It was a sketch of him in bed, lying on his back with his arm over his head. He had nothing on except the duvet draped over his hips, hiding his manhood. Judging by the surroundings, it was the night they'd spent at Charmley Manor.

Despite knowing little about art, Adam recognised the talent in the drawing. The shading of dark and light was confident and bold. It was an exquisite piece and Adam vowed to treasure it forever. He might even have it framed and hang it in his bedroom. Wherever his next bedroom turned out to be.

Adam turned his attention to the letter. It was brief, only four short paragraphs. His heart beat faster and his breathing was shallow. Please don't let this be a Dear John letter.

Dear Adam

I am writing this with a heavy heart. As I haven't heard from you since the will reading and you haven't answered my calls and texts, I can only assume that we are now over, and you are staying with Rosamund.

I have always known what we had together wasn't forever, but the time I have spent with you was the happiest of my life. Despite the horror of the drug dealers, the tyranny of Rupert and being branded a tramp and a prostitute, I would go through it all again, gladly, if it meant I could have my time with you again.

If I was the romantic type I would describe you as my soulmate, my other half, the only man I've felt completely comfortable and happy with. You fulfilled me and completed me in a way I've never experienced before. I'll be completely honest now, Adam, and tell you that I love you. I know you don't feel the same, and that's okay, I have never expected you to fall in love with me. But my feelings for you are real and I'll never forget all the things you've done for me, and for Nora. You have truly been my knight in shining armour if you'll forgive the cliché.

I don't want anything from you, you've done enough already. I just wanted you to know how much you mean to me. I wish you well, Adam. I hope Meredith Motors thrives and that your marriage is happy.

Always in your debt

Colleen

Adam sat staring into space. He picked up the drawing Colleen had done and studied it. She loved him. She'd been brave enough to pour her heart out to him. And the drawing, which was more precious than ever, was something he would cherish forever, as he intended to cherish Colleen. He needed to do something about the situation instead of sitting there like a lump. But just as he was about to get up and start being proactive, Rosamund burst into his office.

'Oh, so this is where you're hiding, is it? There's no time for just sitting there you know, we've got so much to do.'

Rosamund was power dressing again, in a turquoise skirt and jacket and a white blouse. She had her hair up and subtle make-up. Adam had to admit she looked the part. But looking the part didn't mean you knew what you were doing and Rosamund was just making noise for the sake of it.

'This is my office, Rosamund, where else would I be on a weekday morning?'

'Actually, it isn't *your* office anymore, is it? It's *our* office. We share it, so I have every right to be here.'

'Of course. But we can't both sit in this chair at the same time.' Adam realised he was slipping back into the habit of having ludicrous arguments with Rosamund that made them sound like a pair of children, not mature, professional adults.

'We need to establish some ground rules,' Rosamund said as she wandered nearer to the desk, picking up documents, pretending to read them, and putting them down again. She picked up the drawing and her whole demeanour changed.

'What the fuck is this?' She had gone red in the face and

her jaw clenched tightly. Adam wished he'd put the drawing away, but it was too late now.

'It's none of your business and I'd be grateful if you'd put it down. It's private.'

'Fancies herself as a Picasso, does she, your tart?'

'She isn't a tart and, since you ask, she's an accomplished artist.'

'Accomplished in bed but little else. I told you to get rid of her. She has no place in your life now, Adam. I fired her hoping that we would see the last of her.'

'Well bad luck, I've reinstated her.' Or at least he would when he saw her.

'You what? How dare you undermine my authority! Once someone is fired, they stay fired. And if I hear that you've been seeing her again behind my back, there will be serious trouble.'

'Put the drawing down, Rosamund.'

'Means a lot to you, does it?'

'Yes, as a matter of fact, it does.'

'Well, tough.' Rosamund took the drawing and slowly tore it into two, then four, and threw the pieces on the desk. 'Like I said, she's history.'

Adam clenched the arms of the chair to stop himself leaping up and stabbing her with the letter opener. He closed his eyes and breathed deeply, but it was no use, he had to get out of there before he really hurt Rosamund. He had never hated her as much as he did in that moment. His beautiful, precious drawing had been destroyed by an empty-headed, vapid, entitled bitch and he felt rage the like of which he had never experienced before.

In monetary terms it was worth nothing. But it was a symbol of Colleen's love for him, and he felt that Rosamund had tried to destroy that love. Well she hadn't succeeded. She would never succeed. Nobody would. Ever.

He took the letter Colleen had written to him before Rosamund discovered that as well, folded it into four and stashed it in his inside pocket next to his heart.

Then he stood up and without glancing at Rosamund or uttering another word he left the office.

―――――

Adam went straight to his penthouse apartment, packed a small suitcase, and changed into casual clothes. He bought a rail ticket from Euston to Piccadilly, Manchester, online, then requested that Davis drive him to the station.

'Bye the way, Davis,' Adam said as his chauffeur took him through the London streets, 'I think you are owed a rather long, paid holiday and when you return, there will be some changes. I can't explain what they are at the moment, but I'm hoping they'll be for the better.'

'Very good, sir,' said Davis. 'I'm overdue a holiday in Cornwall, staying with my sister. I'll leave tomorrow.'

'Sounds like a plan. What part of Cornwall does she live in?'

'St Ives.'

'Nice part of the world.'

'Indeed, sir.'

As Adam waited for the train to pull out of the station, his thoughts were on Colleen. His biggest fear was that he had left it too late, and she'd refuse to see him. But that wasn't Colleen. She'd told him she loved him and all he wanted to do was throw himself at her feet and beg her forgiveness for not treating her like the beautiful, gracious, kind, and sexy woman that she was.

Adam wondered if he should ring or text her and tell her he was on his way to Manchester. But what if she, or her mother, didn't want anything to do with him? It would be better to surprise her then she would have less chance to reject him. Not that he didn't deserve it, but the way he felt at the moment, it would break his heart if she did.

Chapter Twenty-Seven

It felt strange to be back in Manchester. It was good to walk the familiar streets and visit her favourite shops and coffee bars. It was good to be home and she felt happy that Auntie May had left, leaving her mother and herself to enjoy each other's company without her stressful presence.

Colleen hadn't decided what her next move would be. Her mother had told her to take her time, do nothing for a while, relax and get over the awful ordeal she had gone through. Nora was safe and getting the help she needed, so it was time for Colleen to think about herself and her future. The world was her oyster, her mother said, and she could do anything and go anywhere she chose.

But Colleen missed London, the crowds, the hectic toing and froing of people in and out of the underground train stations, the red buses, the tourists, the feeling that she was part of it all and belonged. And more than anything, she missed Adam and working at Meredith Motors.

Would Adam write her a reference if she asked? Or maybe Doris would. She had to account for her time in

London on her CV as prospective employers would want to know what she had been doing in the months she had been away from Manchester.

Colleen strolled through Piccadilly Gardens and, feeling hungry suddenly, she bought a sausage roll to eat as she was wandering around. With all the exotic and tasty food on sale, cuisine from all over the world, she had chosen a sausage roll. That said more about her state of mind than anything else.

What was she doing anyway? Wandering aimlessly. Not even shopping. She made her way towards Spinningfields, thinking she might call into Waterstones on Deansgate on the way to have a look at the books on sale. If she was having some downtime, she may as well use the time wisely and catch up on her reading.

———

Adam got a taxi outside Piccadilly station and told the driver to head for Withington. Adam had got Colleen's mother's address from her personnel file. One of the perks of being CEO was that he had access to all the staff's records.

Adam rehearsed what he would say to Deirdre O'Shea, Colleen's mother, when she opened the door. Being at a disadvantage as he had no idea what Colleen had told her mother about him, if anything, he would have to wing it and see how the conversation went. But he would try his best to be honest, even admitting his feelings for Colleen if necessary.

Adam rang the doorbell and waited. He could see a woman's figure through the glass and when she opened the door, Adam put on his best smile.

'Yes?' she asked looking him up and down.

'Hello, are you Mrs O'Shea?'

'Yes.' She held the door as if she intended to slam it shut if necessary, having opened it only a fraction; enough to peer around it.

'I'm Adam Turner, Colleen used to work for me in London. I wonder if she's in at all?'

'Adam! You're him,' cried Mrs O'Shea, flinging the door wide. 'Come in, come in, I'm pleased to meet you. Call me Deirdre.'

Deirdre drew him into the house, her attitude now welcoming instead of suspicious.

'Thanks. I don't want to intrude.'

'Not at all, not at all. After everything you've done for my daughters, the least I can do is welcome you into our home. Now would you like a tea or coffee?'

'Tea would be fine thanks,' said Adam following her in.

'You have your case with you I see, would you like to leave it in the hall?'

'Thanks. I'm booked into a hotel in the centre, but I wanted to find Colleen first before I checked in.'

'No, you'll be staying here with us. We'll look after you, don't you worry. You don't want to be spending money on hotels. Not at all.'

Adam followed Deirdre into the kitchen, looking around at the house with interest. There were photos in the hallway of Colleen and Nora at different ages, and one big picture of the four of them together when the girls were quite small.

It was a cosy house, warm and inviting. A typical family home and spotlessly clean and tidy, but not the kind of place that made you hesitant to put a mug down or wonder if shoes needed to be removed before moving further in from the hallway.

'Colleen's out at the moment, but I'm expecting her back any time. She went to town shopping and said she wouldn't be too long. She's at a bit of a loss, not sure what she's going to do with her life.'

'Right.' Of course, she would be. Colleen had effectively lost her job, her apartment, her relationship, and her sister, although that was only temporary and would be for the better in the end. All of that because of him. He'd given her the job and apartment and then taken them off her again, albeit unintentionally. He had a lot to make up to her for.

'Come through to the living room, we'll be comfy in there.'

'Thanks. Can I carry the tray for you?'

'That would be splendid, thank you. Colleen told me you're a gentleman and she was right.'

Adam wondered what else Colleen had told her mother and, after Deirdre had poured them a cup of tea each, in the best china by the look of it, Adam realised he owed her the truth. She was treating him like a prince, and he didn't deserve it.

'Have you lived here long?' He cursed himself for asking such a stupid, banal question, but it appeared Deirdre was pleased that he was taking an interest.

'Over thirty years now. We bought it when we got married and have lived here ever since. I've always tried to make it a proper home, you know, for the girls and for us too of course.'

'Colleen mentioned an Auntie May was staying with you.'

'Oh, the minx has been telling you all the family secrets.' Deirdre was laughing and Adam couldn't help smiling at her. She was a homely body, but he guessed that she wasn't a stupid woman and would see through insincerity.

'Well, not everything—'

'Oh, I'm only teasing. We don't have much to hide and with Nora and her little problem, I think you've probably heard the worst.'

'Nora's in the right place. She'll get the help she needs and be back with you soon.' He didn't know if that was even accurate as he'd taken little interest in the girl since she went into rehab. Another thing to feel ashamed about. He'd been neglectful and wasn't proud of himself.

'Yes,' Deirdre sighed, looking sad, 'I don't know how that came about. I just hope it wasn't something I did or didn't do, that made her chose that path...'

'Deirdre, you mustn't think like that. London is full of temptation for young people and Nora was just unfortunate to fall in with the wrong crowd. It was no one's fault, least of all yours. Colleen's always singing your praises.'

'Is she?' Deirdre brightened up at that. 'She's a good girl, my Colleen. Not that Nora isn't you understand, I don't mean that, but... well, Colleen has always been a friend as well as a daughter.'

'I understand.'

'Well, she's not turned up yet, and if you haven't got anywhere else to go, would you like another cup?'

'Actually, I'd like to discuss something with you if that's alright.'

'That sounds serious. I hope it's nothing bad. I don't think I could take any more bad news, not after hearing all about Nora and the drugs.'

'It's nothing bad. I hope you'll be happy with the news.'

'Well, that's very mysterious I must say. So, I'll put the

kettle on again and then we can settle down and you can tell me everything. Tea or coffee?'

'Tea please.'

'You're a man after my own heart.'

Once Deirdre had returned and had a cup of tea to hand, she looked expectantly at Adam.

'It concerns Colleen—'

'Oh, I do hope you're not going to tell me something bad about my Colleen, Adam. She's a good girl and has been wonderful with Nora, going to London and snatching her from the jaws of the drug dealers.'

Adam couldn't help smiling at the thought of Colleen fighting off Rupert single-handedly.

'She is wonderful, I couldn't agree more. In fact, I've never known anyone like her. She's beautiful, brave, loyal…' Adam trailed off as Deirdre was watching him with a suspicious look.

'She is all that and more. And she's lucky to have a friend like you. You're a married man yourself, aren't you? What does your wife think of all the business with the drugs and everything?'

Deirdre was on to him. It was time to come clean. 'My marriage is over and has been for a long time. Way before I met Colleen. My estranged wife knows nothing about it and won't as it's none of her business. I need to talk to you about Colleen. The thing is… I love her and want to spend the rest of my life with her—'

'But how can you when you're still married? Colleen's a good Catholic girl and won't want anything to do with a married man.'

'Deirdre, I've already instructed my solicitor to start divorce proceedings. As soon as the divorce comes through, I hope that Colleen and I can marry.'

'What does my daughter say about all this?'

'I don't know, I haven't asked her yet. That's the main reason I'm here.'

Deirdre swallowed her tea and put the cup and saucer down. 'I think you might be jumping the gun a bit, Adam, if you don't mind me saying so. What if she doesn't feel the same way about you?'

'I'll be heartbroken, but I'll just have to work harder at winning her round. I love her, Deirdre, more than I've ever loved anyone and will do anything it takes to win her love in return. I think she feels the same way about me.' Adam wasn't going to tell Deirdre about Colleen's note confessing her love for him as that was private. But he didn't want to come across as cocky, saying he knew she loved him.

'Well, all I can ask is you treat her gently. She's been through a lot recently with Nora and the worry of it all. She's fragile at the moment.'

'I promise. If she does feel the same way about me, do we have your blessing? It would mean everything to Colleen as she thinks the world of you. And it would mean a lot to me too.'

Deirdre smiled and her eyes were dancing. 'So long as Colleen feels the same way and you promise to treat her like the angel she is, then… yes, you have my blessing.'

'I promise. And thank you.'

'You're a good man, Adam. It's obvious that you are sincere, and you've done so much for my girls already. Colleen needs a strong man by her side. You have my blessing.'

'Thank you. That's all I need. And Colleen to say yes of course.'

Colleen was bored wandering around the Manchester streets. She wasn't in the mood for shopping and knew she should do something about getting herself a job but couldn't drum up the enthusiasm. She'd check online when she got home to see if there were any suitable jobs going.

She found herself in St Peter's Square and sat on a bench, staring at the town hall. It was a lovely building and had always fascinated her. She'd been inside a few times and loved the stained glass windows and the busts of influential figures that sat on plinths.

As she sat there, she remembered that she hadn't been to confession for months. She wasn't ready to go yet, either, but she could light candles for her father and Hugo.

She made her way to St Mary's, the Hidden Gem off St Peter's Square. As soon as she entered the church, she felt a weight lift off her shoulders. She sat for ages with bent head, just letting her thoughts wander. She prayed too, in her own way, which amounted to a "chat" with God, as if she was talking to a friend in Starbucks. She'd never been very good at the formal prayers.

She asked God to bless and look after Nora and her mother. It wouldn't be right to ask for things to work out for her and Adam. He wasn't hers in the first place, being already married. Even though the marriage was one in name only. But he was married in law and in the sight of God.

Some people might think she was wrong and a hypocrite to even think God would be interested in her after the things she'd done. The almost strip and sleeping with Adam for money. But Colleen thought that God would understand. She hadn't done it for herself, but for Nora, to get her away from the drug dealers.

What if Nora hadn't been in the equation and Adam

had offered her all that money to have sex with him, would she still have said yes? That was a question she wasn't able to answer. She hadn't been in that situation, had she? She ended her prayer by giving it all to God and went to light her candles.

As she strolled to the bus stop to go home, she felt more peaceful. Whatever happened it was out of her control. What will be, will be.

Colleen put her key in the door and went in. She noticed the suitcase and heard voices at the same time. The suitcase looked very much like the one Adam had taken to Charmley Manor for the wedding. She stopped and strained to hear the voices. Her mum's and a man's. A man that sounded like Adam.

Was she dreaming? Had she fallen asleep on the bus and slipped into a dream about meeting Adam again? But if she had, wouldn't she have chosen a more romantic setting?

When Colleen pushed open the living room door, the sight that greeted her almost made her want to go out and come back in again, it was so improbable. Her mother was sitting on the couch with a photo album on her knee and Adam was sitting next to her, holding a cup and saucer— the best bone china tea set by the looks of it—and gazing at the pictures, her mother pointing out all the places they'd been on their holidays.

'Here she is,' said her mum. 'We were expecting you back ages ago. Adam's been entertaining me with stories of his childhood, so I reciprocated and am showing him ours.'

'Right.'

'Hi, Colleen,' said Adam who looked settled sipping his tea and grinning as if he was perfectly at home.

'Adam grew up in the working-class area of London. He's just like us.'

'Yes, Mum.'

Colleen sat down in an armchair and stared at Adam as if he was a mirage and would disappear at any moment. Adam gazed at her with a look in his eyes that was unmistakable. But what was he doing here?

'I'll make some more tea and give the two of you the chance to say hello.'

'Right.' Colleen was lost for words, so said nothing. Adam could do all the talking now.

He put his cup and saucer down and patted the couch where her mum had been sitting. 'Come and sit next to me.'

Adam took her hand and brought it to his lips. As he kissed her knuckles, the warmth started, but she ignored it, as this wasn't the time for sex, it was the time for talking.

'Why are you here, Adam? Does Rosamund know where you are?'

His face darkened for a second as if a cloud had moved across the sun.

'Rosamund is no longer part of my life. We're getting divorced.'

'But... the will, and—'

'Listen. Can we go for a walk? There's a lot I want to say to you.'

'Is it good news? I don't think I could bear any more bad.'

'If what you said to me in your letter is true, then it's the best news.'

'Everything I said to you is true, so let's go.'

Chapter Twenty-Eight

They strolled hand in hand in the local park, listening to kids laughing as they played, putting their faces up to the blue sky and feeling a gentle breeze on their skin.

'First, I want to apologise to you for not answering your messages. I wasn't deliberately ignoring you, I promise and with hindsight, I should have spoken to you first, but I wanted to get everything in place before I asked you.'

'Get all your ducks in a row, you mean?'

Adam laughed. 'You could say that, but my ducks were a stubborn lot and had to be tamed.'

'Are they tamed?'

'They are now, yes.'

'Right, so now you can ask me.'

'I want to tell you something first. I've bought a property in Suffolk. It used to be a filling station and MOT centre. It has a small area for cars, but it's big enough to start with. I'm hoping, if we become successful in a few years, we could expand to a bigger place and have a proper showroom.'

'So you're not staying at Meredith Motors? Not staying with Rosamund?'

Adam stopped and pointed to a bench in the sunshine. 'Let's sit.'

'Okay.' Colleen's heart was beating fast, and she took deep breaths to try and calm herself. What Adam was about to tell her could turn out to be momentous.

'I'm finished with the Merediths. I've always wanted to run my own business, start from scratch, and build it up slowly, making my own decisions and mistakes, but learning from them. It'll be hard at first and I'll have to work twenty-four seven to get it up and running, but I haven't felt as excited about a project for a long time. I learned a lot from Hugo but it's time I worked for myself now.'

'But you would be if you stayed at Meredith Motors. It would be yours and Rosamund's. You would be working for yourself.'

Adam turned and gazed at Colleen. 'That part of my life is over, and the next stage is about to begin. And I want you to be part of that if it's what you want too. In your letter you said—'

'I said I love you, and I do. I think I fell for you that first night when you were so kind to me and when we spent the night together. But I never expected you to fall for me, Adam. I know I was just your mistress.'

Adam kissed her tenderly and the heat started again.

'Maybe at first that was the way I was thinking. But you soon became more to me than that. I wish I could express myself eloquently so I could tell you how I feel.'

'Let's walk.' Colleen felt too restless to sit in one place. She needed to understand what Adam was saying but was still confused. He had everything with Rosamund and

Meredith Motors, but he'd decided to throw it all away for a petrol station? It didn't make sense.

They stood up and ambled along the path towards the pond, still holding hands.

'You've become the most important person in my life, Colleen. I love you too and I want us to be together. I want you by my side in my new venture, working together for the future.'

'Right. So you want me to work for you again?'

'No, not work *for* me, work *with* me as an equal.'

'But how can I do that when I know nothing about cars or business?'

'I'll teach you.'

'So, what's Suffolk like? Where are you going to live?'

'Suffolk's a great place, you'll love it. There's country-side, the sea, and quiet villages. And as far as where we're going to live is concerned, the business I've bought comes with a four bedroomed house. It's a nice place.'

'But what about everything you're leaving behind to start again? I can't get my head around it, Adam.'

They stopped in the middle of a pathway with decid-uous trees on both sides providing a shady spot known by the locals as lovers' lane.

'Meeting you changed everything for me. I realised I was living a lie. I hated the fact that I was pretending to be happily married to Rosamund just so we could sell more cars. You were so brave, doing dangerous things like strip-ping in front of inebriated men so you could help your sister. I sensed there was more to you than the things people called you.'

'I've been called a lot of things, but they're just names, Adam.'

'Exactly. The more I got to know you the more I

admired your spark, your love for life and when we made love it was... I can't find the words.'

'Oh, I know. I had my first orgasm with you. I'll never forget that night. I'm so grateful to you, Adam, for everything you've done.'

'Well, I want you to stop being grateful. I'm the one who should be begging your forgiveness for not recognising sooner that you are the person I want to spend the rest of my life with.'

Colleen was startled as Adam dropped to one knee.

'What are you doing? Have you lost something?'

'Yes, Colleen, I've lost my heart to a wonderful woman who I love more than I've ever loved before. Will you marry me, Colleen, and make me the happiest man on earth?'

Colleen couldn't help it, she squealed. 'Oh my God, are you joking?' She put her hands to her face in shock.

'I've never been more serious. I love you so much. You're funny, sexy, loyal, loving, kind—did I mention sexy?'

'Oh stop it, I can't bear it.'

'Well, put me out of my misery then and let me put this ring on your finger.'

Colleen hadn't even noticed the small black box Adam had been holding. He opened it but she could hardly see the ring for the tears that streamed down her face.

'Yes, of course I'll marry you. Oh, my goodness, wait 'til I tell Mum.'

'I like your mum,' said Adam getting to his feet. 'I think we'll get on fine.'

'Let's go back and tell her.'

They strolled home, arms around each other, talking about Suffolk, about Doris and how he was going to break the news to Rosamund.

'Doris isn't far off retirement age, so I was thinking of

offering her a job working from home. She could do the invoices, letters, and other admin stuff on a part-time basis. What do you think of that idea?'

'It sounds good. I'm sure Doris won't want to go on working at Meredith Motors with you gone.'

'And you. She told me how fond of you she was getting.'

'And I her. I loved working with Doris.'

'And Davis. I'm going to offer him a job, but if he says yes, we'll have to work out his job description between us. He lives alone and his only relative is a sister in Cornwall. I think he'd love Suffolk.'

'You've thought of everything, haven't you?'

'No, but at least I've got a plan. Whether it works out like that, only time will tell.'

'I think it will. I've got a good feeling about this.'

When they got back home, her mother was waiting for them. Colleen flashed her ring at her, and her Mum squealed. Like mother like daughter.

'You said yes! Congratulations! Oh my goodness I'm so happy. We've got no champagne but there's a bottle of Prosecco left over from Christmas. Let's open it.'

As her mum bustled about, still talking and grinning equally, Adam and Colleen stood together gazing at each other. Colleen couldn't believe this was happening to her, it was like a dream that she never wanted to wake up from.

'Is it too early to talk about the wedding? How long does it take for a person to get divorced? When are you getting married? And where? I'll have to buy a dress and a hat. Must look my best as mother-of-the-bride. Oh, Colleen, I've dreamed about my girls getting married for so long and now you are and to a wonderful man like Adam. I'm so happy I could cry with it.'

'So am I, Mum, so am I.'

When they were settled on the couch and her mum was on her mobile to Auntie May to tell her the good news and gloat, Colleen remembered something.

'Did you like the drawing?' He hadn't said anything about it and maybe he hadn't liked it which is why he hadn't mentioned it. Adam sighed deeply.

'I loved it, Colleen, but I'm sorry to tell you that Rosamund didn't. I was going to cherish it, and have it framed, but she was furious when she saw it and ripped it up. I'm so sorry.'

'She was jealous probably. Never mind, I'll do you another one, a better one this time.'

'There's something I've been meaning to ask you. You are such an amazing artist, have you never thought of going to art college?'

'Me? Go to college? No way. I'm not clever enough. You've got to be good to get into art college.'

'You are good. In fact, you're more than good. You're great. Why don't you apply? Nothing to lose.'

'Oh, I don't know…'

'Goodbye then… yes I'll let you know when the wedding is and yes, you'll need a hat. No… auntie of the bride is not as important as mother-of-the-bride. No, May, I'll not be cleaning your house again and I'm sorry about your back. Take some painkillers. Bye now.'

Her mum ended the call and collapsed back in her chair.

'That woman. Anyhow she sends her congratulations to the pair of you.'

'Deirdre, we were just talking about Colleen applying for art college. What do you think of the idea?'

'Colleen? Going to art college? I think it's a splendid idea. I always told you, didn't I Colleen, when you were in school and you did those lovely sketches of animals and trees, I told you that you were good.'

'Yes you did, Mum. But going to college isn't like being in school.'

'No, it's better. You'll be doing the art all the time and not just for a few hours a week. Go for it, Colleen, you're in a good place now, with Adam at your side. There's nothing better than the support of a good man.'

Adam looked pleased with himself. 'You should listen to your mother, she talks a lot of sense.'

Colleen's phone rang which, thankfully, stopped her from having to answer.

'It's Nora. Hi, darling, how are you getting on?' Colleen looked at her Mum and Adam as she spoke to her sister. They looked as if they were waiting breathlessly for news. 'That's fantastic news, Nora. Well done. When will you be home?'

Deirdre squealed at that and clapped her hands.

Colleen ended the call after sending everyone's love to her.

'She's being discharged from residential care and is going to be seen on an outpatient basis. They're pleased with her and she's coming home!'

'That's fantastic! Oh, I can't believe all the good news we've had today. We are truly blessed that's what we are.'

'That's great news, Colleen,' Adam said quietly. 'I love you.'

'I love you too.' They kissed gently, aware that Colleen's mum was watching.

'Oh, you two are so perfect together. Remember me telling you, Colleen, that all I wanted was my girls' happiness? Well, today is the day that I have everything I could possibly want. I feel the need to go to Mass and give thanks. Are you coming, Colleen?'

'Do you know, I think I will. Do you mind being on your own for a bit, Adam?'

'Not at all. I've got some phone calls to make.'

So Colleen and her mum strolled arm in arm to the church. Her mum chattered away about the wedding and Colleen thought of how far she had come from that day she'd arrived in London. Nora was on the way to recovery, she and Adam were in love and engaged to be married and she might—just might, as she hadn't quite made her mind up yet—be going to college to learn how to be a proper artist.

What more could she possibly want?

Lost for Words: Chapter One

It was Monday morning again. Esme McBride stepped through the door of the medical centre with a familiar swirl of anticipation and dread in her stomach. She shook her head a little. Dread was too strong a word she told herself sternly. But sometimes the anxiety she'd been suffering with for the past ten years made things feel worse than they were. Her heartrate increased as she nodded and smiled at the two old ladies in the waiting room who greeted her.

'Good morning, Sister,' they said cheerfully.

'Good morning,' she replied before continuing down the corridor to the treatment room she used to see her patients.

The feeling of anticipation was always there, however, as she loved her job as senior practice nurse at the medical centre. With each day being different, she never knew what was in store.

When she reached the kitchen in the middle of the corridor, she heard laughter emanating from the propped open door. It should be shut when the clinics were running, to keep the noise level down. But, propped open, any loud laughter would be heard by the two patients already in the waiting room.

The laughter continued. It was obviously a very funny joke. Should she ignore it and get ready for clinic? But the professional Esme was annoyed and she had to speak out.

She walked through the open door to the sight of Patricia, one of the registered nurses, Sally, the youngest receptionist, and a man she had never seen before standing in the middle of the kitchen. The laughter died as soon as they saw her. She must have had a serious look on her face to match her mood. Granted the clinics didn't start for another half an hour, but the staff knew better than to behave like school kids on a day trip when they were on duty. They were professionals and should behave with decorum at all times.

'Morning, Sister McBride,' said Sally as she squeezed passed her to return to the reception desk carrying a mug of coffee in each hand.

'Good morning, Sally.'

'Esme,' said Patricia, 'good timing. This is Dr Whittaker, our new GP. He was just telling us a funny story of when he was a medical student. Right, I'll leave you in Esme's capable hands.' Patricia left the kitchen and Esme turned her attention to the man who was standing in front of her with his hand out to shake and a smile on his lips.

'Good morning, nice to meet you. Shall I call you Esme or Sister McBride?'

Esme looked at his hand—strong with beautifully manicured fingernails—then took it in hers. He was looking directly into her eyes, his blue eyes seeming to reach into her soul. She dropped his hand quickly.

'I'm old school, Dr Whittaker, I think we should be professional at all times, so Sister McBride will suffice.'

Esme knew that many nurses her age weren't concerned with titles but she preferred to be called by hers. She may be only thirty-two but she was an old-fashioned girl at heart and she'd worked hard for her title.

'Absolutely,' he said with a smile. An open, happy smile which reached his blue eyes. Esme imagined that Dr Joel Whittaker smiled a lot.

'But welcome to Leytonsfield Medical Centre, we're very pleased that you're joining us, and I hope you'll be very happy here.'

'I'm sure I shall.' Dr Whittaker spoke slowly, enunciating each word clearly and he hesitated slightly before he pronounced some words.

Esme hoped she hadn't annoyed him, that was never her intention. She came across as quite stern and serious—she'd been told enough times by both her family and her colleagues to lighten up—but she was serious about her job and liked things to be done just so. It was unfortunate that, in the modern world in which they were all forced to reside, most people preferred informality. She'd lost count of the number of times she'd had to complain about the recep-tionists using their mobile phones when the clinics were running. It created such a bad impression for the patients.

'Would you like me to show you to the room you'll be using today?' Esme asked in an attempt to make up for her earlier abruptness.

'Thank you, that would be very kind.' Dr Whittaker spoke politely but Esme couldn't lose the feeling that he was laughing at her in some way. It wouldn't be the first time someone mistook her desire to behave appropriately for stuffiness. His blue eyes were twinkling far too much for her liking.

As they walked down the corridor to the room Dr Whittaker would be sharing with two part-time GPs, she realised that she had to look up to meet his eyes. At five feet eleven inches tall, Esme towered over most women she met and a lot of men too. But Dr Whittaker must have been over six feet tall. It made a refreshing change. Not that she had a problem with her height, she rather liked being tall.

'Right. Here we are. Georgina, our practice manager, will be along before clinic starts to show you how to navigate the patient software and set up passwords and the like. I can give you a brief tour before she arrives.'

Dr Whittaker sat down and Esme stood next to him, leaning over slightly to use the mouse and show him how to move from one piece of software to another. She was aware of him as he stared at the screen, a tiny frown creasing his brows. It had been a long time since she had been this close to a man and she knew her cheeks would be cherry red if she didn't back off and keep her distance. Damn these blushes. She'd been plagued with them all her adult life and wished she knew how to control them. No matter how cool and detached she wanted to be, her red cheeks always gave her away.

'Good. It looks similar to the one I used at my last place, so I'll be able to hit the ground running.' He turned his head to look up at her and the smile was back in place.

'Where were you working before?' Not that she really cared but small talk had never been her strong point.

'A small health centre in Manchester.'

'Oh, so what made you move to Leytonsfield? It'll be a lot quieter here than what you were used to in the big city.'

'Peace and quiet sounds good at the moment.' He sighed and looked away, staring at the computer screen again. 'I've moved in with my brother who is a psychiatrist at Leytonsfield General. He bought himself a fixer-upper and finds now that he has neither the time nor the skills to do the place up. I needed a change, so I offered to help him.'

She was tempted to ask him why he needed a change but feared it might be too personal a question. Stick to the mundane and avoid affairs of the heart.

'Do you know anything about house renovation Dr Whittaker?'

His smile this time was barely perceptible. 'I did a lot of work on my own house in Manchester, so I'm not a complete novice, and anyway, there's plenty of advice on the internet.'

Esme had run out of questions to ask him and was keen to get ready for clinic. 'I see. Well, good luck with it all.'

'Thank you.'

The door flew open, and Georgina, the practice manager, rushed in. 'Sorry, sorry... the bus took ages this morning. I'm here now anyway and I'll take over. Thanks, Esme, for looking after Joel. I'm so sorry I wasn't here to welcome you. Well, I'm here now.'

'Right.' Esme backed away from the desk to avoid Georgina elbowing her out of the way. 'I'll go then.'

'Yes, go, clinic's starting soon and some of your patients are already here.'

Esme left the two of them together, Georgina still talking and Dr Whittaker—Joel—frowning at the screen, trying to keep up with the cascade of information Georgina was no doubt imparting.

As Esme reached the small clinic room she used to see her patients, Patricia was coming out of it.

'Esme, I'm sorry, I forgot what day it is. No wonder you were a bit tetchy earlier on. Are you going to the...?'

Tetchy? She was merely expressing an opinion. But at

least Patricia had the grace to apologise. 'Yes, I'm going after work today. Thank you for remembering.'

'Oh, you're welcome. It must be... well, I know how hard this day is for you. If there's anything you need, please just shout.'

'Thank you, Patricia, I will.'

'Right, better get on.'

When Esme was alone, she took a deep breath and closed her eyes, trying to calm her thoughts and her fast heartbeat. Then she turned her attention to the list of patients she was seeing that clinic. Professional at all times. Personal things would have to wait until later.

After spending the morning performing routine procedures such as cervical smears, pregnancy tests and dressing changes, Esme took a quick break for lunch.

Two of the younger nurses were in the kitchen as Esme made herself a coffee and ate her sandwiches.

'What do you think of the new doctor?' Matilda asked Ebony. 'Bit of a hottie, eh?'

Ebony glanced at Esme. All the nurses knew that she disapproved of gossip, especially when they were discussing other members of staff. Idle chat about which reality show or soap opera they had watched the previous night, or something equally innocuous was acceptable. But talking about colleagues behind their backs certainly wasn't.

On this occasion, Esme said nothing and pretended she hadn't heard. She continued to eat her sandwiches and scanned the front page of a tabloid newspaper that someone had left on the table.

'I've only seen him briefly so I couldn't really say.'

'Oh, go on, you have seen him. I think he's sex on legs. What do you think, Esme?'

'I think you shouldn't be having this conversation, you know how I feel about gossip. But if you must know, I think he's very pleasant and yes, he is also attractive, but whether he's a good doctor and will fit in here remains to be seen.'

Esme had her back to the door and hadn't heard it open. She did, however, note Matilda's eyebrows rise almost as high as her hairline and her eyes widen. Too late, Esme realised that she was trying to signal the need to stop talking.

'Right, come on Ebony, back to work.' The two nurses rushed out of the kitchen as if devils were chasing them.

Esme felt the heat rise to her face and knew, without having to look in a mirror that her cheeks would be bright red. She also knew who she would see behind her. She turned around slowly but couldn't meet his eyes.

'Ah, Dr Whittaker. I'm so sorry you had to hear that—'

'You surprise me, Sister McBride. This morning you were telling me how you believed in being professional at all times. And now, I find you gossiping about me with two nurses.'

'Dr Whittaker, I don't know what to say.' Esme's face burned with humiliation. She felt sick and stared at his shoes.

When Esme finally forced herself to look up, she expected to see thunderclouds, but the doctor was smiling, the skin around his eyes crinkling attractively and his blue eyes shining with mirth. He was enjoying her discomfort, that much was obvious.

'I think you've probably said enough. It's gratifying to know you find me attractive and I'll do my utmost to prove to you that I'm a good doctor and can fit in here.' His tone of voice was almost gentle as if he knew how bad she must be feeling. But also slightly mocking as if he found the whole thing a hoot.

'Dr Whittaker… please accept my apology…'

'Apology accepted. Enjoy your lunch.'

Then he was gone, and Esme was alone. She threw her sandwiches in the bin. She had lost her appetite. After making herself an extra strong coffee, she took a deep breath, then groaned. *Damn the man.* Today of all days she had to make a complete fool of herself. Maybe she should have asked for the day off, but then she would have been moping around at home feeling sorry for herself. Since it happened Esme had taken refuge in work, finding the act of helping others went some way to allay the pain that she carried with her constantly.

Esme went back to her office and her next patient.

Joel survived his first day at the medical centre without any mishaps. The patients he saw were a mixed lot; elderly people with arthritis, heart conditions and diabetes, a young man with suspected gall bladder problems, a child who had got a bad cough and a runny nose, and a woman in her forties with a lump in her breast.

Joel had written prescriptions, referral letters to specialists and listened to the patients closely to ascertain their real problems. Sometimes they were too shy or embarrassed to tell the doctor what was really troubling them. Occasionally they only got to the point of their visit when they were about to leave the surgery. They'd say things like, "While I'm here, doctor, I thought I should just mention…" then they'd admit to a lump, or rash in an intimate place, or bleeding and try to shrug it off as not really worth mentioning, or they'd look at him with frightened eyes and Joel would know that, really, they were worried sick. It was part of a GP's role to recognise the serious symptoms.

It had been a long day and Joel was glad to head home. As he was saying goodnight to the receptionists, he bumped into Esme, who was also taking her leave.

'How was your first day?' she asked as they walked towards their cars.

'It was fine, actually,' Joel said, 'I think I'm going to like working here. And I hope I can prove to you that I'm a good doctor.' He smiled to show that there were no hard feelings about the earlier incident.

Sister McBride blushed which softened her features and made her look more vulnerable. Joel felt strangely protective of her.

'I am sorry about the gossip in the kitchen, it's not like me at all.'

'It's fine,' said Joel, 'I've forgotten about it already.'

'Good.'

They stood together, Esme looking at the ground and Joel wondering if he should ask her if she fancied a quick drink in the pub at the end of the road, which, he had been told, was the medical centre's local. She intrigued him and he'd like to get to know her better. Just as colleagues, of course. But Sister McBride was clutching her car keys and looked eager to be off.

'Right then,' he said, 'I'll see you tomorrow. Goodnight, Sister McBride.'

'Yes, goodnight, Dr Whittaker.'

He walked away and got in his car. Sister McBride did the same and she pulled away from the carpark, turning right. Joel turned left heading for his brother's house. They had an exciting evening planned—stripping the old wallpaper. He knew from the experience of doing his own house up how thrilling that was. But Noah was letting him live there rent free. It was a fair exchange.

He wondered what Esme McBride would be doing tonight.

Lost for Words: Chapter Two

'Hello, David, I'm here again.' Esme took the dead flowers out of the vases and replaced them with fresh ones. Gerbera, dahlias, allium and rudbeckia or black eyed Susan. There was also some white gypsophila which reminded Esme of weddings. She had bought them from The Little Flower Shop, her favourite florists. She usually bought David's flowers there. Occasionally she brought flowers from her own garden, from the house she shared with Scarlett and Maria.

Once the fresh flowers were arranged to her satisfaction, she stood in front of the gravestone and wondered what to talk about this time. This was a special visit as it was the anniversary of David's death. It had been ten years to the day since the road traffic accident that Esme had survived and her fiancé had not.

'We have a new doctor at the medical centre, and I made a complete fool of myself today. He overheard me telling the nurses that I thought he was attractive. Well, he is. Not that looks matter. He didn't seem annoyed, just amused. I have a feeling I'm going to struggle to get him to take me seriously now.'

Esme usually found a lot to tell David and had got used to their one-sided conversations, so they came naturally to her. She didn't even care if anyone walking passed heard her talking to his gravestone. She missed him so much and longed to hear his voice again. The next best thing was being able to talk to him as if he could hear her. It may be daft, as several members of her family thought, but it had always brought her comfort and kept the connection with him alive, even if that was only in her mind.

Today, however, she was finding it hard to focus on David. All she could see when she closed her eyes was Dr Joel Whittaker and his sparkling blue eyes. When she added in his sexy smile that made her heart race faster than she was comfortable with, she realised the truth of what she had said to the nurses in the kitchen. Their new doctor was an incredibly attractive man.

But David had been her fiancé, the only man she had ever loved, and she missed him like crazy. She shouldn't be thinking of another man when she was visiting him. She needed to concentrate on him and think of how happy they had been together, at least at the beginning.

Esme shivered, even though the air was warm. She glanced at her watch and saw that she had been standing at the graveside, daydreaming for nearly half an hour. It wasn't like her to feel sorry for herself and she stood up straighter and smiled.

'Right, David. I'd better get back before they send out a search party. Goodbye, my love.' She walked briskly back to her car.

Joel cursed and brushed bits of plaster and dust out of his hair from the large piece of wallpaper he had ripped off the wall, the plaster coming away with it.

'There's no doubt about it, Bro, you'll have to get these walls replastered before you do any decorating.'

'Yes, I know. I don't think anyone's changed the décor since the house was built in 1899. Or it seems that way. This wallpaper's awful.' Noah coughed as the dust settled on both of them. He brushed the dust from his short, dark hair.

'Strange how fashions change. Anyhow, more importantly, when are we stopping for tea? My stomach thinks my throat's been cut.'

'Me too. Right, which would you prefer? To nip out for fish and chips or stay here and finish stripping this room. We've nearly finished here anyhow. Then we can start on the floorboards. Another dirty job.'

'It's a dirty job but someone's gotta do it,' Joel said in his best American accent.

Noah laughed and put down the steamer he was using to loosen the wallpaper.

Joel looked his brother up and down, then glanced down at himself. 'Seeing as I'm the one who's copped for most of the plaster and other unidentifiable muck, I think you should go and get our tea. I'll just finish up here, then have a wash and put the kettle on.'

'Sounds like a plan. What are you having? Fish, chips, and mushy peas?'

'You know me so well. Lots of salt and vinegar on mine.'

Noah laughed and went into the kitchen to wash his hands and face.

When he was gone, Joel got stuck into removing the last

of the wallpaper. He sang as he worked. It had been the right decision to come to Leytonsfield and help his beloved big brother rather than stay in Manchester moping because Julie hadn't wanted to marry him. Joel hoped he'd be able to carve out a brand new life for himself in the Cheshire countryside.

Joel triumphantly pulled the last piece of wallpaper off the wall, then started clearing up. By the time he had done this as best he could, Noah was back with the food.

'Ah, that smell! The best aroma in the world—fish and chips with salt and vinegar—heavenly,' Joel said.

'What, better than the smell of roses or coffee, bread fresh out of the oven?'

'Sorry, Bro, but they're a poor second to fish and chips when a man's hungry.'

Noah laughed and Joel was reminded how much he had missed the company of his brother after Noah left Manchester. The easy banter, gentle teasing and shared confidences had been the background to his life, and he missed all that. It was great to be living with Noah and he was determined to help him turn the old house into a palace.

They sat down at the small pine table in the almost empty kitchen. They were definitely roughing it while the renovations were being carried out. Only essential furniture, bare floorboards, bare lightbulbs, cheap and cheerful crockery; a plate, bowl, and mug each.

Joel sighed with pleasure as he savoured his first mouthful of food. 'This is good. We'll have to eat there again.'

'One of the best things about living in this town is the amount of great places to eat, including the fast food joints.'

'I'm looking forward to having a good look around. I'm liking what I see so far.'

Noah took a drink from his mug of tea. 'How was your first day in the medical centre?'

Joel took a swig of his own tea before answering. 'It was good. Everyone seemed friendly and welcoming. All except one, that is.'

'Oh, who was that?'

'Her name's Esme McBride, she's the Senior Practice Nurse. She was quite standoffish at the beginning of the day. She said she believed the staff should be professional at all times.' Joel couldn't help smiling as he pictured Sister McBride trying to put him in his place, then blushing like a teenager when he caught her gossiping about him.

'Weren't you being professional? What the heck were you doing?'

'I had just met another of the nurses and one of the receptionists and I was telling them the story of my first day as a junior doctor. I was just trying to break the ice and be friendly, but Sister McBride didn't approve.'

'You'll win her over. Just use the old Whittaker charm and she'll be putty in your hands.' Noah stuffed more chips into his mouth.

'Well, listen to this. I went into the kitchen to make a coffee and she was gossiping about me with two other nurses. She knew I'd heard her and did have the grace to blush. Fire engine red.' Joel had felt quite sorry for poor Sister McBride.

'Terrorising the nursing staff on your first day isn't the way to make friends in a new job.' Noah scrunched the chip shop paper up and threw it into the bin. 'Slam dunk.' He grinned.

'I'll make it my business to be extra specially pleasant to her, whilst being professional of course.'

'There's a nurse in the unit called McBride—Scarlett. She's got sisters who are nurses. I wonder if they're related.'

'It's a common name. You could ask her though.'

'Yes, I will.' Noah looked away then up at the ceiling. He usually did this when there was something he didn't want to talk about. Or someone.

'So Scarlett is a friend or something else?'

'She's a colleague.' Noah wouldn't look at him.

'Is she pretty?'

'Extremely. Red hair, green eyes, alabaster skin, always laughing.'

'And just a colleague?'

'That's right.'

'So why don't I believe you?'

Noah was quiet for a while, staring into space. Then he sighed. 'No comment. Right, I'll wash up, then we can make a start on the floorboards.' Noah had always loved red heads. But he wasn't going to get any more out of his brother tonight. The floorboards awaited.

'Whoopee do,' muttered Joel.

Lost for Words: Chapter Three

When Esme arrived home to the house she shared with Scarlett and Maria, she expected to be able to smell the aroma of food cooking. They knew she was visiting David's grave that afternoon and she had been sure that one of them would have, at least, started preparing the evening meal.

Scarlett came running down the stairs as Esme was about to go upstairs to get changed.

'Hi, we've been summoned, so you've just got time for a quick shower. Maria's home, so we can all go together.'

'I do wish she'd give us more notice. It's lovely to be invited for a meal, of course, but I could have made other plans for tonight,' Esme said irritably. Then she sighed. She should be used to Mum and her impromptu gatherings by now.

'But you haven't though, have you? I mean, you never do after you've been to the cemetery. You never go out on the anniversary, do you?'

Scarlett studied her face as if searching for clues. Since becoming a mental health nurse, her sister was acutely aware of people's "tells", the little clues that gave away how they were feeling, or whether they were telling the truth.

'No I haven't but that's hardly the point. I'm going up for a shower.'

'Okay, Esme. I'll drive so you can have a drink.'

Esme got into the shower and let the hot water run over her. All she wanted at the end of a busy Monday that just happened to be another anniversary of her fiancé's death, was the chance to chill. She wanted to get into her PJs and slump in front of the telly, then have an early night and cry herself to sleep. But instead, her mother decided to host a dinner party. Well, okay, it was just the family and perhaps Dot, her mother's best friend, but still. It would involve polite—or not so polite—conversation, being interrogated about the slightest detail of her life, and hearing about how wonderfully well everyone else was getting on.

Esme stepped out of the shower and wrapped a towel around herself. She wiped the condensation on the mirror so she could see herself through the narrow gap. *I'm being a bitch aren't I?* She studied her reflection. *It's okay, you can be honest.* Her reflection nodded mournfully. Esme sighed. She needed to stop feeling sorry for herself and count her blessings.

When they were all ready, they piled into Scarlett's car. She loved big, powerful cars, that she drove far too fast for the family's liking. When she traded her last car in, she compromised and bought a second hand Honda Accord. Scarlett had confided in Esme that she had her heart set on a Ford Mustang that cost about two year's salary. Esme promised not to tell their mother.

When they arrived at the house, Esme hung back while their mother hugged and kissed Scarlett and Maria.

'Here's my girls, come and give me a hug.'

'Hi Mum,' said Maria wrapping her arms around Candy.

'Hi there,' said Scarlett and hugged them both which made them laugh.

Esme took deep breaths and plastered a smile on her face as they all made their way into the house which had been the family home for thirty-five years. All four of the McBride girls had been conceived in this house, although they had all been born in the maternity unit of Leytonsfield General Hospital.

The house was full of memories, but instead of calming Esme, it reminded her of everything she had lost. The innocence of childhood, her father, Frank McBride, who had died five years previously of a heart attack, and David. Always David.

'Aren't you going to give me a hug?'

Candice McBride, who liked to be called Candy, was nearly as tall as Esme and at fifty-seven, was an extremely attractive woman who made the best of herself. Her ash blonde hair was cut in a fetching bob and her blue eyes were framed by false eyelashes which, on some older women would have looked silly, but on Candy looked chic.

'Yes, Mum, of course. How are you?' Esme, not being fond of public displays of affection, put her arms around her mother as they hugged each other, but was the first one to break the hug.

'I'm fine, dear, but you're looking a bit peaky. Are you getting enough sleep?'

'It's the anniversary of David's death. Had you forgotten?' Esme snapped at her mother.

'No, darling, of course I hadn't forgotten, but it was ten years ago.' Candy moved to hold Esme, but she avoided her and stood with her face averted. 'Don't you think you should be trying to move forward? I know you'll never forget him, as you loved him so much, but you're wasting your youth mourning him after so long. It's time you started living again.' Candy reached out to her eldest daughter, but she backed away.

'You don't understand. Just because you've managed to get over Dad so quickly, doesn't mean we're all cut from the same cloth.'

Esme turned away from her mother and went into the living room. Scarlett followed her in.

'That was nasty, Esme, I think you should apologise to Mum. She hasn't got over Dad, she just keeps her feelings to herself. Next year will be their thirty-fifth wedding anniversary. You were only with David a matter of a couple of years. There's no comparison.'

Esme turned on Scarlett, her face hot and no doubt as red as a pillar box. 'What difference does that make? Love isn't measured in years and anniversaries. I will never get over him no matter how long I live, and the thought that I can just move on like that, as if I have the choice and can turn off my feelings...' Esme couldn't say anymore as the tears came, fast and hot. She wished she could make her family feel what she felt and understand the depth of despair she experienced, especially on the anniversary of the accident.

She sat down on the couch and sobbed. Scarlett was beside her immediately.

'Oh, my darling, I'm sorry, please don't cry. Forgive me. We all need to stick together, that's what Dad would have wanted.' Scarlett rocked her, and Esme cried harder to think she had upset her darling mother who she loved so much.

Mum came into the room and sat on the other side of Esme. Then Maria came in and sat quietly in the armchair, not speaking, but looking anxiously at Esme.

Esme felt as if she was at the bottom of a dark pit and a tiny beam of light was drawing her upwards out of the pit, back into fresh air and sunshine. Her family was the light and Esme shuddered to think of how she would have coped without them over the past ten years.

Surrounded by her family, all loving, concerned, and supportive, Esme slowly calmed down, then felt stupid for losing it with Mum. She didn't deserve to be spoken to like that.

'Come on now, dry your tears,' said Candy, 'we all know how much you loved David, and it's admirable that you still have deep feelings for him, but I'm your mother and my concern is for your happiness. I hate to see you tearing yourself apart year after year. You're such a lovely young woman, I want you to be happy, that's all.'

'We all do,' said Scarlett.

'I know. I'm so sorry. Sometimes I get these feelings and I can't control them.' She knew her family wanted the best for her and she vowed that she would try harder to keep her darkest feelings hidden from them to prevent her lashing out and hurting the people she loved the most.

The sound of footsteps running down the stairs and the door bursting open announced Connie, the baby of the family, although she was twenty, who still lived at home.

'Hi! I'm starving—oh, what's wrong?' Connie came and knelt in front of Esme and tried to hug her. 'Are you okay?'

'It's the anniversary,' said Candy, holding Esme's hand in her own and stroking it gently.

'Oh yeah, sorry Esme. I'm really sorry.'

Esme sighed. 'It's fine. I'm okay now. Thanks everyone and I apologise for acting like a complete fool.'

'Well, not a *complete* fool,' said Scarlett and Esme smiled.

'Right, let's take our seats shall we before the meal is ruined?' Candy got up and held her hand out to Maria. 'Would you help serve? You can open the wine.'

'Of course,' said Maria who took her mother's hand, and they left the living room.

When they were all seated around the dining table and were enjoying Candy's homemade chicken and asparagus pie, with steamed vegetables, Esme silently gave thanks for her family. They were always supportive and loving; no matter how appallingly she behaved, and she knew she did, they understood and forgave her. What would her life have been like if she'd had to endure the last ten years without them?

When they were eating their dessert of Eton mess, Candy asked, 'Dot's spending Saturday with her family as it's her daughter's birthday, so if any of you can spare a few hours to help in the shop I'd be grateful.'

'Working, sorry,' said Scarlett between mouthfuls. 'This is gorgeous, Mum, is there any more?'

'There's some left, yes. I'll get it in a minute.'

'I'll get it.' Scarlett left the dining room.

'I'm working, too, Mum, sorry,' said Maria.

'I'll do it.' Esme enjoyed working in the cake shop. She was a reasonable baker, having been taught by the best— her Mum—and liked the idea of the two of them spending some time together without her sisters there too.

'Thank you, sweetheart, that's kind of you.'

'You're welcome.' Maybe it would make up for being cruel to her earlier on. Guilt weighed heavily on her for hurting her mother. She knew how much her parents had loved each other and that her mum kept her grief hidden to protect her daughters.

Scarlett came back carrying a plate with what was left of the Eton mess and fresh strawberries. 'Right, who wants seconds?'

Lost for Words: Chapter Four

The following day, Joel resolved to get to know Sister McBride and break through her ice queen persona. Use the Whittaker charm, his brother had advised. He didn't think they had any. He'd never had much success with women and the thought that the frigid Sister McBride would be bewitched by his so-called charms was a joke.

She was already at the medical centre when he arrived, making coffee in the staff kitchen. She looked tired and pale as she waited for the kettle to boil. Joel wondered if she was anaemic or wasn't getting enough sleep. Then realised she was a senior nurse and didn't need him to diagnose her. It was none of his business.

'Good morning, Sister McBride, how are you today?'

'Good morning, Dr Whittaker. I'm fine thank you. Did you have a pleasant evening?' She took another mug down from the cupboard and put some instant coffee into it.

'My evening was taken up helping my brother renovate his house. Hard work but satisfying.' She gazed at him, waiting for more details perhaps. Or just killing time until the water boiled. He marvelled at how dark brown her eyes were, and her hair was almost black. Cut short and neat it emphasised the heart shape of her face. 'What about you? Did you have a pleasant evening?'

'I did, thank you. I had a meal with my family.'

'Great,' he said, then remembered Noah's mental health nurse. 'By the way, do you have a sister called Scarlett who works in psychiatry?'

'I do, why?'

'My brother, Noah, is a consultant psychiatrist and mentioned her. We were just wondering if you're related, that's all.'

'We are. I have three sisters, all younger. Maria is a carer in an old peoples' home and Connie is at university, studying nursing.'

'Wonderful, a nursing family.'

Sister McBride stirred the mugs of black coffee. 'Do you take sugar and milk?'

'Milk, no sugar thanks.' He took the mug she offered after she'd splashed some milk into it.

'What do you do in your spare time, Sister McBride, if you don't mind me asking? I'm new to Leytonsfield and am eager to make my home here. Any advice about social activities in the area would be welcome.' Joel was determined to get to know Sister McBride. She fascinated him. Still waters run deep as the saying goes. He'd love to know more about her.

'I think you're asking the wrong person, Dr Whittaker, as I don't have an active social life. I tend to stay at home and read. I spend a lot of time in the garden.'

How could it be that such an attractive woman spent her weekends reading and gardening? Why wasn't she out dancing or partying? There was something behind this and he wanted to know more.

'So, no husband or boyfriend then?' He hoped he hadn't upset her by his questions, but she intrigued him.

'Not any more I'm afraid. You see, my fiancé died in a road traffic accident, and I haven't been very sociable since then.' Esme turned her face away, but not before Joel saw the pain in her eyes.

'Oh, that's awful, I'm so sorry. If I'd known I wouldn't have said anything. How long ago did you lose him?' The poor woman. Recently bereaved and trying to put a brave face on it. He felt awful for things he had called her, even if they were only in his mind.

'He died ten years ago. In fact it was the anniversary of his death yesterday which is why I wasn't really myself.'

Ten years? She had mourned him for ten long years.

'Ten years is a long time to miss someone.' And far too long to still be in mourning. She must have been very young when he died.

'I miss him just as much now as I did then. In fact, the pain grows every day. I still love him you see.'

'Yes, I see. I'm so sorry for your loss.' But he didn't really see. How young was she when she lost him? And why hadn't anyone helped her to move on? He felt so sorry for her but sensed that she was a proud woman and wouldn't welcome a stranger offering assistance.

'Right, better get on. Have a good day, Dr Whittaker.'

'Yes, thanks. You too.'

Joel carried his mug of coffee to his room, ready to start the day. He couldn't get the image out of his mind, of a young woman locking herself away from the world, denying herself love and marriage, children, and a family, still trying to give her heart and soul to a dead man. Poor Esme. He wondered what he could do to help, but he couldn't think of it anymore. Clinic was about to start and he had patients to see.

Grab your copy...
vinci-books.com/lostforwords

About the Author

Jax lives in the NW of England with two cats - George and Cloud. She spent the last twenty years working in a cancer hospital as a secretary and retired in the middle of the pandemic. Her colleagues still managed to give her a decent send off.

Jax writes contemporary romance novels set in a small fictional town in Cheshire. All her stories have a happy ending which is hard won. She doesn't shy away from serious subjects - her characters have a lot to cope with! But that makes their happy ever after all the sweeter.

When Jax isn't writing or plotting a new series, she listens to music or reads. She can sometimes be found doing a sneaky cross-stitch whilst listening to an audio book.